<u>Ragweed</u>

A novel by Kent Detweiler

Prologue

The fluorescent light flickered on, and rodents scattered, invisible but definitely audible. Goosebumps raised the blonde hair on the back of Benzler's neck and arms. He yanked off his wire-rimmed glasses, and wiped at the fog with a bandanna. His gaze fixed on the tractor parked in the middle of an otherwise deserted corridor. His breath made a misty cloud before him as he exhaled. Benzler hesitated, and his eyes darted from the tractor's propped up hood to the dark office at the far end. He already knew that was where he needed to go.

Forcing his heavy foot forward, the boy deliberately placed his boot on the dirt floor, first one and then the other. His parka made a swishing sound as he walked, and it drowned out everything else. He balked, and his senses strained to gather information. He cocked his right ear, hoping for any sound from within. Some cows lowed and shifted their massive girth in their pens to his left. By now he had grown immune to their rich stench. But he heard nothing unusual.

He reached the outside of the door, and came to a stop. He grasped the icy round handle, and the metal latch slid stiffly with a click. The door creaked as it opened, and he peered inside.

"Hello?" he called out. "Dad?"

His eyes adjusted to the dim light that came through an outside window. This enabled him to glimpse just enough in the shadows. Benzler jumped, startled when he recognized the limp form slumped over the desk.

His head whirled, and he groped the paneled wall in search of the light switch. The dark red pool confirmed what he somehow expected he would find. He crumbled to his knees and cried, "Why?"

*   *   *

Chapter 1

Benzler brooded while seated alone in a brown metal folding chair in a secluded corner of the church. A quiet din of chattering townsfolk buzzed in the background. One expected the somber atmosphere at a funeral, even though this one was different.

I had watched Benzler all day, but stood clear of him. What could you say to your best friend when his Dad died? Especially so sudden. I finally worked up enough courage to approach, and then stood in silence before him, my legs apart. He held his head down in his hands, and his stringy mop of straw-like blonde hair draped over his fingers. Even seated he looked awkward in his ill-fitting powder blue leisure suit.

I couldn't think of anything to say. I just blurted out, "Benzler, you OK?" My high voice screeched like fingernails on a chalkboard, but at least that interrupted his trance. How could he possibly be OK?

His head moved up in slow motion, and he looked at me slowly, a grave, hollowness in his eyes. At least I didn't see any tears behind his glasses. His eyes drifted to the empty spot right up there by the altar where Mr. Benzler's closed mahogany casket had lain not more than two hours ago. Nobody'd tell me why they kept it shut.

"Hey Digger," he responded. "Yeah, I suppose I'm OK. This ain't fun, you know." I relaxed some; he didn't bite my head off or melt down. Under the circumstances, I felt obliged to comfort him, but I didn't really know how. We didn't just lose a ballgame or a girl. This was serious. He reset his head in his hands.

I turned my attention through the wide open accordion doors to the next room. Benzler's ancestors have resided locally for many decades, farmers in a farming community. His Dad worked as an ag engineer over at Landmark, a solid good paying job. Though well-liked by most, Mr. Benzler wasn't exactly a pillar of the community. He had a reputation of living beyond their modest means, for example the big bass boat that usually sat in their drive. And he always had a brand new Ford pickup truck. Nothing outrageous, but things like that sometimes made waves among plain and humble farmers. Nothing that explained this though.

Otherwise, the family seemed normal mostly. Folks here didn't much appreciate gossip. But when a boy found his thirty-five year old father dead in his workshop... Yes indeed, this funeral was a little different than most.

"Where's your Mom?" I continued after a minute.

He looked back up and shrugged, "She's 'round here someplace." He mumbled out of the side of his mouth like an old movie gangster.

"David and Nancy?" His nine year old brother David looked nothing like him, but unfortunately his six-year old little sister Nancy was his spittin' image.

5

"I don't know." He shook his head, and seemed irritated by my questions. "Probably with Grandma and Grandpa."

With a squeal of laughter, Nancy ran out of a Sunday school room, chased by my ten year old brother Lester.

"That should answer your question," Benzler said.

He stood up. His tall, gangly frame loomed over me. I cast a sidelong glance at his hawkish nose and slight under bite. Physically, Benzler was a klutz, and overall he wasn't really good at anything. He showed a lot of cockiness for a twelve year old, but Mom said that's 'cause he's insecure. That annoyed me, but he was still my best friend. Since kindergarten in fact.

Schoolmates at Waldo Elementary, we made an odd pair, the stork and the bulldog. Besides our outward appearance, he acted loud and ornery, while I tended to be more bookish and serious.

I spotted Benzler's Mom over in the church kitchen, where a small flock of townies fawned over her. I pointed across the floor at a woman with thick blonde hair and glasses like her son, though hers had large plastic frames.

"There's your Mom." She carried a few extra pounds over her big bones. That once made her a good match for his Dad, a burly and hairy man. But not anymore.

6

Earlier that day we buried him down at Waldo Cemetery out on Park Street. The funeral party paraded through town past the G & R Tavern, famous for its fried bologna sandwiches. We ran the town's two stoplights, bearing our little purple flags. The caravan of vehicles stretched a quarter mile. It seemed like half the town lined up there. The other half likely could be found in the bars. Right across the street from the G & R sat the Village Tavern, and finally, at the edge of town where Marion street darkened into Rt. 47, a red neon "BAR" ran vertically along the front door, and identified the third establishment.

We followed Jack Klingel's snow plow out to the graveyard, and the car tires crunched on the fresh salt he spread on the icy roads. During the interment, I could hardly hear the words Pastor Brown spoke because of the wind and the driving sleet that stung my face. I reckoned this weather befitted a funeral, bitter, dreary, and gray. It'd be a shame to bury someone on a sunny spring day.

Then we came back to the church for the wake. The Marion Street United Methodist Church rested squarely in the middle of Waldo, Ohio, population 500. That number remained steady for the past three decades. They built this church a hundred years ago in the traditional Western Reserve style with a standard steeple and a bell tower on top.

Folks of various Protestant faiths attended because there weren't enough people out here to divide a congregation into denominations anyway.

They held the wake in an assembly room, just off the main sanctuary. I suppose you could say that the building served many purposes, more like a Community Center than a church.

"What're you gonna do now?" I asked, and looked back at Benzler. "I mean about the farm and all."

Benzler's mouth gaped. I could tell the thought had never occurred to him. "What about the farm? You think we'll have to give up the farm?"

"No, no, no. I'm not saying that. But you remember Jimmy and Jonny." Our friends Jimmy and Jonny Rausch moved to Iowa after their Dad died. "It's just that times are tough with the recession and all." I suddenly felt hot. With the back of my suit sleeve, I wiped the sweat off my forehead.

"I don't know," Benzler dismissed me. "That was different." The idea gnawed on him though, and in a couple of minutes he hurried over to his Mom and butted into her discussion. He asked her the question, and I could read by her desperate brush off that she told him something like, "Not now honey, we can talk about that later."

Watching him suffer, I shifted my weight in my stance. I couldn't imagine not having a Dad. Mom always said, "A boy needs his father." What would happen to Benzler without his?

"She doesn't want to talk about it right now," he said when he returned. "But I can tell she's scared. Thanks a lot. Now I'm worried."

"Sorry. Guess I opened up a can of worms." I tugged at the shirt collar that chafed my neck. "Look, I'm sure you'll stay. Like you said, that was different. Besides, your Grandma and Grandpa live next door."

"Yeah, but those are Dad's parents. Mom's from Indiana."

We silently stared at the people around the room. I licked my cracked lips. My mouth felt stuffed with cotton. I tried to think of something else to talk about. Somehow I sensed that just making normal conversation would help him, or maybe me.

"You coming to school tomorrow?" was all I could come up with.

"Yeah," he responded, defensive. "Why wouldn't I?" His voice cracked.

"I don't know," I grumbled, defensive myself. "Your Dad I guess." I felt as if everything I'd say would upset him.

"Well, if I don't have to I won't," he replied, calmer this time. "But if I stay home I'll have to deal with all of my relative's bullshit."

"So what?"

"Well, my Grandma and Aunts'll just be sitting there at the house bawling, that's what. I'd rather be at school."

Over at the buffet table, folks had spread out potluck items brought from all over: turkey, ham, mashed potatoes, green beans, every type of vegetable. They loved having potlucks around here. Normally this place smelled stale and musty, but the aroma of all this home cooking replaced it now.

"The food line's gone down." I elbowed Benzler in the ribs. "Let's go get some."

"Nah," he declined. "I'm not hungry."

"You gotta eat." I again tried to encourage regular behavior. "They got a terrific spread over there."

"Yeah. Maybe later. I'm just gonna sit here awhile," he responded.

"OK. I'm gettin' some food. I'll be back in a bit." I wandered away from him over to the long table, feeling relieved of a burden. I grabbed a floppy paper plate from the stack, and added another one underneath to beef it up and prevent spillage. I piled on vittles, and then found my Dad, knees together, his own heaped up plate in his lap. He shoveled down his grub while he talked with our pastor. Dad often talked with Pastor Brown, and as the church deacon he did so at length every Sunday.

At forty-two years, Dad kept fit for his age from hard physical labor on the farm. He didn't farm as his primary occupation, he wrote for the local newspaper, the Marion Star. But we lived on the old family farm and he constantly worked on projects on the house, the barn, and grounds. He had a full head of straight brown hair and striking hazel eyes. Neither of my parents were good friends with Benzler's parents. But they knew each other well in such a small town, and always acted friendly toward them.

"…nobody really knows what happened. The boy found…" Dad stopped talking as soon as he saw me.

"Donny, come sit with us." I pulled up a chair next to them, and Pastor Brown greeted me. The warmth of the meal passed right through the flimsy plate to my thighs.

"I saw you sitting over next to Marshall. How's he doing?" Dad asked with a raspy, gravelly voice. Marshall was Benzler's first name, but only adults used that. Around here we typically called each other by our last names unless, you had a nickname. There was Billy Essenheimer, whom we called "Heimer" for short. And then, of course, there was me, Donny Eidegger. Everyone called me "Digger."

11

"OK, I guess. Kinda quiet." I looked sideways at my Dad's profile as he chewed. "For Benzler anyway." I dug into the Ambrosia salad, my favorite. I savored the sweet marshmallow and coconut. It was like eating dessert first.

"What were you all talking about?" I asked.

"Don't worry about it." Dad took another bite of ham, and didn't say any more. What else was there to say in times like these?

Folks in small towns like ours didn't really know how to handle these kinds of tragedies. Believe it or not, acts of God were easier to understand. Tornadoes? Tragic but understandable. Death like this? Hard to fathom. The townsfolk carried on, but it left a scar, not just on the family, but on the town itself.

When the party ended, people passed out of the church into the damp darkness. The winter night came early, and the icy drizzle cloaked the emotions of the town. I returned the few short miles home with my family. Later, I looked out my bedroom window, and couldn't help wondering why nobody'd tell what happened. Not even my best friend. I watched the white lifeless ground below. Snow buried everything, but life went on. In the spring the snow would melt, the grass would turn green, and the ragweed would bloom.

Chapter 2

""Set her loose Jim! We're all right now!" But there warn't no answer, and nobody come out of the wigwam." Ms. Sponseller, our sixth grade teacher butchered the hillbilly accent from *Huckleberry Finn* by Mark Twain. The youngest and prettiest teacher on the faculty, she looked like Cher with her long, straight black hair, and short dresses. Though all of us boys had a bit of a crush on her, I thought that she liked me best.

Ms. Sponseller had never been fond of Benzler, since he acted up in her class; or maybe because he always hummed "Half Breed" around her. As far back as I could remember he had disrupted classrooms. That made the rest of us laugh, but drove the teachers crazy. His father's death hadn't changed much, but Ms. S did treat him more gingerly in the month since. In fact, most kids walked on eggshells around him now. I myself still wondered how he was really doing, though on the outside he put up a good front. He had to be feeling something inside, but he covered it up. I guess when your life changed drastically like that you were expected to suck it up and go on. But I felt

13

like we were all ignoring the signs of a storm coming. I couldn't shut my mind of it.

While I listened to Ms. Sponseller's lilting voice, Benzler dropped a folded up piece of wide-lined paper onto the hardwood floor. Stained with a hundred coats of lacquer, these floors have been vomited on, peed on, and bled on over the years. Scratches, scuffs, and scars showed the age. Originally built as Waldo High School in the twenties, they turned the run-of-the-mill brick schoolhouse into an elementary in the sixties. You could still read, "Waldo High School Est. 1926" clearly etched into the stonework above the front double doors.

Benzler slid the paper back to me with his lumberjack boot. The alphabetical seating chart put me directly behind him. We sat in the last two seats on the left hand side of the classroom, whereas Ms. Sponseller read from her desk clear over on the other side. The giant green chalkboard, the one with a cursive alphabet track that ran across the top, spanned the distance between us.

Benzler sneered at me over his left shoulder, a snaggletooth grin on his face. He nodded his head downward to direct my attention to the floor, but I ignored him, just to get his goat. He sure hated to wait. I'd have even rather listened to *Huck Finn* than pick up his childish note.

14

Ms. Sponseller droned on, part of her daily ritual to try and calm us down after morning recess. I figured I'd tortured Benzler enough, so I finally reached down and picked up the note. I quietly opened it, glanced over his scrawl, and then pushed it back. "I can't read that chicken scratch," I whispered.

He shoved it back at me, and said a little too loudly, "Read it!" He never could whisper.

Sensing Benzler's urgency, I took a closer look. My face flushed, and prickles ran up the back of my neck. Along with his usual nasty remarks primarily about me, he targeted Ms. S with his silly but vicious humor. Across the page he had scribbled a spread-eagle picture of her. The words rape and kill jumped right out at me. This wasn't funny, not even by Benzler's standards. I tried to keep my cool, and just refolded the paper, opened the lid of my desktop, and simply placed it inside.

Benzler craned his neck to look back for my reaction, his mouth open, left eyebrow raised.

"C'mon wuss. Write something back," he demanded.

"I'm not in the mood for your pussy note passing," I countered, trying to hide my embarrassment.

"Marshall. Donny," Ms. Sponseller interrupted. "Be quiet!" Benzler sulked, and turned back around to face the front. The rest of our classmates stared at us. Then he jerked his right leg backward, and hammered my shin with the heel of his boot.

"Ouch," I cried out. The sharp pain shot up my leg.

Ms. Sponseller paused again. "Donald, is there something you'd like to share with the rest of the class?"

"No Ma'am," I replied as I rubbed my shin.

"Well, be quiet then."

"Sorry," I mumbled.

As soon as she got back to the story, I punched Benzler in the meat of his shoulder, but unfortunately, Ms. S. spotted me.

"Donald Eidegger. You stop that now!" On her feet, she raced toward us in the back corner. Her eyes blazed, and her heels clicked like a typewriter on the hardwood floor. Red faced, I sank into my seat, head down, numbed by her angry expression. She grabbed me by the left ear, hoisted me onto my feet, and led me to the front of the class, past the coatroom and out the door.

Benzler snickered, and growled a prolonged, "Digger." The door slammed behind us, and Ms. S. dragged me to the principal's office.

Her perfume sure smelled nice, and despite the rough tug on my ear, I could feel her soft, warm hands.

The principal's office was offset on a split-level mezzanine between the first and second floors. Just inside, an administration counter ran nearly the length of the office.

"Sit down." She directed me to one of two armless, hard-backed waiting chairs. As she walked toward the office, she turned back to me. "Donald...." She shook her head, and turned away.

Alone, outside of Mr. Steinhauser's office I trembled, feeling a little nervous. Though I was no goody two shoes, I got straight A's, and I didn't get into trouble. I listened to a muffled conversation behind the door, but couldn't make out any words.

I braced myself for the worst from Principal Steinhauser. Kids called him Salamander behind his back, and had for as long as I could remember. I never knew where it came from, but he didn't find it complimentary.

In a minute he stepped out of the office wearing a white shirt with a skinny black tie. Tall and thin, with a thickening waist, he combed over his slick black hair to cover his balding head. His nose protruded like a Roman statue, but it was those eyes that stood out. Piercing, sharp, they drilled right into me when he spoke.

17

"Donald," he rumbled slowly, with his deep bass voice. A flick of his hand ordered me in.

I trailed behind him, my tail between my legs. Steinhauser proceeded to sit in his green, leather, high-backed chair, and I took yet another standard school issue wooden chair. These chairs made a student more uncomfortable, but I guess that was the point. Ms. S. stepped out, and passed me without even a glance. I guiltily watched her dress waft by. So much for being her pet.

Mr. Steinhauser swiveled around to face me. I fidgeted in my chair, and kept my head down to avoid his eyes. "Donald, look at me." I looked up, but still eluded his eyes by watching his pudgy fingers clutch a cup of coffee. He went on, "I'm going to be blunt. You punched a classmate." He stopped and took a sip from his steaming mug. "Under no circumstances is that kind of behavior acceptable. Do you care to explain yourself?"

I stammered, "Uh. Well, Marshall is my friend. And, um. We were just messing around. I didn't hurt him." I licked my lips to fight my cottonmouth.

"That's no excuse. Striking another student is strictly forbidden. And I most definitely do not encourage horseplay of any kind. Is that clear?" Salamander stopped and glared once more into my skull.

18

I mustered out a weak, "Yes sir."

He hardly recognized my response. "Now, since you're not typically a troublemaker, I'm just going to give you a strong warning." The principal got up, and walked to the window. "But, I will also make an example out of you. You are to stand in the corner outside of my office during the lunch period." His index finger pointed out the emphasis of each command. "You will keep your face in the corner. You will not look at or speak to anyone. When the final bell rings, you will report back in here to me." He paused for effect. "Is that clear?"

"Yes," I answered softly, relieved by the small penalty.

"Is that clear?" he asked again like a drill sergeant.

"Yes sir," I repeated more firmly.

"One last piece of advice," he added with a creepy smile. "I recommend that you stay away from Marshall Benzler. He IS a troublemaker, and will definitely lead you down the wrong path. Go on now, get out of here." He whisked me away with the back of his hand.

Out in the hallway, I stuck my nose into the corner by the stairwell outside of the principal's office. From two inches away, I stared at the green plaster walls, and just waited. My mind drifted back to the note. What the hell was with Benzler? Had he lost it? He'd

19

always been a bit off, but that's what I liked about him. Now, I felt a strange and awful churn in my stomach.

The noon bell officially kicked off the lunch hour. The quiet hallways filled with muffled voices and shuffling feet. Eyes front, I could hear the voices of small children from downstairs. As sixth graders, Benzler and I came from upstairs. The mob of lemmings approached, but I curbed the urge to look around.

I felt the movement of bodies behind me as the commotion peaked. Most kids knew better than to mess with a Steinhauser victim, let alone a sixth grader, so they left me be. Most kids, but not Benzler.

"Digger. Surprise, surprise, surprise," I recognized Benzler's voice immediately as he mimicked Gomer Pyle. "What the heck are you doing here?" I didn't acknowledge him, especially since I could see Mr. Steinhauser out of the corner of my eye.

Benzler put his hand on my left shoulder and whispered in my ear, "Ha ha, they got you this time, buddy."

Mr. Steinhauser pounced. "Benzler, what do you think you're doing?"

Benzler didn't care much for Mr. Steinhauser, and in defiance he kept talking to me. "Did that asshole Salamander give you any whacks?"

I didn't have time to reply, because Steinhauser rushed out of the office, his forehead vein ready to burst. He jerked Benzler by his skinny arm back into his office. The glass rattled with the force of the slam. His secretary looked at me with a surprised "oh no" look on her face. I couldn't help but chuckle, and shake my head.

Around that time, Ms. S returned. She brushed by me briskly, her forehead furrowed deeper than I'd ever seen. As she turned I noticed that she clutched a piece of folded paper. My breath stopped. She'd found Benzler's note. With all it contained.

Shortly thereafter, despite the closed door, I could hear the high-pitched smacks as Salamander gave Benzler repeated whacks, too many to count. Obviously, Benzler's Dad's death hadn't softened him any.

By the sixth grade, Benzler got whacks for almost nothing. I don't know if they kept records, but he surely held the one for the most whacks in a career.

The hallways cleared out meanwhile, and I kept my face in the corner and waited. Eventually, Benzler skulked out of Steinhauser's office. His head faced down, but his angry eyes lightened up when he saw me. He winked as he passed me by.

Whenever you got into trouble at school, a letter went home with you. Your parents needed to sign it, and then you brought it back to school the next day. That evening I procrastinated telling my parents, and I anxiously watched the clock as the time to tell them ran out.

I found my Mom down in our living room, ironing clothes in front of the television. Then I fetched my Dad from his downstairs workshop. When he entered, he immediately fiddled with the TV reception, wiggling the rabbit ears, and banging on the top.

"Just turn it off," Mom said. "Donald wants to speak to us." Once I had their attention, I fumbled through my rehearsed speech. "I need you guys to sign something."

"Get your feet off the couch Donald." My Mom interrupted because I'd pulled my legs up in front of me as a defensive barrier. I put them back down, and started over.

"I got in trouble at school today." I went on to finish my story, and sat still, tense, awaiting the firing squad.

Then, after all of that worrying, they didn't even give me any grief. None whatsoever. They laughed at me, for goodness sakes. I guess since I rarely got into trouble, and tended to be so serious, they actually liked it when I got ornery, though they never said so. Dad gave me his patented lecture about the importance of an education, but that was all.

The next morning, Benzler missed the school bus. Then he didn't attend first or second period. I finally ran into him in the hallway, as he came out of the office. When he looked up at me, I saw his bloodshot, sunken eyes, and the puffy face.

"Where've you been?" I asked.

"I don't wanna talk about it," he grumbled. It looked like his Mom didn't take the trouble yesterday very well. When Benzler's Dad was still alive, his family shared the same "boys will be boys" attitude of my parents. In the month since the tragedy, Benzler told me how his Mom's been acting weird. She just sat on the couch, cried constantly, and hardly paid attention to anything, including her kids.

"What happened? What'd they say about the note?" I had to ask. Thinking about that note freaked me out, also since Ms. S. found it in my desk.

"I said I don't wanna talk about it."

Then his mom came out of the office. She looked worse than he did, unkempt, sloppy clothes, hair a mess. She stared right at me, but said nothing, as if I weren't even there.

"Gotta go," Benzler said, and turned away from me. I just stood there with my mouth open, and watched the pair escape. I could only guess what happened that night, but obviously it wasn't good.

Chapter 3

Marshall Benzler stifled his contempt for his mother. You just weren't supposed to hate your mom, and that was that. But he didn't really hate her, he was just pissed that she was making him see a psychiatrist. Now she treated him like he was rotten, like some leftover compost. All because of those silly, dirty pictures he drew of his teacher. Well, that and she blamed him for his Dad.

He watched her switch on the windshield wiper knob with her chubby fingers. Dime sized drops of rain pelted the Chevy Suburban as his mother steered the car down Newmans-Cardington Road. She hadn't always been fat. He could still remember her lithe frame from when he was younger, and how she would pick him up for a cuddle. He couldn't remember the last time she'd hugged him. Not since his Dad died. Somehow all this was embodied in her fat, sloppiness, which upset him even more. She needed the shrink, not him.

After her husband's death, many concerned folks close to the family gave her well-intentioned, though unsolicited advice. A few suggested counseling for her and the children, which just made her angry. Not to mention the financials with the current economy. She didn't even know if insurance covered any of this. But this latest school incident was the last straw, and she finally gave in.

Mrs. Benzler pulled onto two-lane State Route 423, which headed right into the southern end of the town of Marion. She drove slowly, so that other cars constantly passed on their left.

Since Waldo didn't have any psychiatrists or even psychologists, Mrs. Benzler sought out the nearest opportunity. Located about a 10-minute drive north of Waldo, Marion looked strikingly similar to thousands of villages across the Midwest.

After she reviewed the short list of options, Rosemary selected Dr. Randall Stevenson. Though he had settled in this fairly remote rural outpost, he ranked as one of the most accomplished and reputable psychiatrists in the state. So she arranged an appointment for Marshall to meet him.

Filled with dread on the drive to town, Benzler thought of ways to get out of this, but he found no escape. "So what's this guy like?" the boy asked, and his voice cracked at the end. His mother's flowered hat and scarf blocked his view of her face, and she wore sunglasses, though the dark skies made that unnecessary.

"Don't you worry about him," she curtly replied. "He's a very nice, very smart man who can help you."

"I don't need any help," he groused under his breath.

She jerked her head toward him like a bird, cocked up her sunglasses, and gave him the evil eye. But she made no further response, and he asked no more questions.

They arrived at the office, a stately Victorian mansion that rested where Delaware Avenue split in a "Y" into Main and State Streets. In a more prosperous time, it used to be the residence of one of Marion's elite citizens. But nearly all of the grand homes of that era had evolved into businesses over the years.

Benzler followed his Mom to the receptionist, a small, bespectacled woman who directed them to the waiting room. Though the reception and waiting areas used to be someone's living room, the alcohol smell made it seem sterile, typical of a doctor's office. It felt like a neat freak's house, where you weren't allowed to touch anything in fear of making a smudge. Benzler did nothing while they sat, and his anxiety peaked. A chilly numbness flooded his heart. *"I don't need any help,"* echoed in his mind. But he knew he really did.

When the receptionist signaled to them, Benzler sheepishly tailed his mother into the office.

"Come on in, Mrs. Benzler. Marshall."

"Good afternoon, Dr. Stevenson," Mrs. Benzler greeted him cordially. "It's so nice to see you again. I'm anxious to get this started." Her energy surprised Benzler, who hadn't seen her get off the couch in weeks.

The doctor motioned his hand toward the chairs. "Please have a seat." Tall, middle-aged, with a finely groomed gray-black beard, he sat down in the chair across from them. He crossed his leg, grasping his knee with his hands, while his kindly eyes surveyed them both.

"Hello Marshall. I'm Dr. Stevenson," he began. "I've heard a little bit about you and your situation from your mother. I'd like to spend today just getting to know one another." Benzler just scowled, and slumped in his chair, arms crossed. The doctor proceeded to review some basic therapy ground rules, and meeting details. Benzler's Mom excused herself shortly after the doctor's opening spiel. Benzler noticed that she hadn't even removed her hat or glasses.

"Alright then, now it's just us," said Dr. Stevenson, who sat up and clapped his hands together. The pit in Benzler's stomach pushed bile into his mouth. Though angry at his Mom, he wished she'd stayed.

Though the doctor sat not two feet from him, he felt completely alone. "Now, we can really get down to business." The doctor cleared his throat, and stared at the boy's right knee, which bobbed like a mini jackhammer. Benzler caught the focus of the doctor's attention, and stopped it. The doctor went on. "Marshall, can you tell me how you feel right now?"

Benzler shifted in his chair, and a puzzled look came over his face. His knee again hammered away, but Benzler couldn't muster any words. The doctor spied on him over the top of his glasses. "I could sit here, and lecture you the whole session, but I'll be honest with you, that'll get us nowhere.

Benzler clenched his jaw shut tight. If he started to talk, perhaps the flood would break down his dam. He had so much to hide.

Neither the boy nor the man spoke for awhile. The doctor stood, and ambled over to the window. Benzler steadied himself with the constant ticking of a clock that rested on the small, wooden table in front of him. The clock faced so that only the doctor could see its hands. Soon, Benzler knee bobbed in time with the tick.

"C'mon Marshall. Talk to me. Tell me why you're here."

"Look man, I don't need to be here," Benzler burst, then he quickly shut down again.

28

Unfazed, the doctor grabbed hold of this. "OK, let's work with that." He stood behind his chair, and held its back. "Let's assume you don't need to be here, OK? But your mother does. I can help you work better with your Mom."

This approach calmed the boy somewhat, and he searched the doctor's face. "OK," he agreed.

"Great," the doctor said, excited. He returned to his seat. "Let's start over." He stroked his beard as he leaned forward. "OK, we're just talking now. Marshall, describe to me, in any way you can, how you feel right now."

The boy's knee hammered away again. "I don't know. Pfft. Bored I guess." *Bored, ha!* He didn't mention that he felt like he'd been skinned alive, completely exposed.

"That's OK, that's OK." The doctor chuckled. "I'd like to think that, over time, you'll see some benefit from our meetings. At a minimum you shouldn't be bored." Dr. Stevenson paused to allow Benzler to comment, but he didn't.

"How about school? Can you tell me how things are going at school?" Benzler thought, here it came. He prepared for the lecture on how sick and depraved his pictures were.

"School's OK." Benzler looked down at the doctor's black dress shoes, and avoided any eye contact.

"Grades?" With soft eyes, the doctor pleaded with Benzler. He spoke carefully, as if he tried to coax a trapped animal out of a hole.

"Not that good." Benzler stole another glance at the doctor's face, but quickly diverted to the clock.

"What's that all about?" the doctor asked, finding a point to dive deeper.

"I don't know," Benzler said blandly, and he reached over to pick up the clock. He noticed a dark spot on the wood, where it had stood.

"Are you having trouble with any particular subject, or all of them in general?"

Benzler didn't respond right away, and fixed his eyes on the clock in his hands. He put it up to his ear and listened. The ticking steadied him.

"Marshall?" the doctor prodded. "Put that down please."

Benzler looked up straight into the doctor's eyes and said, "Look, maybe I'm just stupid." He replaced the clock roughly back onto the table surface facing him.

"Whoa, whoa, slow down," Dr. Stevenson rebuffed, hands up in a weak surrender. His smile beamed, but his eye betrayed a hint of tension. "I'm not saying you're stupid at all." He picked up some transcripts from his desk and raised them up. "In fact your school records indicate quite the opposite."

The doctor thumbed through the records. "Sometimes troubles in school, changes so to speak, are indicators, or signs of something other than a lack of intelligence, that's all I'm saying." Benzler looked out the window. Outside the rain came down hard on the glass, and thunder grumbled in the distance like an empty stomach.

Dr. Stevenson oriented the clock back into its designated place, as he foraged on. "Can you describe your relationship with your mother?"

Benzler immediately responded, "It's good. Good." His eyes flickered for a moment then again died. No way would he ever talk to this guy about his Mom.

The doctor observed closely as the boy continued to look outside. "Can you tell me about some of your friends?"

"They're good. No problems." The doctor continued to ask open-ended questions, and Benzler quickly realized that he wasn't going to be confronted on the pictures. He replied to each one of the questions

31

with a coiled, flippant response. Pause, question, brief response. This game went on for the remainder of the session. The two boxed and danced around the ring, the doctor with his thoughtful jabs, the young patient valiantly defending himself. Throughout Benzler constantly squirmed in his chair, visibly uncomfortable with the interview.

As they approached the end of the hour, Dr. Stevenson stroked on the tender underbelly of the family troubles. "I know some of the details around your father's suicide." Benzler flinched as if in pain. "What I don't have is your version of the story. I'm not sure you're ready to tell it. Are you willing to talk about it?"

"Nope," Benzler stated bluntly. His arms crossed, wrapped around him as if to keep him closed tight.

Dr. Stevenson grinned as he had through most of the session. "That's fine, that's fine. I don't want to push you. Later on though, that's something that we're going to have to address." He looked at Marshall closely to check his reaction. Marshall just looked down, sullen, expressionless.

"OK, Marshall. That about does it for today." Dr. Stevenson rose, and extended his hand. "It was nice to meet you and begin our adventure together. I'll see you next week."

Benzler weakly shook his hand. "Some adventure," he grumbled. "Can I go now?"

"Yes, of course. Your mother should be waiting for you."

Benzler's Mom picked him up when the session ended at five, and they walked out to the car together. He hunched down, and pulled the collar of his jacket up. For now the rain had stopped, but one look up told that wouldn't last.

Once they were seated in the car she asked him, "So how did it go?"

"OK," he replied in the same tone as he had with the doctor.

"What does that mean?"

"All we did was sit there and talk."

"Well, you better get something out of this." Her white knuckles gripped the steering wheel. "I'm not paying this quack for nothing."

*   *   *

Chapter 4

I pedaled my bike hard down Whetstone River Rd. The road, in fact, wound along the banks of a river, but the map called it the Olentangy. I guess the name Whetstone came years ago from locals because of the hard limestone and shale riverbed. From Whetstone, I biked the five straight and flat miles that separated Benzler's house from mine. Probably only a dozen or so farms inhabited the route, scattered among the cornfields and woods filled with ragweed.

Ragweed got its name from farmers because they always used rags to wipe their noses while they worked the fields during pollinating season. Ragweed sounded much easier. We had them all over our land, but because they looked so common and ordinary most people didn't even notice them. Unless you suffered allergies. Luckily, I didn't, but Benzler had every allergy imaginable. Spring, summer, and fall he carried his own stupid snotrag that hung from his back pocket. The allergies suited him somehow.

My chest heaved as I turned down Benzler Road for the stretch run to his house. Many families in the county had owned the same property for a hundred years, so a lot of my friends lived on roads named after them. That wasn't uncommon anywhere, only here the families still lived in the same places.

The first thing I saw as I got closer was the big white barn with a twenty foot Mail Pouch chewing tobacco ad on the side. Benzler came out of their barn in overalls and workboots. I swore sometimes he only invited me over to do his work for him. His family owned at least a hundred head of Black Angus, and they needed tending.

While we worked, I couldn't help but notice his Dad's old office down at the end. Farm machinery lay stacked in front of the door in a feeble cover up. Benzler did his best to not even look in that direction.

My shovel slid under another cow paddy, and I tossed it aside. I never minded cows much. I preferred them to pigs at least. Benzler's neighbors, the Wertzes kept pigs which stunk to high heaven.

"Been down to hang out with your Miss Piggy lately?" That was the Wertz's daughter, and I liked to needle him about her. They named her Becky, and she looked pretty decent for a pig farmer. Her Dad acted a bit crazy though.

"Shut up." He blew his nose into his rag again. "Why do you always keep up with that crap?"

"Because it's so obvious." I chuckled and shoveled some more crap. "I don't know why you won't admit it."

His face reddened like a blonde Raggedy Andy. "Well, knock that shit off."

35

"Yeah, sure," I said. But I stopped.

After we finished the chores, we headed upstairs to the loft. Hay and straw bales stood dozens of feet high on all sides. We each took a couple of turns swinging on a rope from the rafters, and release ourselves into the loose stuff below.

"Mom says we gotta move," Benzler utters.

"What? I thought your Grandpa and Uncle were helping out."

"She want to move to my other grandparents."

"In Indiana?"

He didn't answer. He just climbed on up to take his turn. This time he went up higher than our usual launching pad. "Digger, watch me," he called out as he held the rope.

"I dare you." I stood and watched from the floor. "You're gonna kill yourself."

The grin disappeared from his face, he set his jaw, and kicked off. From this height he made a tremendous arc, which curved gracefully until he let go. His body flew, and crashed into the stack of bales on the far side. I gasped, and started over to him. He jumped up with skewed glasses, but unhurt. "Your turn man."

I climbed up to our usual spot, and grabbed the rope.

"C'mon man. Go up higher," he called. Sometimes I felt pressure to follow his lead and risk life and limb, but I always stopped short. I couldn't leave my senses the way he could. I shoved off from the usual place, and Benzler blew a giant raspberry at me.

The next time he climbed as high as he could, so that his head almost touched the rafters of the barn roof. "Watch this, wimp."

"Benzler, stop." I felt embarrassed showing my fear. But this went beyond his normal daredevil stunts. At this height, he could get seriously hurt. He stopped and observed me from on high. I watched him think it over for what seem like an eternity. But then he dropped the rope, and climbed back down.

He walked past me, shaking his head. It reminded me of my father, the coach when I made a mistake in sports.

Sun streamed through the open barn door, and thousands of dust particles floated in it, and made it smoky. We left the barn, and fresh air washed over me. Though only May, the hayloft had probably hit at least 100 by now. We walked toward the house, both of us covered with straw and hay, the grainy particles stuck to our sweaty faces and arms.

"I'm thirsty," I complained. "Let's get something to drink."

"Where do you think we're going, pussy?" He scratched at the red blotches all over his arms.

I knocked him off balance with a push. "You're the pussy."

He shoved me back and took off. "Race you to the house," he called back from his head start. His long limbs flailed as he ran, knock-kneed. I raced past him easily. My Dad always said he was slower than molasses in January, whatever that meant. I waited for him at the house, where he hacked and gagged for at least a minute.

"Beat you again, loser," I said when he recovered. I victor should never miss a chance to taunt the loser. Especially after his smugness back at the barn.

Benzler threw a harmless elbow at me as we approached the house, which was white with black trim to match the barn. A picket fence marked the border of the yard. A Colonial eagle made of iron sat in the peak above the front door atop a "D" insignia.

We climbed the trio of stairs into the screened back porch. Kukla, Benzler's big Husky, laid in the middle of the floor, the mop of hair rising with each pant. His tongue stretched out onto the floorboards. We stepped over the dog into the kitchen, and the stench from a ripe trash can hit me like a slap in the face. Benzler grabbed a couple of sodas out of the fridge. Kukla jumped up and followed us into the house.

"You're lucky, Benzler. My Mom never lets us have pop," I exclaimed.

"Hell, we're lucky there's anything in the fridge at all." He handed me one of the cans, the cheap kind, RC Cola. We both pressed the cold containers against our sweaty foreheads. "Yeah, it's nothing but paradise around here." Benzler kicked over a stack of newspapers, disgusted. "Look at this place. It's a pigsty." I scanned the kitchen. Flies buzzed over dirty dishes stacked up in the sink. Junk cluttered the table and counter tops. As we left the kitchen, my shoes stuck to the linoleum like in a movie theater.

"So what's this about moving?" I asked. He shushed me with his finger to the lips. We whisked the Cokes upstairs, stepping gingerly so as not to unsettle his Mom. A fan whirred in Benzler's bedroom window, and the cool air felt good against my moist, itchy skin. Benzler climbed to the top of the unmade bunk bed, which he shared with his little brother. A giant *Aerosmith* poster papered the wall next to where he slept. His long legs dangled down, and swung back and forth. The messy room matched the kitchen.

"What's up with your Mom?" I whispered.

"I don't know. She's just not the same," Benzler finally answered, and his voice trailed off. "I guess that's why she wants to move back home."

I opened the pop, and shoved the pull tab into the can. I guzzled until the liquid burn forced me to stop. I knelt down at his desk and pulled a book out of his bookcase. "Fourth Down Showdown," by Bill Hogan. Sports books dominated his bookcase selection. Right next to his desk a Cincinnati Reds trash can served as storage for balls of all kinds.

"So, you can read?" I asked in fake surprise. I checked his reaction, but he didn't take the bait. I couldn't see him sit still long enough to read one book, let alone all of these. "Are you even going to pass this year or what?"

He picked up my serious tone. "What do you mean?"

"Man, I sit right behind you." I pushed the novel back into its slot. "I've seen the grades you've been getting."

Benzler looked down at me with a curious smirk on his face. "But.."

"But nothin'," I cut him off. "You just need to do some work, lazy ass."

"Screw it," he said, and something odd in his eyes made me uneasy, a glazed over look.

"I can help you," I pleaded, but he looked away. "Suit yourself then."

I turned my attention to a half-finished model B-17 bomber in the middle of his desk with glue spattered all over the place. "This sure is a lousy job," I jabbed at him. He threw a pillow, which barely missed me and instead knocked over a stack of cans from his meager beer can collection.

With the clatter of the metal, Benzler froze. He raised his hands to stop action, his ear cocked. We waited for a word from his Mom, but heard nothing but the hum of the fan.

When the threat passed, I picked up another model, this one a sleek, red corvette. "Pretty nice."

Silence smothered the room, finally interrupted by Benzler's meek, "My Dad did that one." As much as I tried to avoid it, I stepped right into that one. Everything pointed back to his Dad. I wanted to know more about what happened, and then again I didn't. In either case I felt too awkward to ask him about it. It seemed like we'd slipped right back to the funeral, and I still didn't know what to say.

"He's the one who liked doing models," Benzler spoke up again. "I think it's boring, but the doctor says it's a good idea." Benzler's eyes softened and his cheeks slumped.

"Doctor?" I asked. "Are you sick or something?"

"Nope," he replied. I rolled the Corvette back and forth across his desk, and his eyes followed the car.

"What's the doctor for then?"

"Mom makes me go," he answered.

I stopped the car, and looked directly at him. "Yeah, but what for?"

He held my gaze for a moment, and then turned away. "I don't know. My Dad I guess. And the trouble at school."

"No shit? So what's new about that?"

"You know. My grades, and like the other day."

"What?"

"C'mon man. Those pictures I drew. The suspension."

I thought about the disturbed note, and his punishment. I took another sip from my soda, and then stared at the can in my hand. I asked, "What's a whack feel like?" At this, Benzler broke into a cocky smile.

"You never got one?" I shook my head in the negative. "Never ever?" he repeated, only this time with an edge.

"I said no!" It came out too loudly. My face flushed, and a buzz climbed the back of my neck.

"Christ calm down, man." He looked down at me with disdain.

"He only made me stand in the hall that one day. That was your fault too," I replied.

"My fault? You were the one who got caught." He had it right again. For my part in that incident Mrs. Sponseller blew her stack a little, but still, I more or less got away pain free compared to Benzler. He added, "Man, you should have seen your face when Sponseller had you by the ear. I thought for sure she was coming for me." I didn't laugh, as I didn't think it was funny.

"So, what does it feel like?" I asked again.

"What?"

"The whacks, numbnuts."

"Stings like a bitch. Especially when Old Sal uses the paddle with the holes." His legs kicked more with his enthusiasm. He leaned so far forward, I thought he might fall off.

"Holes?"

Benzler rubbed his chin as he thought for a minute. "Yeah, he's got different paddles: wood ones, metal ones, some with holes, some without."

"What are the holes for?"

"I don't know. What am I? A paddle expert?"

"Well, you've been whacked by enough of 'em." We both laughed at that one. The laughter cut the tension immediately, and the old Benzler smile emerged briefly.

After the mirth died down, I went over to his window and looked over the top of his fan down into his front yard. The spinning blade vibrated through my hands and up my arms. The blue light of clarity lit in my brain. I spun and looked at him. "You're seeing a psychiatrist."

His smile vanished. "Look at the fuckin' genius. Nice going, Sherlock."

"What for?"

"I already told you. My Mom makes me go," he snapped back. "I don't want to talk about it."

Silence cloaked us again. It was hard to imagine our laughter just a moment ago. I decided to push on.

"What do you do at the shrink's?"

"Nothing much." He sighed, not wanting to go there. "We just sit and talk."

"About what?"

"He just asks me questions, and I answer them."

"What kinds of questions?" His pauses between answers grew along with the tension that again filled the room. He stopped bouncing on the bed, flopped down on his back, and remained quiet. The window fan roared behind him.

"Just questions, for Pete's sake," he squeaked. "Now you're the one asking me questions."

I waited another minute then repeated, "No really, what kind of questions does he ask?"

He flung the other pillow on his bed at me, and I caught it. "He asks me why all of my friends are such wusses, especially you. Now shut up about it."

"All right, all right." I retreated again to the window, and looked out at the sun setting. The beautiful soft purple melted to gray. My eyes rested on a solitary dandelion, the only blemish on the dark green lawn. It dawned on me then how late it had gotten.

"Damn, it's late, I gotta get home."

"You're always late, Digger." Benzler looked at me dejectedly, upset over my leaving. He forced a smile. "Your Mom never does anything to you." Usually when I was late, I figured I might as well be really late and make it worth my while. Today Mom said I could come over here for an hour, but I'd already stayed all afternoon.

"Yeah, but I can only push her so far," I said and hurried to his door.

45

He followed me down the stairs, and out to my bike. "You want me to come over tomorrow?" he asked. I looked up at him, his face drawn. I thought of his Mom back inside on the couch, and understood.

"Yeah sure." I threw my leg over the banana seat on my red Schwinn five-speed. "After church."

His eyes brightened up, and his fake smile became more real. "Hey Digger," he called. "You won't tell anyone will ya?" I shook my head no.

Kukla barked after me as I wheeled down the driveway. Benzler stood and waved at me like a stick figure. My mind raced in pace with the twirling bike tires. I just had to get out of there fast. I worried about Benzler. I worried about him needing a psychiatrist. And what about his Mom? His Dad definitely screwed up their lives. But he would get over it wouldn't he? He had to. My legs burned as I pumped them harder through the familiar five mile ride home, past the stench of the Wertz farm, through the rustle of the corn. I rode home to the buzz of the locusts.

*   *   *

Chapter 5

"I can't wait for tonight," I told Benzler as we slowly strolled out of the school. The littler kids ran past us in a race to be the first outside for recess.

"Yeah, me too. It's gonna be great." Those were his words, but his shallow eyes betrayed them.

The end of the school year drew near, and summer break loomed. As 6th graders we faced our last days here at Waldo Elementary, and one of the final recesses of our lives. Next year we'd be in Junior High. At recess, the faculty restricted students to the back of the school. Blacktop ran the length of the building and then some. Beyond that, a sizable grass lawn stretched all the way to a chain-linked fence that bordered Highway 23, and marked the boundary of the school property. On the south side of the grounds sat an outdoor full basketball court, and on the north, a baseball diamond.

Billy Essenheimer tracked us as we walked, and grabbed Benzler from behind. "Did you see Hank Aaron's home run last night?" he bubbled too loudly. We let "Heimer" tag along with us sometimes, though he could be loud and pushy, and he and Benzler argued a lot. As tall as Benzler, he was pudgier, a big kid. He also wore glasses, but Heimer had greasy brown hair and already had pimples. He lived two

47

miles from me in the opposite direction from Benzler on Firstenberger Road.

"So what?" Benzler shot him down. He wiped his nose with his ever-present rag. The smell of fresh cut grass filled the air, which always got Benzler's nose going. That, and the unkempt field of weeds on the other side of the fence.

"Whaddya mean so what?" Heimer rebutted, alarmed by the icy reception. "You do know that he beat Babe Ruth's record, don't you?"

Benzler stopped. "You think I live on Mars?" he yelled in Heimer's face.

Heimer pulled his hands out of his pockets, and raised them in surrender. "Easy man. I'm just talking here."

I stepped between them, irritated by Benzler's attitude. "You don't have to get so uptight about it." They both stood a half a head taller than me, though Heimer surely outweighed Benzler. Hell, I probably weighed as much as him.

"I know," Benzler replied, calmer. "It's just not that big of a deal to me right now."

We ducked into an alcove on the east side of the school building to escape the clouds and drizzle that filled the June sky. A door entered into the gymnasium there, but it always remained locked. Benzler and I liked to hang out in this niche, out of sight of the playground monitor, Mrs. Riggles. Inside, we sat down with our backs pressed against the jagged bricks. Heimer stood and leaned against the entrance wall.

"What do you mean it's not a big deal?" he kept after Benzler. "You're the one's always boring the shit out of us with baseball trivia."

"Yeah, Benzler, you love baseball," I added.

Benzler rolled up the sleeves on his denim jacket, and proclaimed, "I love the Reds, not the Braves numbnuts."

"I know that," Heimer said. "But still, it's a big record and all. It deserves mention."

"So you mentioned it. Big whoop," Benzler replied. "Besides, he beat Ruth's record two months ago. Now beat it." Heimer shook his head, tucked his chin in, and left us.

Once Heimer got out of earshot, I said, "What's the matter with you, man? You're being a jerk." Benzler frowned but didn't respond. He pulled a pack of Marlboros out of the front pocket of his denim jacket. "What the hell are you doing?" I gasped. "Put those away." Sure, we'd experimented with smoking out in the barn and stuff. Still, he didn't really smoke.

I watched him put the cigarettes away with a sour look on his face. He finally spoke. "I guess some things are just more important than baseball."

"No shit. Like since when are you dumb enough to smoke at school?" I asked.

"Well, maybe it's not my last year here, that's all." He stated this matter-of-factly, as if he were telling me that he'd had eggs for breakfast. He tended to drop bombshells like that.

"What the hell are you talking about?" I replied.

"Mrs. S. told me I might flunk," he explained. "Then I'll be held back." Have some bacon with those eggs, sir.

"How can you flunk?"

"I don't know… grades I guess."

I rolled my eyes. "Of course it's the friggin' grades. But only dumbfucks flunk. You get decent grades."

"I used to, but not lately." He pulled a crumpled test paper out of a pocket and tossed it to me.

I spread it out over my knees to smooth out the wrinkles. Math.

"Another F?" I turned to him, and could tell he was embarrassed, despite his wry smile. "You didn't even fill out half of the answers. Man, this is easy stuff…" My voice trailed off as I could see he took offense.

"I guess I'm not the brain like you," he replied with sarcasm.

A pumpkin-sized red rubber ball bounced into our alcove, by accident. A small blonde-haired third grade boy hustled over toward us to fetch it. When he came close, Benzler jumped up and kicked the ball as hard as he could. The ball sailed up and smashed square into the boy's nose.

The kid stopped and stared fearfully at Benzler, then began to cry.

"Go on. Get the hell outta here," Benzler shouted, and waved him off. The boy ran away holding his nose. Benzler chuckled.

"You're such an asshole," I told him.

"What? For that? That kid's a punk," he replied in self-defense.

"But you didn't have to do that," I scolded.

He ripped the test paper out of my hands. "Who cares?" He crumpled it back up, and threw it in the corner.

I stared at the paper, and neither of us spoke. A dump truck rumbled down Highway 23, making a helluva racket.

"You boys come on out of there." Mrs. Riggles's rich alto voice cracked our stalemate. Her knee length overcoat nearly met her dry rain

51

boots at the knee. The small blonde boy trailed behind her. A rim of dried blood caked to the rim of his left nostril. "Marshall, Alan says you kicked the ball in his face on purpose. What do you have to say for yourself?"

We came out of the cave, and Benzler scowled. "I kicked the ball, but it hit him by accident." Alan recoiled at this, and he looked from Mrs. Riggles to Benzler and back. A gust of wind blew, and Mrs. Riggles clamped her hat down more tightly over her bright red hair.

"Donald?" she asked. All three of them locked in on me.

"I don't think he did it on purpose." My answer satisfied Mrs. Riggles.

"Very well. Marshall, in any case I feel Alan is due an apology."

"I'm not apologizing to that twit," he cried. Mrs. R's austere look changed Benzler's tune. "Oh, all right," he mumbled. "I'm sorry."

The boy did not appear appeased, but that ended the drama anyway. As she walked away, Mrs. R pointed at her eyes, then at us and mouthed "I'm watching you."

Once we retreated back to our hiding place, I continued our discussion. "Does your Mom know? I mean about you flunking."

"She doesn't care. You've seen her. She just sits there all day," he complained while he paced. "She doesn't even know I'm alive except

52

to bitch me out from time to time." He gestured wildly with both arms. "She'll just take this as one more reason for us to leave." His voice drifted off.

"Is there any way you can still pass?" I asked.

"I don't know. Maybe." We viewed some kids swing back and forth on the swing set. Old and worn tractor tires, of various sizes, and faded colors served as an obstacle course of sorts. A group of students played kickball on the ball field to our left. Though the district couldn't afford new equipment, they kept the old stuff pretty well-maintained.

"There's finals in each subject," he resumed. "I s'pose if I ace those, I'll be OK."

"I can help you." I jumped up, excited to help my friend.

Disinterested, he shrugged, "I don't know."

"Man, do you want to be back here next year?" I pleaded with him.

"It's not so bad."

"Not so bad? Are you shittin' me? We treat flunkies like dirt. You wanna be like that? What's the matter with you?" The din of the other children resounded. The shouts and laughter contrasted to Benzler's blank, drawn face. I choked out, "Is it your Dad?"

I hadn't had the courage to bring this up before, but the leap in Benzler's eyes told me I'd hit it spot on. He kicked a pebble across the asphalt playground.

"I don't know," Benzler said, then stopped. "He used to help me with my homework." Then more animated he blurted out, "I hate my life." He dropped his head down into his hands. "And my Mom. You've seen her." In a voice I could barely hear, he said, "I don't want to talk about it."

In fact, I didn't want to talk about it, either. Once more, I couldn't think of anything to say. I wished I was one of those people like my Mom, who just talked and talked, and always knew the right thing to say. But I wasn't. What did you say to someone about this? My friend fell apart right in front of me, and I couldn't do a thing about it.

"How 'bout your doctor, can't he help?" Benzler didn't even look up at me, he just shook his head.

"Man, that guy's worthless." We remained in silence until the bell rang. The noisy playground mellowed as the kids formed lines at the breezeway to go back inside. One by one the children filed into the school, youngest classes first.

Benzler made no movement to go back towards the school. I started to walk out of the alcove when he mumbled, "I found him you know." His voice sounded like an opening crypt. My skin tingled.

I slowly turned back to face him. "What?"

"My Dad." He rubbed his eyes and nose with the back of his hand. "I found him."

"What do you mean?"

"He blew his friggin' head off, that's what I mean. Blew it off with a twelve gauge." He marched off the other way, abruptly while I reeled in shock. No one had ever told me that his Dad had committed suicide. Scenes rushed through my mind, the closed casket, the barricaded office in the barn, the look on my Dad's face at the funeral.

"Benzler, hold on a minute," I called, but he kept walking. "C'mon man, wait up." I sprinted after him. "Hey man, I just want to help. I can tutor you or something." What a stupid thing to say, I thought.

"I don't need your help. Just leave me alone." I let him go, and he never even looked back. I turned and joined my other classmates in line. Mrs. Riggles flashed her disapproving look when I walked up late. Benzler didn't return to class the rest of the day.

Later that afternoon, Heimer snuck up behind me at my locker. "Did you hear? Benzler got kicked out?"

"What?"

"Yeah. For the whole last week." Heimer's grin showed me that he enjoyed this a bit too much. "Riggles caught him smoking after last recess." Heimer always seemed to get the dirt first, and then spread it like wildfire.

Smoking? What the hell was Benzler doing? I just warned him about that. And at school? What an idiot.

I finally caught up with him on the bus after school. By the time I boarded, he already sat all the way in the rear. His surly and cool expression left no trace of his earlier sadness. Now he just looked mean and smug, as he stared at me while I walked back.

"What the hell happened to you, man?" I asked.

"I guess I'm coming back here next year after all," he said dryly. He laughed, a loud, forced laugh.

I took the seat beside him, but ignored him the rest of the ride. My terrible feelings about his Dad were overwhelmed by my anger with him about his expulsion. He quit. He just gave up. And he wouldn't even let me help.

56

As the bus neared Benzler's house, he rose to exit. He stepped over me and asked, "You're still coming to my house tonight, aren't you?" He spoke in a businesslike tone, definitely not conciliatory. The campout had to be the furthest thing from my mind. How could he even think about that?

I crossed my arms and said, "I guess so." He disembarked from the bus, and I watched him walk up his driveway. Kukla ran out to greet him. It wasn't going to be any fun tonight. Not now anyway.

* * *

Chapter 6

That night I arrived at Benzler's house about 5 pm. My Dad drank beers at the G & R Tavern every Friday after work, and that made me the last one there. As I stepped out of the car with my duffel Benzler's dog, Kukla ran out to me, but nobody else. The events from earlier in the day hung over me like a thick cloud. The lack of any kind of greeting didn't help.

Kukla joined me as I searched for the rest of the guys. I headed around the storage shed that Benzler's Dad had built, and also as a small workshop. The barn, which housed his main workshop, provided too far a walk to be practical in the winter.

As I rounded the corner, I ran straight into Benzler as he exited the shed door. His shoulder nailed me in the jaw, and he dropped an armload of fireworks all over the cobblestone walk. Benzler's Dad always staged his own family show on the 4th of July, and stored loads of them in the shed. All kinds of them now were strewn on the lawn. M80s, bottle rockets, but even some of the lame ones for little kids as well. Sparklers and those black snakes that turn a small tablet into a black ash.

"Nice going dipstick," Benzler yelled at me.

"Sorry" I muttered. I dropped down to help pick up the mess. He grabbed what I had collected and walked off. I couldn't tell if he was mad at me or just intent on his task.

Since his father's death, Benzler's Uncle and Grandfather had taken over the extra duties needed to run the farm smoothly. The Benzler family farms covered over two hundred acres in Marion County. They had operated the business jointly, even before the death of

Benzler's father. In this day and age, solo farmers had a tough go of it as it was, with the economy and all.

Soybeans and corn topped the list of Ohio's two primary crops. The Benzlers grew both, and also owned livestock, though agriculture served as the first function of the farm. Their livestock consisted of Black Angus cows mainly, plus a couple of goats. Benzler helped out with a heavy load of chores after school and in the summer.

We always looked forward to events at Benzler's, like tonight's campout. In the country, we had plenty to get into: the barn, the woods, streams... the neighbors. We didn't plan anything; spontaneity was part of a 12 year old's life.

I trailed Benzler and his explosive treasure back to the rest of the gang, who sat on a picnic table by the barn. Four of us made up tonight's guest list. The typical customers: Heimer, Benzler, and me. Additionally, Timmy Klinefelter joined us tonight. "Felt" came from a rich family with a big, new house and yard on the edge of town. That meant the city to rest of us. Smaller in size like me, Klinefelter acted somewhat like a follower, and he had a pleasant enough disposition. We all gave him a hard time just for the heck of it. A smart student, a decent ball player, he was an all-around nice kid. Benzler said that if Felt were a girl he'd "go" with him. Lastly, Benzler's Alaskan Malamute Kukla hung out with us usually too, and served as our protector.

We usually staged these events at Benzler's or my house. Heimer's parents thwarted us with their strict Biblebeating, and Klinefelter wasn't a regular. So we stayed out here in the country, out here in nowhere. In a couple of years as girls, cars and parties would become priorities; the town will hold more fun. But for now bugs, rocks, dirt, and dares grabbed our attention more than that stuff.

Nightfall came later now with daylight savings, so we still had a couple more hours of light out. The hint of a warm breeze in the still chilly night promised that summer would arrive soon. Moist, earthy smells signaled spring's fresh growth everywhere. The season brought a sense of freedom and hope. Freedom from school, freedom from confinement indoors, freedom to shed winter's clothes, to let loose all of a twelve year old's troubles. And hope, of adventures, of growing up to become men. Someday. Someday not too far down the road.

Benzler distributed firecrackers to the rest of us, and we ran rampant like banshees blowing up the landscape. His Dad never would have stood for this. Tonight though, I doubted he even asked his absentee Mom for permission. But she probably wouldn't even have noticed us, we hadn't seen her at all.

Benzler turned his attention toward the innocent Kukla. As he terrified the dog with the loud noise, I could tell by his pet's reaction that he'd done this sort of thing before.

"Benzler, leave Kukla alone man," I said.

He stared at me with a dead expression, then chased after me with one of the lit firecrackers. I laughed at him, and easily outraced his feeble attempt to blow me up. When I slowed down to turn back toward the group, he tried it again.

"Knock it off asshole," Heimer called to him. Benzler then went after him, and Klinefelter too. We scattered like flies, and our laughter and whooping filled the air. But though we laughed, meanness lurked below the surface with Benzler that disturbed me.

Unable to catch any of us, Benzler gave up, and took a seat at the picnic table. After he caught his breath, he lit a couple more firecrackers, then daringly held them up to the last second before they went off.

"You're crazy Benzler." Klinefelter swept his brown hair out of his eyes. "You're going to hurt yourself."

Benzler ignored Felt and lit another one. This time he set it on smack dab on his crotch, and let it explode.

"Ouch," he screamed, and jumped around the table. "Goddam mutha!" He stopped and inspected himself closely, but his Levis prevented any serious bodily damage.

"Stop it Marshall, you're scaring me," Klinefelter again voiced his fears. The rest of us agreed but remained silent, not sure if we should be amused or scared.

He repeated his trick. Our laughter stopped now, and we all stared, amazed at our friend.

He finally noticed our genuine fear.

"C'mon you guys. I'm just foolin' around." He looked around at us, as we stared back in silence. "It doesn't even hurt."

I had to say, "Benzler, man, you're nuts."

"What do you know?" He glared at me defiantly.

"What's your problem?" I replied, and we stared one another down. It went no further, and the evening passed quickly to the next action.

At dusk, we erected a tent beside the Benzler barn. We found a relatively soft area, full of grass and ragweed. With the four of us working together, we got the sixteen square footer up in no time. We tossed our gear inside, and headed up to the house for some grub.

The sun had set by now, and our stomachs grumbled with hunger. Just like last time the kitchen looked like a pigsty. I truly had never seen a house this messy. Historically, Mrs. Benzler kept this place spotless. Compared to last time, I think it looked even worse. My Mom would have killed me if I brought friends over with the house in this shape.

Two unopened packages of Armour hot dogs lay on the dining room table. No buns or anything else at all. Benzler grumbled under his breath, "Where the fuck is she?" He stomped off to look for his Mom. With Benzler's hyperactivity and bent for orneriness, she used to hover over us like a hawk tracking mice. But not this night.

While we waited, Heimer broke into the familiar Armour theme song, "Fat kids, skinny kids, kids who climb on rocks..."

Felt and I jumped in, "Tough kids, sissy kids, even kids with chicken pox love hot dogs, Armour hot dogs, the dogs kids love to bite."

Our voices trailed off as Benzler thundered back into the kitchen. Without a word, he ripped open the package of hot dogs and tossed them into a pot of water.

We all stared at him dully. "Where is she?" I asked.

He looked sullen. "Sittin' her fat ass on the couch watching fucking 'Happy Days,' that's where." His angry remarks seemed to be directed toward all of us as much as his Mom. "'Happy Days,' and we're sitting out here with nothing to eat."

"Isn't she coming?" asked Klinefelter, astounded that she might not. Benzler didn't even answer. I looked around the corner into the living room. His Mom slumped in a chair in front of the television in a near catatonic state.

But we persevered without her. Hot dogs remained the staple at our sleepovers, it seemed. Benzler overcooked them tonight, so they split and turned gray. I liked them better roasted over a fire. But, no matter.

I pulled a dog off the paper plate Benzler had stacked them on. Wonderbread served as buns. I slathered on mayo, mustard, and ketchup and topped everything off with relish.

We all ate quietly, and the soggy bread squished in my fingers like a paper towel. "Benzler, this kitchen is messy," Felt said with a mouth full.

I kicked him hard under the table.

He jerked back, "Ow, what's that for?"

"Shut up, man." I glared at him. "I don't see you organizing anything.

"What'd I do?"

"Why don't you invite us all over to your house, Mr. Tidibowl?" I responded. Timmy flushed as he genuinely didn't mean any harm by his careless remark. But he didn't expect my backlash either.

"C'mon." Benzler slammed down his knife and fork. "I'm sick of this mess too. Let's get outta here."

The rest of us scurried after him, back to the freedom and freshness of the great outdoors. By then, stars filled the clear night sky. Back at the tent, moths flapped and buzzed around the hiss of a kerosene lantern, which sat atop the picnic table.

Once we'd undressed and climbed into our sleeping bags, I propped my head on my elbow. "Ghost story time. Who's got one?"

"I do," Heimer volunteered with excitement.

"Well, go on then," Benzler piped up, and pulled himself into and Indian style position.

Heimer stood and began. "This is the story of the Hootchiepucker."

"The Hootchie what?" Klinefelter yelled.

"Shut up and listen. I said Hootchiepucker, moron." Heimer continued, "A long time ago these very woods were much thicker and darker than they are today. One day a farmer found one of his cows killed. I know that happens every day, but this cow was decapitated and

65

completely drained of all blood. Nobody could figure out what happened, so eventually they forgot all about it. Then later it happened again to another farmer's cow across the county. And it kept on happening again, and again. And again. People started to talk about it, and get concerned. After awhile even some people went missing."

Klinefelter interrupted, "Is this a true story?"

"I said shut up and listen." Heimer's face reddened. Benzler and I laughed in the background.

Heimer glared through his thick glasses at Felt, and then went on. "People seen some strange sights. Some folks said they seen a creature with the body of a man with a gigantic head."

"Bigfoot," I said. The others agreed.

"No, no, this one had a great mane of hair, like a lion," Heimer countered. "It was nothing like Bigfoot. People spotted a creature with a snout like a dog, and big, sharp teeth, and a thick muscular body. And this thing was fast as lightning and strong as a bull, and it could jump as high as a house."

"It could leap tall buildings?" Benzler busted in this time. "Sounds like Superman,"

Heimer stopped and looked at him with a frown. "You want me to finish? Then shut the fuck up and let me finish." We all razzed him,

66

so he said "Screw it, I'm not telling you the rest." We had to beg him to finish.

Eventually we talked him into it. "One rancher witnessed the thing attacking his prized bull. He said its strikes were quick and silent, but deadly. The weirdest part though, was that when it finished the kill, it howled. The howl sounded something like a freight train in the distance. Well, that's the Hootchiepucker. Anyway, nobody ever caught it or anything. Folks say it's still around here, and comes and goes from time to time, killing animals and sometimes people." Heimer told the story with much dramatic effect. He whispered softly sometimes, and then raised his voice in just the right spots. What made the story that much eerier was the nearby Amtrak line. Every once in awhile, one could hear trains from off in the distance.

When he finished Benzler mocked, "Ooh, that's scary."

"Heimer that story sucked," I added. "Let's do something else."

Klinefelter asked, "So where'd the name Hootchiepucker come from?"

Heimer looked at him with disdain. "How the hell do I know? That's just what my Mom calls it."

In fact though, Heimer's story put us in the exactly right frame of mind for our next game, truth or dare.

We spun an RC Cola bottle to determine the first caller, and the first victim. It turned out to be Benzler, and Heimer respectively.

"Let's get started," Benzler kicked off the game. "Heim, truth or dare?"

"Truth."

"Truth it is." Benzler paused to think. "OK. Did you kiss Angie Thomas that one time in school?"

"No way, man!" he screamed, and shoved Benzler's shoulder.

The rest of us yelled in unison, "Liar!"

"I saw the whole thing, man," Benzler added

"I'm not lying," Heimer insisted. "I hate her frigging guts."

"You don't convince me." Benzler spoke firmly like a judge. "Now you have to do a dare to make up for your lie."

"C'mon guys," Heim pleaded fruitlessly.

Klinefelter and I agreed with Benzler, which according to rule meant he had to take the dare.

"OK, OK," he finally conceded. "What's the dare?"

Benzler leaned back, cross-legged. "Let's see. What's a good one?" He rubbed his chin thoughtfully. "OK, I got one. Go into the barn. In my Dad's workshop is his hunting jacket and his hat. Put 'em on and come back here."

"No way, that's creepy," cried Klinefelter.

Heimer looked at us all, eyes wide.

"C'mon and do it," I said and shoved him.

Despite all of his whines, Heim completed the dare without incident. No spooks in Benzler's barn apparently. But as he walked back, a train whistle blew in the distance. Heimer let out a scream, and bolted the rest of the way. We looked at one another eerily. The sound startled all of us, but we laughed.

The bottle stopped, pointed at me next.

"OK, Digger. It's your turn. Truth or dare?" Benzler gloated.

"Hold on a second," Heimer complained. "Why do you get to give all the dares?"

"You're right," Benzler replied to Heimer. "You just did the dare, it's your call."

"OK, Digger. It's your turn," Heimer said.

"Ah man. No fair. You have to spin again," I wailed. "Fuck you guys." They all stared at me with goofy grins.

I didn't even want to be asked about my love life, so I went straight for the dare.

"All right, a brave soul." Heimer clapped his hands and rubbed them together. "OK here it is." He looked at me with his squinted eyes, while he cleaned his thick glasses. "Run up and touch the security pole by the back of the house."

"That's too easy," Benzler interrupted.

"Let me finish, asshole," Heimer cut him off. "Get this, you have to streak." Streaking, the latest fad, involved running naked in public. Though very far from the public, I still felt somewhat uncomfortable.

The pole seemed a mile away. The bright security light on top illuminated the entire back lot between the house and the barn. Already undressed except my briefs, I stripped them, and took off across Benzler's sizable backyard.

Heart pumping, I sprinted as fast as I could, all the way past the damned blazing security light, and then back to the tent. My eyes darted to the back door constantly, expecting to see Mrs. Benzler appear at any moment. I barely felt the cold dew on my feet as I flew. I raced back to the tent, and these guys laughed and whooped it up.

"Did you see that lil' feller flappin' in the wind?" Benzler laughed.

"Screw you guys," I yelled back as I put my underwear back on. "It's cold."

"Runnin' scared, baby," added Heimer. Everyone laughed again.

"Why don't you do it then, wuss?" I challenged. And so he did it.

Then one by one, all four of us did it. I even did it again. Gradually, we became more comfortable with our public nakedness. Streaking was in, and the freedom and wickedness of the act exhilarated us.

After that, Benzler convinced us that a naked jump off the barn roof would be a good idea. Draped in white bedsheet parachutes that we snuck out of the house, we all climbed up onto the roof of the barn. Overall, the barn stood three stories to the peak atop the hayloft. But an addition on the west side had a flat roof only about ten feet up. Still daunting, but not deadly. We leapt off nearly together, and our chutes flapped uselessly. Nobody got hurt, so Benzler searched for a bigger challenge.

He climbed back up, but this time he continued to climb all the way up to the second tier of the barn, which measured two stories. The rest of us begged off.

"Benzler, get your ass down here," Heimer demanded.

"Why don't you get up here?"

"No way man," piped in Klinefelter. "It's too high."

Benzler kept going all the way up to the top of the barn.

"Benzler," I hollered. "Come on down." He didn't speak. "We're waiting for you down here."

"You don't think he's going to jump do you?" Klinefelter whispered to me.

"What? No way," I said. "He's not that friggin' crazy." But to myself I wondered the same thing.

We waited anxiously for Benzler for about twenty minutes. When he finally climbed back down, however, he was upbeat and that conflicted with his weird behavior of a minute ago. I went along with it, not sure what that was about.

With the late hour, the darkness of the night, and the aloneness of the country, you couldn't pick a better time to explore. Benzler had few neighbors. His Grandma and Grandpa Benzler lived next door to the south, but at least a quarter of a mile away. The Wertzes and their hogs raised their stink to the north, probably at least a half mile.

"We could go down to see your lover, Miss Piggy," I directed to Benzler. He gave me another dirty look.

"No way we're going down to that hog haven." We looked at each other for a moment. "Let's go across the street to the Lanfear's," Benzler announced. "Mrs. Lanfear's hot, man."

Cattycorner across Benzler Road lived a childless couple in their early thirties, the Lanfears. And Benzler was right. Few adult women in our community possessed the sex appeal of Mrs. Lanfear. But she had married Mr. Lanfear, a strapping, mean-looking man with a rough reputation. But no matter. We agreed to go and check out the house.

Covered still only in our white sheets, we drifted like ghosts in the moonlit night. We crossed the unpaved gravel country road. The lawns met the road at the same surface then dove down into deep ditches along the barb-wired fields.

The Lanfear's house sat away from the road maybe fifty yards. Oaks, maples and a couple a willows outlined a well-manicured front lawn. At night the trees all looked the same, and in the full moon they cast eerie shadows.

Our troop tromped across the yard toward the house, Benzler in the lead. At first glance, the house appeared dark, but closer inspection showed some internal lights still on, though it was about midnight. We crept along through the hedges, and stopped before a side bay window.

Benzler poked his head up first, while the rest of us crouched low by the bushes.

"You gotta see this," Benzler spoke recklessly, and much too loudly. "It's Mrs. Lanfear. And she's playing with herself!"

"Sshh," I said, while we fought each other for window space. Inside, Mrs. Lanfear sat alone on the sofa, and watched television. She seemed to be looking right at us. Her fingertips tucked into the front of her jeans as she slouched, but I would hardly call that "playing" with herself. Benzler always exaggerated.

"Man, I'd like to get a piece of that," Benzler said, again much too loudly. It made me wonder if he'd done peeping tom bit before.

I shushed him again, "You friggin' loon. They'll hear you."

"Shut up," he almost yelled at me.

As we bickered, a deep bass voice boomed in the night. "What the hell is goin' on here?" All four of us froze, and then in unison sprinted back across toward Benzler's house. The man, presumably Mr. Lanfear, ran faster than us, and caught up to the slow-running Benzler first, and tackled him on the dewy lawn. The rest of us didn't stop to rescue Benzler; instead we scattered, every man for himself.

When I reached the road, I turned to run down it. The gravel bit at the bottom of my bare feet. Headfirst, I dove down a few yards into the ditch. I laid flat on my belly, naked except for the sheet, among the weeds and grass. Dammit! The white sheet would be easily visible even in the dark. I quickly balled up the sheet to hide it under me, and rolled deeper into the longer and thicker weeds. The cold, damp grass and weeks prickled the skin on my soft underbelly. My heart pounded in my throat, and I listened carefully, all senses on high alert. I heard some muffled talk back in the yard. It sounded like Mr. Lanfear's voice, too deep to be Benzler's. I giggled to myself, and shivered uncontrollably with cold and fear. I bet the sight of the four apparitions gave Mr. L. a start. He must've been relieved to find out it was only us, and not something supernatural.

In any case, I lay in this terrified state for what seemed like an hour. Once again I heard a train whistle off in the distance, and thought of Heimer's story. That creeped me out even more. I almost jumped out of the ditch as I preferred to be with the other humans than risk it with the Hootchiepucker.

After some time, a strange sound startled me. *What the hell is that? Did I fall asleep? It sounded like shotgun shells being dumped out of a cannister. Mr. Lanfear must've gotten out a shotgun. Holy shit!*

I mustered the courage to pull myself up into a crouch, and then I dashed away in the direction opposite of Lanfear's. That also took me farther away from Benzler's. I hopped a barbed wire fence, and cut across the corn field. In June, the fields consisted of one foot corn stalks in rows. I plowed through for 100 yards or so, which was not exactly easy in bare feet. Then I turned and headed back toward Benzler's. I stopped every few moments to listen, but didn't see or hear anything.

As I approached the tent, I saw the light inside and heard voices. I opened the canvas flap and peered in, and all three of my friends looked up at me.

"Where the hell have YOU been?" Heimer asked.

"Hiding," I replied. I breathed hard. "What happened?"

"You've been hiding this whole time?" Heimer continued. "Christ! Where? We've been back here for a fuckin' hour."

"C'mon, just tell me what happened," I demanded, embarrassed but curious.

"Nothin' much. Lanfear caught me," Benzler said without any emotion. "Damn he's fast. He just chewed me out, though. Told me if he ever caught me doing that again he'd call the sheriff. After he let me go we came back here. No big deal." Then after a pause he asked, "So where were you hiding?"

"In the ditch."

"For a fucking hour?" Heimer chimed in again. "Are you out of your mind?"

"I fell asleep," I told them, and tried to shift the focus off of me. "When I woke up, I swear to God I thought I heard Mr. Lanfear with a shotgun."

"You're such a wuss," Benzler said with much disdain. "That must've been us. We lit off some sparklers and firecrackers." All three of my friends stared at me, awaiting a response that I did not supply. "Anyway," Benzler continued, "I say we go back over there."

Together the rest of us said, "No way, man, you're crazy."

After we all talked him out of his crazy scheme, we settled down into the tent. A kerosene lamp hung from the center pole, and gave off a pale light, along with the ever-present hiss. Each of us fought off the fatigue, not wanting to fall asleep first.

I just about drifted off myself, when Benzler nodded off. Heimer jabbed me gently with his elbow. Heimer dangled a light string onto Benzler's cheek. The rest of us broke into giggles with each swipe at the string from Benzler's sluggish hand. Finally, Heimer leapt onto Benzler with all of his weight, and slammed him hard, like big-time wrestling. Benzler jerked awake, startled, and glared at us, wild-eyed as we laughed hysterically.

When he realized what happened, Benzler lunged at Heimer, and grabbed him around the throat. Klinefelter and I needed to pull him off. Though the fight didn't amount to much, it still killed the mood of the evening. I lay wide-eyed for a long time, no longer worried about falling asleep, only about Benzler and his craziness.

*   *   *

Chapter 7

We played little league baseball on Tuesday and Thursday evenings. That Thursday, Dad and I left our house and drove to pick up Benzler at his. Heat and humidity ruled the day, and as the day wore on that humidity looked to bring rain. The air thickened with it.

We drove down Whetstone and turned onto Cardington Rd. Cardington wound down by the river, and crossed by bridge in two places. Cornfields covered most of our county, but the river provided a

78

scenic break in the view. We took another right on East River Rd., a left on Newmans-Cardington Rd., and finally another right onto Benzler Rd.

"Dad, did you know that Benzler sees a psychiatrist?" I asked on the way.

"No I didn't know," he replied. "Doesn't surprise me though. He's been through a lot." We continued to drive, windows down, wind blazing in. Dad went on, "How's he been acting to you? Does he seem OK?"

"What do you mean?" I put the pocket of my mitt up to my face. I loved the smell of the leather.

Dad answered me with more questions. "I mean is he acting any different? Does he seem himself?"

"Well, yeah, I guess. He's always been a little crazy." I looked out the window as we passed the Lanfear's house. "Lately he's been a little worse. Doing wild things, you know."

"Just be careful. Keep an eye on him," he said, and closed the discussion.

Our station wagon pulled onto Benzler's cobbled driveway at 5:00PM, Dad blaring the horn. Our Little League baseball game started at 6:15, and all the players needed to be at the park by 5:30.

"I bet that kid's not ready again," Dad said. As I hopped out and ran up to the porch, I could hear Benzler's Mom inside yelling at him.

"Marshall!" she screeched. "They're here Marshall. Hurry up or you'll be late."

"Hi Mrs. Benzler." I spoke warily through the door screen. I couldn't recall the last time I saw her mobile. I guessed that was a good sign.

"He's coming, just late again. Don't know what I'm gonna do with that boy." She still looked awful. Not normally an attractive woman, now her hair stood awry, and dark bags circled beneath her eyes. She appeared to have slept in her wrinkled clothes.

"He's coming Dad." I walked back out to the car. We always picked up Benzler and he always ran late. His parents used to come to every game, but this summer his Mom hadn't attended a single one.

Dad glared. Considered one of the best coaches around, he insisted on being the first one at the park. He sat tight behind the steering wheel, and nervously finished his cigarette. Then he jammed it into the already full car ashtray.

All arms and legs, Benzler finally came down the stairs and out to the car. By the looks of his uniform his Mom must not have washed it after last week's game.

"Where's your glove son?" Dad hollered. Benzler stopped in his tracks, dropped his arms down to his sides in disgust, and then retraced his steps back into the house. "That boy'd forget his head if it wasn't attached," Dad said, and lit up another cigarette. I leaned on the car, and dug my toe in the gravel. Benzler returned with his glove, his hat and his bat, all of which he'd forgotten.

Benzler approached the car and climbed into the backseat. Dad winced as Benzler inadvertently banged his aluminum bat against the door of the car, metal clanging on metal.

"Slow down boy, be careful," Dad admonished.

"Careful and Benzler are not often in the same sentence Dad," I chided my friend.

"Shut your face." He punched me over the seat.

"Boys, boys, knock it off," my Dad yelled, agitated. We settled down for now.

Benzler lived for sports and thought he was good too. But the fact remained that he was one of the worst players on our Little League team. My Dad let Benzler play first base. Physically, Benzler looked like a first sacker, but the resemblance ended there. I played shortstop and he dropped half of my throws to first. Uncoordinated and lazy, he also got distracted by anything and everything during a game.

Our car pulled around the circular gravel drive around the gas tank that most farms have. We pulled onto Benzler Road, paved just five years ago in '69, and drove south. Storm clouds darkened the west, and cut the sky in half, splitting up the once beautiful day. Benzler resided only about five miles from the tiny hamlet of Waldo.

We took Benzler Rd. to Rengert Rd. to St. James Rd. The path led us out of the cornfields into a heavily wooded area. Even during mid-day the dense forest kept everything dark. We turned out onto Waldo-Fulton Rd., which came to an end right at Main St. in Waldo.

We played ball at the park on the edge of town. Two adjacent diamonds ran along a cornfield behind the backstops. A dilapidated barn rested, haunted and unused yards away from the fields. The community had built a snack shack between the fields a couple of years ago. Benzler had gotten into trouble recently for breaking into the locked stand during a practice and stealing candy. Though he knew nothing of it, Dad took hell since he was the responsible adult of the practice. He also lost what little trust he had left in Benzler on that day.

The Eidegger station wagon ignored the usual entrance to the park. Coach E., which was what everyone called Dad, steered the car into the second dirt pathway, which he followed around the back rim of the park, around the ball field where he parked about 20 yards behind the backstop. No one else could park here, just the coach.

We had a pretty good team that year, mostly returning players from the previous season when we went 12-4. Heimer was our ace pitcher, and I was no slouch. Most of our lineup consisted of pretty good athletes. Except Benzler.

Olentangy Sand and Gravel Incorporated sponsored the team. Fellow teammates Joey and Jamie Krupenauer's dad managed at the mill there. Benzler sported a dark blue "13" on his navy blue and white pin stripe jersey. I wore number "10". Heimer wore number "5" because his favorite player was Reds catcher Johnny Bench. Benzler pulled his white and blue pinstriped hat down tight on his head, so his ears stuck out. The letters "OSG" spread across the front of our uniforms. Our pants went to the knees, and we pulled our stirrups all the way up tight. My bushy hair stuck out on all sides.

Upon arrival, we found Davey Himmer sitting alone, head down, shoulders hunched inside the white, paint chipped dugout. He was a shrimpy, malnourished looking kid. His parents had never attended a single game, yet constantly harangued my dad over Davey's lack of playing time. A correction from earlier, Himmer surpassed Benzler as the worst player on the team. None of the boys really liked Davey. We didn't actually dislike him, it was more as if he didn't really even exist.

We piled out of the car, Benzler again banging his bat against the side of the car. Dad yelled over the metal-to-metal clang almost as if he anticipated Benzler's clumsiness, "Dammit Marshall, be careful. For the love of Mike."

"Sorry Coach." Then as the two boys entered the dugout, Benzler giggled, "Your Dad cussed."

"Shut up, Benzler. You're such a klutz." I grabbed a dirty ball out of Dad's canvas bag. "C'mon, let's play catch." I noticed Benzler's playfulness. Maybe that was a good sign.

Ignoring Davey Himmer, we began to toss the ball back and forth. Playing catch with Benzler could be a challenge. His first throw sailed too high, but I leapt up and snagged it. My return throw fired straight to Benzler's chest with a pop.

Dad hauled the second canvas bag from the car, and dumped an assortment of wooden and aluminum bats along the chain-link fence. Dad grabbed a ball and glove himself and yelled to Himmer, "Come play catch Davey." The coach usually played catch with this lonely boy. Perhaps that was why Davey always arrived first...to avoid the embarrassment of being the last one chosen by the other boys.

Benzler's next throw bounded into the dirt, but I easily dug it out. I began my return throw, but stop half cocked seeing Benzler looking the other way, his attention drawn to other boys arriving.

"Wake up Benzler," I hollered. My throw again fired right in the middle of Benzler's number thirteen.

The four of us are lined up two by two, Benzler side by side with Davey, Dad and I on the other.

Benzler's next throw flew clear over my head, so I had to chase it down.

The rest of the players showed up one by one, some in pairs. Essenheimer, Klinefelter, the Krupenauers, and the rest. The other team arrived soon as well, tonight's opponent, Caledonia Farmer's Exchange. Quite a few fans attended the game tonight. Parents of course, but also many of the locals supported our team. A small bleacher section stood behind either dugout, and the fans segregated accordingly.

Larger by a hair than Waldo and located 10 miles to the northeast, Caledonia supported two Little League teams. The Farmer's Exchange always sponsored the better of the two. In the same high school district as Waldo, Caledonia had become a natural rival. We knew most of the kids on the other team from other sports, camps, and such. One particular ballplayer named John Rustin played catcher for them. A square-faced stocky boy of average height, his arrogant and pushy demeanor meant none of us liked him. He and Benzler especially had staged an open on-going feud.

The dark portion of the sky continued to consume the lighter side. The wind kicked up dust devils on the infield. Players grabbed their caps and covered their eyes.

"Play ball," cried the umpire.

The game began and the parade of batters, strikes, and balls followed.

By the fourth inning Caledonia led 5 to 2. Most of their runs came due to our pitcher, Essenheimer's lack of control, and a crucial but typical Benzler error. Our two runs came when I drove them home with a double in the bottom of the third.

In the bottom of the 6th, the final inning in little league, Benzler came to the plate with the bases loaded and two outs. Rain sprinkles started, the wind whipping them sideways.

Not usually a good hitter, Benzler overswung and so struck out a lot. Anxiety filled the dugout and bleachers.

"Come on Marshall, hit the ball," someone yelled from the stands.

The pitcher delivered the first pitch, right down the middle.

"Strike one," called the umpire.

Benzler looked back and Rustin wore a smart aleck grin. Benzler flailed badly at a high fastball out of the strike zone.

Rustin chuckled. "Nice swing."

Benzler glared, a long, mean stare back at him.

Rustin hollered, "No stick here."

Benzler dug in, turning his glare toward the mound, and waggled his bat behind his head. Both benches and the stands came alive, cheering or jeering respectively.

But Benzler worked the count full, and then he somehow caught all of one and drove the ball deep into the left center gap. With two outs the runners were moving as Benzler began his slow stride around the base paths. The first runner scored, and as Benzler rounded first base, the left fielder bobbled the ball in the outfield.

As the second runner scored, Benzler rounded second and the third base coach waved the third runner home. The throw from leftfield sailed way off the mark over the second baseman's head, allowing the third run to score tying the game. As Benzler rounded third the coach threw up both arms palms out, signaling him to stop there. The errant throw wound up behind first base, but the Caledonia first baseman recovered it quickly. Excited, Benzler ignored the sign and raced for home. The rain really began to pour.

Caledonia's first-baseman fired a one hopper to home, and the catcher, our favorite John Rustin fielded it cleanly. Rustin had plenty of time to block the plate. With his slow stride, Benzler would clearly be out by a mile. However, Benzler didn't even slow down, he just put his head down and rammed straight into the unsuspecting catcher. Benzler bowled Rustin completely over, and the two boys rolled in the sandy mud in the lefthanded batter's box. Rustin hung onto the ball, and the umpire called Benzler out.

Despite being out, Benzler stood up over the writhing boy and taunted him. This unsportsmanlike behavior outraged the entire Caledonia team. The players on the field rushed toward the boys. Rustin jumped up and put his face into Benzler's, yelling at him. Benzler took a big swing at the kid, clocking him square in the jaw.

Both benches cleared, coaches too, but no other players got into the fight, just Benzler and Rustin. I raced up to Benzler, and tried to pull him from behind out of the melee. Rustin retaliated from his blow, dive-tackling Benzler, forcing us all three of us to the ground. The coaches and umpires at this point pulled all of the players apart. The plate umpire ejected Benzler from the game.

Players, coaches, and fans alike stood and stared as Benzler walked off the field. He headed for the dugout, and shoved Davey Himmer out of the way.

Dad bawled out Benzler. "Hey, hey. Get over here." Benzler walked away from him into the dugout.

Dad chased him down and continued yelling, "That was the stupidest play I've ever seen. We were holding you up at third! Didn't you see that?" Again Benzler turned his back on my Dad, walking away. Infuriated, Dad pursued and continued his uncharacteristic yelling. "Son, I've had it with you. You are off this team."

Benzler, covered in mud sat down in the dugout, and angrily focused his eyes on the playing field, puddles splashing with oncoming raindrops. By now the umpire had called the game, a 5 to 5 tie. Benzler picked up his gear and began to walk through the rain across the field.

As he walked past the visitor's dugout on the first base side of the infield, the Caledonia players razzed and jeered at him. "Benzler, you crazy asshole." Their coaches quieted them down. Benzler gave them the finger, and then head down continued walking onto the gravel path that splits the two ball diamonds.

*　　　*　　　*

A half hour later, the field emptied and most people had gone. The rain continued in a steady fall. Dad and I finished picking up all of the bats, baseballs, catcher's equipment and all, and loaded up the station wagon. The dirt turned to a sandy mud, and stuck to everything.

"Where's Marshall?" Dad asked.

"He walked off after you kicked him off the team," I replied.

"Christ," he said disgusted. "Get in the car."

We pulled out of the lot and soon were on Park Street. We searched the length of the street to no avail. Park ended where it met Main at the G & R Tavern. The windshield wipers slapped on high as the cleansing rain fell more heavily. I rolled down the window to see better.

"Where the hell is he?" my Dad muttered, frustrated. I really began to worry about him. We turned the car around.

As we back tracked down Park Street I spotted Benzler. "Dad, there his is!"

In the rain, Benzler sat in the Waldo cemetery cross-legged in front of his father's headstone. He was completely soaked and covered with mud from his scrap.

90

The rain fell, wetting everything on earth. The rain soaked the soil, providing life to all things, flowers, weeds, plants, and animals.

Dad pulled the station wagon down the curving gravel drive toward Benzler. I stuck my head out of the window. "Benzler, come on, get in."

He didn't reply, and continued sitting, his hard gaze piercing the black granite stone. He sat where the hole lay a few months ago. The grass still had not filled in completely so you could easily see the outline of the grave.

"You can't walk home from here. It's at least 5 miles," I said. He still didn't reply.

Dad pulled the car off of the driveway and got out.

Walking over he said, "Marshall. I promised your Mom I'd bring you home."

Benzler looked up. Tears streaked through his dirty face. "She doesn't give a shit about me."

Dad knelt down beside him. "Look son, I'm sorry about what happened back there. Come on, let us give you a ride home. It's raining."

"I'm not riding with you. You kicked me off the fucking team." Benzler looked my Dad right in the eyes and glared.

This show of emotion and threatening tone briefly shocked my Dad. Watching from the car it shocked me too.

Dad stood up and took a step back. "Marshall...."

"Get away from me," Benzler said emphatically. "Leave me alone."

"Look, I know you're upset right now. I would be too," my Dad replied.

"Shut up," Benzler screamed his reply. "You don't know anything."

"C'mon son. Maybe I was too tough on you back there. I can let you back on the team," my Dad responded, grasping desperately for anything to help.

"I don't care about the fucking team," Benzler screamed.

Dad, perplexed, stood silently in the rain before the sobbing boy. Benzler, head hanging, remained kneeling in front of the grave. Dead flowers surrounded the stone.

"Marshall, I'm sorry about your father," he said.

Benzler didn't reply. He merely shook his head back and forth, squeezing his eyes shut. Dad approached him and knelt again beside him, placing his hand on his shoulder.

"It's not your fault. Your father had problems," Dad said, and then paused. "He was sick. I feel your pain, but this isn't helping." Dad stopped, and then said very deliberately, "Please, just get in the car, and let me take you home."

Benzler's tears and shaking intensified. "Why'd he do it? Why'd he kill himself?"

Dad pulled Benzler to him, hugged him and let him sob onto his shoulder. This was notable because Dad didn't hug often.

"Nobody can answer that son. I just don't know. I just know that it's not your fault." Dad sat there holding Benzler for several minutes, and the rain continued to soak them both.

Eventually, we got Benzler back to the car and tok him home. Silence enveloped the entire car, and what I noticed the most was the dank, wet smell. At Benzler's house, my Dad walked Benzler into the house while I stayed in the car. I sat in the car and listened to the crappy AM radio. He wa gone for quite awhile. Benzler had lost it. The events of the day truly disturbed me. Dad finally returned, crossing the driveway, face grim. We drove toward home.

"What took you so long Dad?" I asked.

He didn't respond right away.

"I tried to talk to Marshall's Mom about all this. She just sat there," Dad began as we drove away. "I put Marshall to bed for Chrissakes. His little brother and sister too. That's what took me so long." He stopped talking for a while then added, "I had no idea what they were going through." We continued the rest of the drive home, staring into the wet darkness.

We pulled into our short driveway, and Dad turned off the car engine. Before we got out, Dad looked at me and said, "I guess that answers my question from earlier about how Marshall's doing." We got out and walked into the house.

*   *   *

Chapter 8

Two days later on Saturday Benzler rode his bike over to my house like nothing happened. I hadn't talked to him since Thursday's incident, and had been worrying quite a bit about him.

When he showed up unexpectedly, I was taking a break from my chores, having an illegal chew outside the barn. My chores today consisted of cutting all the ragweed down in the barnyard and cleaning horse stalls. My family had half a dozen horses, various breeds for various uses but mostly we just rode them for fun. My Dad saw himself as a sort of Midwestern cowboy.

I'd finished about half of the job, the weed part when I spied Benzler pedaling up Whetstone River Road on his metallic green Schwinn Stingray five-speed. He pulled into the driveway, coasted down and dumped his bike at the bottom of the hill.

Our house sat on top of a knoll with a driveway that wound around the house to the garage at the bottom. Our ancestors had lived in the house for decades. Old, red, they originally built the big two-story farmhouse in 1829. The basement of the house was built right into the hillside with the garage and deck extending from there.

My father didn't farm, though our ancestors up to my grandpa owned and farmed all of the surrounding land. Dad sold most of that property to settle the estate when grandma died, an action my Dad later regretted. Now a golf course lay on what used to be acres and acres of our corn and soybeans.

Spotting me, Benzler walked toward the barn. He stumbled as he walked, tripping on a mole hole. Moles. My Dad's bane. We had a lot of them, and they tore up the yard creating small mounds and tunnels just below the surface. Dad put in traps, but they didn't work.

Benzler kept right on walking right through my Mom's vegetable garden, which she kept in a state of perfection, certainly free of weeds. The sweet corn brushed at his waist. "Knee high by the 4th of July" the saying went. I didn't know where that saying came from, but July started the next week and the corn was already way past the knees.

"Great," I said to Benzler when he got near. "You can help me with my chores for a change." He had the lazyman's knack of arriving when the work was already done.

"Cleaning horse shit again? You've definitely found your calling," he spouted off. As I said, Benzler had apparently recovered without trauma from the other day. But I was careful. He started out playfully the other day too, and look what happened.

"Come on, let's do it," I said. "Grab a pitchfork and start at the far end. I'll meet you in the middle."

Benzler raced ahead toward the stalls frightening the horses with his nervous enthusiasm. The animals seemed wary of Benzler, as if they could sense his instability.

"What do I do?" he asked.

"Twelve years on a farm and you don't know how to clean a horse stall?" I jabbed at him.

"Look asswipe. I can pick up the shit, but what do you want me to do with it? Dump it over your head?" he retortsed

I laughed. Yes, apparently he'd recovered. "All right. Cool your jets," I said. "Pick up the horseshit and piss-wet straw with your pitchfork like this, and pitch it into this trailer here." I executed the move. "Make sure you breathe deep too."

Benzler took in a deep breath. "I love it."

"Then put fresh straw down," I finished the demonstration.

We got back into the work. Benzler belted out some current McCartney & Wings tune that I hated.

"Band on the run. Band on the run." He sang horribly out of tune. I didn't say anything though, I just shook my head. If he thought it bothered me he'd never quit.

After a couple of minutes he spooked the horse in his stall. Letting out a fierce neigh, the horse began stomping its hooves.

"What's happening over there?" I called out.

"Sorry, I accidentally poked your horse," he replied.

"Christ. Get the hell out of there before you get kicked" I yelled after him.

As he came on out I said to him, "You'll do anything to get out of work."

Easily distracted, he ran in the other direction and picked up a half flat basketball. Under the best circumstances Benzler couldn't dribble a ball well, but still he comically tried to dribble then shoot the ball through a rusted, netless rim dangling from one of the barn beams.

"Jabbar fakes left, then goes up with his sky hook," Benzler commentated on his fake game. "He scores, yes." Benzler threw both arms up in triumph.

I let him go for a minute, and then asked "Hey Kareem, do you think you can handle feeding the rabbits?" My little brother kept rabbits and showed them for 4-H. He had about a hundred of 'em, mostly Dutch and Lops. Benzler paid me no mind.

"Hey Benzler," I yelled at him to get his attention. "Benzler!" He finally looked over. "Can you feed the rabbits?"

"They're your brother's rabbits. What the hell's he doing?" he resisted.

I looked at him in disbelief. "He's doing different chores today. Do you want to help me or not you lazy ass?"

"Oh all right," he replied.

After about 45 minutes, we finished. If Benzler had not shown up, I'd have been done easily in 30. We kept tools in the empty horse stall on the end. I hung the pitchforks up on the wall, and removed my work gloves. We exited and sat down on two straw bales next to the barn. I pulled out my tin of Copenhagen for some more chew.

Benzler watched me. "Hey, can I have a dip?"

I opened the can and bit directly into the tobacco. I packed it into place with my tongue, and wiped the excess off with my hand. Then I offered the open tin to him.

"No thanks man, you're gross," he replied.

We sat resting for a short time, and Benzler picked a blade of Timothy hay and stuck it in his mouth.

"What time do you want me to come over tonight," he asked. We were having a camp out down by the river tonight.

"Whenever you want," I responded. "Can you bring the goods?" I asked referring to Benzler's portion of the evening's entertainment.

"Yes," he said. "What about you?"

"Just leave it to me, man."

We continued our break in the shade, observing the barnyard. Benzler appeared quiet, but I could see the wheels turning in his head.

"Now what? I asked.

Benzler blurted out, "Let's ride the horses!" Yeah right. Benzler couldn't ride a horse either.

"You think my Dad's gonna let <u>you</u> up on one of our horses?" I exclaimed. "You're nuts."

"C'mon," he plead. "We don't even have to tell him."

I thought for a minute, and spat tobacco juice between my boots.

"OK, but we'll have to ride bareback. The saddles are locked up," I replied, trying to hide my annoyance. Asking my Dad was out of the question. He'd not only say no, he'd give me more chores to do. It was easier to ask for forgiveness than permission anyway.

"That's cool. Saddles are for pussies," Benzler quipped.

I rolled my eyes. "Sure Benzler. Whatever you say." I don't even bother to qualify that remark.

We headed back into the barn where I stepped into the first horse stall. Stall one housed Gypsy, a black and white pinto, getting older but still with spunk. A fine roan named Cinnamon lived in the next stall. Youthful but docile, not even Benzler could spook her.

I led both horses out to the adjacent pasture, bridled but unsaddled. I held both reins as the horses stand calmly, stomping and twitching to shake off flies. Both horses chomped on the pasture grass full of the Timothy hay and alfalfa remnants. Weeds abounded. Already, Benzler was nowhere to be seen.

"Where the hell is he?" I said aloud to nobody in particular. The horses certainly didn't acknowledge me.

"Benzler!" I hollered. No response. "Benzler, come on!" He emerged from the barn like a scarecrow, telltale bits of straw sticking to his hair and flannel shirt. He carried a broken handle from a broom or a shovel. "What the heck are ya doing?" I yelled at him.

"I was just playing with your cats," he responded lamely. We actually didn't own any cats, but strays always lived in the barn.

"Playing with 'em, huh? Torturing more likely." I imagined Benzler poking one of them with a farm tool or whirling them about by the tail. His grin told me I was probably not too far off.

"What the hell is that?" I asked referring to the broken handle. He shrugged his shoulders with a dumb look on his face.

I handed him Cinnamon's reins. Grabbing Gypsy at the mane and haunch, I leapt upward balancing my belly on her back. From there I kicked my right leg over, and spun into bareback riding position. Just as I settled, Benzler smacked Gypsy as hard as he could on the backside with the broom handle. The horse bolted. I catapulted backward, thudding heavily on my back, knocking the wind out of me. Benzler

101

shrieked with hilarity, and knowing my impending rage immediately raced for the safety of the barn.

Unhurt, I gathered my wind. Much quicker than he, I caught up to the laughing maniac, and wrestled him to the ground. I pinned his shoulders with my knees, and still he continued his inane cackle. The harder I tried to stifle him, the harder he laughed.

With his hayfever combined with the laughter, tears streamed down his face, and his nose ran like a sieve.

Preoccupied, we didn't see Gypsy fall across the field. Observing her now, lying on her side, bellowing, I freed Benzler and ran toward the downed horse. As I neared her, my worst fears were realized, as her leg appeared broken. She must have stepped in one of the mole holes and fallen.

Benzler stopped laughing, and sat on the ground like a sack of dirty laundry. Dirt blackened his face, streaked by his tears of joy. I left him alone to watch the injured horse, but didn't part with any warning for him to keep a clear distance. In fact I hoped that Gypsy kicked him.

"Wipe your nose," I said with disdain in parting. I'd never been this angry at an individual before.

I set off to find my Dad, reluctant to break this news to him but in urgent need of his help. Feeling entirely responsible for the incident, I sheepishly entered my dad's basement workshop. Dad loved to work with tools down in his shop, and could be found down there most weekends. He always tinkered with engines or built something like a bookcase with his carpentry tools. Normally the shop smelled dank and dusky, cobwebs sheltered in each ceiling corner. Now, the aroma of freshly cut cedar filled the air as I found my Dad working at the table saw. He wore a white sleeveless T-shirt over his small, wiry frame. Sawdust clung to his summer sweat. He had a gentle but stern disposition. His temper could flare hot on occasions like these. Especially when Benzler was involved.

"Dad?" I said, my voice muted by the buzz of the saw. He finished cutting a board.

"Dad, you gotta minute?" Looking up Dad's half smile erased as he sensed something wrong.

Turning off the saw he queried, "What is it Donny?"

"Gypsy fell and it looks like she broke her leg." I didn't mention anything about Benzler, Dad would be suspicious of him anyway. In the silent pause, without the whirr of the saw we heard the distant cries of the horse. Dad didn't ask any questions. He simply put down the piece of lumber in his hands, and led me out the shop door. As we walked out the barn blocked our view of the bizarre scene.

"I think she must've stepped in a mole hole," I told him.

All he said is "Damn."

We crossed the same field past Mom's garden. I dreaded turning the corner, uncertain of Dad's reaction when he saw Benzler. I dreaded what other trouble Benzler could be into in the short time I left him alone. However, we found Benzler seated calmly next to Gypsy, petting her neck and speaking softly to her. This empathy from him surprised me.

I searched my Dad's face for response. He looked at me with a "What the hell is he doing here?" look on his face. But he said nothing.

Dad ignored Benzler and approached the injured leg, then analyzed it for a few seconds.

Dad mumbled with certainty, "Yep, leg's broken, you two wait here." He walked back toward the house shaking his head.

Once Dad passed out of earshot I said, "Goddam it Benzler. Are you happy now?"

He didn't reply, he just sat on the pasture grass next to the crumpled horse. She stopped bellowing, desperate of breath, her left rear leg cocked up at an impossible angle.

Dad finally returned, stepping with deliberate need, his forehead creased. He carried a Winchester 12 gauge shotgun, the trigger end of

104

the barrel in his right hand. His eyes darted from me to Benzler to Gypsy. The horse looked at my Dad, appearing to understand, accepting its fate.

With the two of us sitting right there, Dad stepped into place behind the horse's white head. He pulled the trigger. The shotgun emitted a loud blast. One final guttural shriek, then nothing. Gypsy was dead.

Dad began to walk back toward the house, lighting up a new cigarette.

"Dad, we can't just leave her here," I pleaded. He stopped and turned.

"Yep, she'll have to lay right there," he stated clearly. He absently rubbed his right shoulder, sore from the recoil.

He continued, "I'll call LAR to come get her, but they won't be open 'til Monday. You boys grab a tarp and cover her." He took a drag from his cigarette then resumed his walk back to the house. LAR stood for Large Animal Removal.

Benzler and I looked after him stunned. I felt mugged by the thick, humid air, and my head buzzed with the sound of locusts. With a blank, vapid stare Benzler followed me into the barn, and helped me pull out a canvas tarp. In silence, we knocked off the rat turds, and hauled it out to cover up the horse.

*   *   *

Chapter 9

"What time are the boys coming over for your slumber party?" Mom hollered down to me from our deck porch. The deck sat on top of the garage so she stood about fifteen feet above me. After ignoring her for a minute, I walked toward her to hear what she said.

"What?" I asked. She repeated her question.

I rolled my eyes, and yelled back, "God Mom. Slumber parties are for girls. We're camping." Leave it to Mom to diminish our adventure. I shook off the horrible vision of a pillow fight in time to catch the end of her retort.

"I'm sorry, I didn't mean to hurt your manly feelings, Dandy Donny honey," she teased. "Anyway, when are they coming?"

"Mom, I hate it when you call me that," I whined. The nickname came from the announcer on Monday Night Football, she had been calling me Dandy Donny since he started. I'd always hated it. If my friends ever caught wind of that it'd be all over. "They'll be here any minute," I answered.

Les and I set up a trailer in the driveway where we got our provisions ready for the big evening. The driveway ran along the side of the house to the rear below my Mom. We packed the trailer full of goods to last us a week, though our stay would only be one night. Dusk settled in and fireflies lit around the yard. Crickets competed with bullfrogs providing background music.

We had planned this campout down by the river a long time ago, and the day's tragedy wouldn't stop us. Les took Gypsy's death in stride as we had quite a few horses, but Dot took it hard.

Benzler had ridden his bike home after the accident, but he would be back later that night. Other than Benzler only Heimer and Lester were coming. Mom made me bring Les, but I didn't mind him tagging along much, and he didn't get in the way.

We worked together silently loading up a 3 by 3 foot trailer. My written packing list for tonight contained:

- two mammoth orange two-man sleeping bags
- foam roll up mats to lay below them
- a propane lantern for emergency light

- an ice cooler filled with food and drinks

- half gallon cans of HiC fruit drink

- potato chips, a brown grocery sack full of popcorn, hot

  dogs, marshmallows, and homemade oatmeal cookies

Just as essential but not written on my list, I smuggled a six-pack of Old Dutch from my Dad, that I had swiped beer by beer over the past 2 months. I snuck some cigarettes from the old man as well. Heimer brought the cards and poker chips. And I was counting on Benzler for the dirty magazines that he pilfered from his oblivious Grandpa. This was going to be great.

Les didn't know anything about the contraband, and he looked up to me so he wouldn't tell on us. Mom woulda killed me if she'd known we had beer and cigs, but she'da killed me twice if she knew I'd let Les have some.

"OK. Ready," I told Les. "Go tell Mom we're heading out. Have her tell the others to just come on down when they get here." I watched Les run off. Everyone said he looked like me, just a few inches shorter and slighter.

I unlocked the trailer brakes and grabbed the front. I pulled the load the couple of hundred yards, across our back field, and down the path through the woods to the river. Meant to be towed by a tractor, still it wasn't that heavy. Some uneven ground posed the only difficulty. I steered clear of the small dirt mounds made by the moles.

Dad let us keep the tent pitched down by the river most of the summer, so it was all set. As a family, we never used it anyway. We never went on vacations anywhere really. My Dad always griped about the oil embargo and how gas cost over 50 cents a gallon. Inflation, recession, you name it and my Dad complained about it.

We set up our camp in a clearing located in a small nook where the river bent around in an oxbow. Heavily wooded, the spring floods regularly deposited enough firewood for a whole summer's worth of bonfires. An old picnic table, red paint flaking and wood bowing aligned with the fire site.

By the time I reached the campsite, Les caught up to me running.

"Mom says to be careful," he reminded me huffing.

"She always says that," I said curtly.

"She just told me to tell you that's all," he said in self-defense.

"Well, if you want to hang out with us down here, stop worrying about Mom," I reprimanded him. "And don't tell her anything about what we do, it's private."

He frowned, and I could tell he was hurt. I felt sorry for being cross with him.

"Sorry Les, it's OK." I rubbed his short hair with my hand. He had a crew cut, and I liked the feel of his fuzzy head. I used to have that same haircut when I was his age, but later Mom let me grow it longer.

We unpacked the load and spread the sleeping bags out onto the floor of the tent. The tent smelled dank and musky. Crickets continued their incessant chirping, and you could hear the flow of the river over the rapids behind us. A mosquito landed on my forearm. I watched it slowly drain blood, then splattered him. That reminded me to pull the bug spray out of the trailer, so Les and I both sprayed "OFF" all over our arms, legs, and faces.

Heimer's "Yeehaw!" holler broke the solitude, and he careened down the path wild-eyed. Since that was his normal behavior we didn't even acknowledge him.

He pulled up to a sudden stop before us. "What's he doing here?" he said, thumb pointing at my brother. He pushed his glasses back into position on his nose.

"Don't worry about it fatass, he'll be fine," I said, sticking up for my brother. I could pick on Les, but no one else could.

"Not if I can help it," Heimer yelled as he picked up Les and threw him over his shoulder. He toted him over to the riverbank and feigned throwing him in. He put Les down and rubbed his head with a rough hand. Les took the episode well, though I could tell he disliked the attention.

"Quit foolin' around. C'mon, help me start the fire," I said to the two of them. I previously had gathered a stack of kindling, and brought down old newspaper to get the blaze going. Dad had taught me to align the firewood into the shape of an Indian teepee. We filled in open spaces with small sticks and twigs, and then shoved newspaper into every cranny. I struck a wooden Ohio Blue tip match against the box, and lit several paper crumples. The dry wood started to burn quickly.

"Where the hell is Benzler?" Heimer asked.

"Damned if I know," I replied. "He should be here by now." After a brief pause I added, "The asshole killed my horse today, so maybe he's too much of a wuss to show up."

Heimer looked at me quizzically. "Whaddya mean he killed your horse?"

"Didn't you see that tarp up in the field?" I asked.

"Yeah, but I didn't think it was a dead horse. What the hell happened?"

I proceeded to tell him the grim tale of the day.

"Holy shit. What a loon. Do you think he got in trouble?" Heimer asked.

"Who knows? He didn't call or anything," I responded.

We got the fire going strong. We intended on building the biggest bonfire possible, but not so big that my Dad would come down and make us put it out.

The sun sank quickly, and in the woods the dark enveloped us. The brightness of the fire intensified the contrast of the dark background. The fire crackled loudly, but the nighttime noise of the woods overpowered. The flames rose about five feet high, and the smoke billowed upward, embers along with it.

Benzler showed up about then, somber and quiet. He sported a fresh bruise on his left cheekbone.

Heimer yelled, "Where the hell have you been loser?" then seeing his face added, "And what truck hit you?"

"It's nothing," Benzler mumbled timidly. Timid? Benzler? Normally he'd have tackled Heimer or at least had some kind of smartass remark. The two of them constantly wrestled and fought.

"Come on man, what happened?" I probed.

"My Mom smacked me a good one," he said, his voice expressionless and flat.

"What for?" Heimer jumped in.

"I told her about the horse," Benzler stated.

112

"Damn Benzler, it was an accident," I exclaimed.

Essenheimer pushed me and added, "Shut up you. A minute ago you were sniveling that Benzler killed your little pony. Crybaby." He elevated his voice at the end and faked a sob.

I pushed Heimer back saying, "Shut up."

Benzler looked at me crestfallen, shook his head, dropped his backpack, and took a seat at the picnic table. His shoulders hunched over, and he stared into the fire. The flames licked the logs, a devilish infernal mouth.

I approached Benzler and patted his shoulder. "Don't worry about that, all right?"

"You told him I killed your horse?" he asked without looking at me.

"I just told him what happened that's all," I explained.

"But you actually said I killed your horse?" he repeated and I could tell his feelings were hurt.

"I didn't mean anything by it," I responded, confirming the accusation.

"Christ, you guys are such pussies," Heimer interrupted and walked away disgusted, back to the riverbank. He fired golfball-sized stones into the water. Benzler and I sat beside one another on the picnic table not speaking. Les sat next to the fire on a tree stump. He looked

happy to be here, like he belonged, not caring or understanding any of

our conflicts.

Heimer stomped back to us "Alright, knock it off. Let's get

things going." He looked around the campsite. "Whaddya got to eat

Digger?" I left Benzler on the bench and helped Heimer find the cooler

filled with goods.

"I brought down hot dogs and marshmallows. And I found some

green branches to roast 'em on," I said pulling out the cooler. "They're

over by the fire."

"All right man," he said, smacking me on the fat of the arm. He

hit me a little too hard, so I wa obliged to punch him back even harder.

"Ouch man, what's the matter with you?" he said flinching.

I said "C'mon, let's cook some dogs. C'mon Lester." I grabbed

four sticks, the ends whittled into sharp points with my red handled

Swiss army knife. I carried the knife all the time. Along with the blade

it hads a file, a saw, a screwdriver, and little scissors.

I tossed each of the boys a stick, except Benzler who said he

wasn't hungry. He remained sulking on the picnic table behind us. The

rest of us lined up around the fire.

Heimer grabbed a dog with his pudgy fingers and shoved it onto the point of his stick longways. His aim went awry and the point poked through the side of the dog halfway down. He cursed, but used it anyway. Les deliberately slid two hot dogs perfectly onto the point of his stick.

"Benzler, ain't you eatin'? Heimer asked, and Benzler didn't reply. Heimer shrugged and watched his dog take flame. I opened up one of the HiC cans with a churchkey, and poured the red fluid through the small triangular openings into some paper cups.

We dug into the dogs, marshmallows, popcorn, and drank the HiC. Benzler didn't eat any of it. He stayed quiet, and we mostly left him be.

At this point I slipped away from the others, returning with my surprise stash of "Old Dutch."

"You stole that from Dad," Les said, eyes wide.

"No kidding jerkoff, do you want one?" I responded offering him the can. His surprise abated and he nodded his head yes. I gave one to Heimer and Benzler again shook his head no.

Heimer couldn't resist, "Benzler, what the hell's up with you? You're being one big pussy tonight."

Heimer nailed it, as usually at overnighters Benzler entertained us all with his boundless energy. He had earned the status of parent's worst nightmare due to his crazy antics. Not tonight.

Benzler simply mumbled, "Just leave me alone asshole."

Heimer started to retaliate, but I stopped him and shook my head.

He stopped, looked at Benzler, and then back at me. He took a sip of the beer. "This damn thing's warm, why didn't you put them in the cooler, numnuts?"

"I had to hide them. Besides I like them warm," I lied, embarrassed. In my excitement over swiping and stashing them, I didn't even think about the proper temperature of consumption. I put the rest of them into the cooler.

After a moment, Benzler stood and walked over to the cooler. He pulled out one of the warm beers, and proceeded to chug the entire contents. The rest of us stared at him dumbfounded. Benzler then opened the second and chugged that one too, spilling a good part of it all over his chin and shirt. He then pulled out the third and final beer, and tipped that one back as well. About half way down, it came back up, Benzler puking all over himself. From admiration to condemnation in seconds. Heimer and I laughed, and yelled at Benzler.

"Nice one pussy," Heimer yelled. Even Les laughed at him. Benzler turned and withdrew into the tent.

"Yeah, go to bed loser," Heimer taunted Benzler, and threw an empty beer can toward him. "You sure are a lot of fun tonight." Benzler looked back out but did nothing.

Without Benzler, we slowly finished our beers. Though warm, the beer felt good going down. I also pulled out the stolen cigarettes from my Dad as well. So there we sat, three pre-teenage boys sitting around the fire, drinking warm beer, smoking stale cigarettes, and roasting marshmallows. We kept the fire roaring by throwing on a continuous supply of fresh logs.

"What the hell's up with Benzler?" Heimer finally said, noting his obvious odd behavior.

I stared into the fire wondering the same thing. "I wish I knew," I said.

We stayed up as late as we could, not quite making it until dawn. Benzler never got back up at all.

*　　*　　*

Chapter 10

Lester watched aghast as Heimer smothered his eggs with Aunt Jemima's maple syrup. "Why are you putting syrup on your eggs? You can't eat eggs like that."

Mom hollered at him "Lester. William can eat his eggs as he likes them. He's our guest. Be polite now."

"Yeah, shut up Les," I chimed in and laughed. Les, humbled again, put his head down.

Wearing a pale blue terri cloth robe, Mom paraded back and forth across the kitchen threshold bringing out food......gigantic helpings of scrambled eggs with pink squares of Spam. Each boy ate his differently. I took mine straight, little Lester poured ketchup on his, Heimer, syrup.

The four of us tired boys hunched around the breakfast table on the Eidegger back porch. Screened in to keep out the flies and mosquitoes, the porch abutted the kitchen. Our family often ate out here on summer mornings and evenings to take advantage of the cool air and avoid the stuffy house. Though only June, this morning already showed signs of becoming another barnburner.

We devoured mouthful after mouthful of our breakfast. Benzler rested quietly at the end of the table eating and saying nothing.

"I'm done first!" I cried out clanging my fork down onto the plate as the winner of the unspoken informal competition. We competed over everything.

Heimer finished a close second earning the red ribbon.

"I had more eggs than you," he complained, a shred of meat lodged in his teeth, visible beneath his sneering lip.

"No you didn't, admit it loser," I argued, defending my title.

We switched gears quickly realizing neither would concede defeat no matter how trivial the battle. Benzler ignored the dispute and frowned, staring blankly into his yellow pile.

Heimer screeched at him bringing him out of his reverie.

"What the hell's the matter with you anyway Benzler? You've been a jerk since last night."

From the kitchen my Mom said, "Watch your language William!"

"Sorry Mrs. E," he apologized.

Stepping back onto the porch she turned her attention to Benzler, "Marshall, you do seem down, what's the matter honey?"

"I don't feel very well," he mumbled.

119

"Would you like me to call your mother?" Mom stepped forward and felt his forehead.

"No Ma'm," Benzler replied.

"Well, you don't have a fever. Just let me know if you feel any worse." Then Mom left us again.

Once she was gone Heimer mimicked Benzler, "I don't feel very well," in a tiny falsetto voice. "Well you're starting to bug me," he continued. "You're boring the crap out of us. Maybe, we should call your Mommy to come and get you," he taunted. A warm breeze blew through the screen across the quiet but tense table.

"Leave him alone," I said, and stood up to Heimer. I added calmly and quietly, "Come on Benzler, snap out of it. It was an accident with the horse. How many times do I have to tell you it's not your fault? Stop worrying about it."

Benzler shifted his gaze up from his eggs. He wasn't wearing his glasses and had that hollow, beady-eyed look that constant glasses wearers have when seen without them. He looked like he'd been crying at some point.

"For crying out loud, are you balling?" Heimer said, again breaching the temporary peace. "Oh my God you ARE a wuss!"

"Shut up already," I said more forcefully this time, again defending one friend against another.

"It's my allergies," Benzler squeaked lowly.

"Allergies, right," Heimer returned skeptically.

"Why don't you let him stick up for himself?" he redirected his attack to me. "You're a wuss too if you let him pull this kind of crap."

"Boys, boys, now quiet down," Mom interjected from the kitchen. "I won't have you raising your voices. Now calm down."

Essenheimer and I glared at one another. Benzler walked out onto the deck, put his head down, and began to cry.

"That does it," Heimer cried, slamming his palms on the table and standing up.

"Sit down," I told him.

"Look at him for Chrissakes." Heimer gestured toward Benzler with this hand. "If you don't agree right now that he's a puss, you're both fags. I'm outta here," he challenged. I deliberated for a moment as Benzler whimpered quietly.

"Go ahead then, get out. We don't need you around here," I finally replied.

"Why don't you make me, fag boy?" he came back.

"Fine!" I jumped up out of my seat.

121

I shoved him and he knocked a juice glass off the table shattering it on the floor. Heimer ducked his head and bull rushed me and we both crashed to the floor of the porch.

Mom rushed back in and broke up the scuffle, grabbing each of us by an ear.

"All right you two, break it up. William, outside now. Donald come in here." She pulled me into the kitchen still holding me by the ear. Benzler stopped sobbing and just looked at us blankly. Les also just sat there staring.

"What are you doing young man?" Mom asked me.

"He was making fun of Benzler," I pled in self-defense.

"I don't care. There is no call for fighting. He's your guest, and that's not how we treat guests," she scolded.

"I know Mom."

"Now go outside and apologize to your friends," she commanded pointing out the kitchen door. I stalled, so she added, "Right now."

I returned to the back porch, and joined Benzler on the deck. We sat on adjacent lawn chairs, and I noticed that at least he has stopped crying.

"Man, you gotta stop worrying about that friggin' horse," I consoled him.

"I didn't mean any harm by it. I was just goofin' around."

"I know, I know," I responded.

"I just feel so guilty. I'm a fucking loser." He started sobbing again.

Frustrated I yelled at him, "Come on, stop crying." Then I settled myself down and tried to soothe him saying, "Everything's going to be OK."

"Why did it have to happen?" he cried.

"Listen to me." I said leaning over and grabbing his arm. "It was an accident."

Brushing my arm off he stood up and said, "I know. It's not just that." He stopped talking as tears again rolled down his cheeks. His face was bright red with embarrassment.

"What then?" I asked.

"I'm not good at anything. I'm stupid, I stink at sports. I can't stay out of trouble." He wrung his hands, pacing back and forth. "Everything I touch goes wrong. Everyone hates me, including my Mom."

"Your Mom doesn't hate you, man," I countered.

"Look at my face," he said referring to his eye.

123

I pondered that a second, and said "Yeah. Your Mom's messed up."

"She thinks I do things on purpose," he explained. "I can't help it. I just can't do anything right."

"Come on man, it's not that bad. You can do a lot of things," I encouraged him. Another pregnant pause followed, as he wondered about that.

"I don't have anything. My Dad's dead. My Mom hates me," he murmured, and another tear trickled down his face. "My life sucks!"

I frowned and bit my lip. I had no clue what to say to him. Watching him struggle, I yearned to help him to somehow fix things, but I couldn't see what to do. I felt helpless. He started to sob again, and I slowly and awkwardly reached my arm over and put it around him. He turned right into me, put his head on my shoulder and broke down with uncontrollable, wrenching sobs. I felt stiff and uncomfortable, but let this go on forever it seemed.

After some time, Benzler stood abruptly. "OK. I'm better. Sorry." He wiped his face off with the arm of his shirt. He set his jaw, and squinted, determined. He rapidly walked into the house. I continued sitting out back, puzzled, my shirt soaking wet on the shoulder.

I looked around to see Heimer out in the yard looking at me. He shook his head disgusted, and turned away. I ran out to chase him down.

"Heimer," I yelled. He kept looking away. "Hey man, look, I'm sorry. Everything you said back there was spot on." Hell, I couldn't find the words to say to him either but I continued. "Benzler's going through some shit right now with his Dad. His Mom. Everything."

He finally looked back up at me, and some of the surliness left his face as it softened.

I continued, "We're his friends. He needs our help."

"What am I supposed to do?" he asked, arms crossed. I ran both of my hands through my hair.

I thought a minute, "Well, at least you can stop hounding him." Heimer turned away, taking a couple of fake baseball swings, and watching an imaginary homerun sail off.

He turned back and said, "Alright. I'll try it."

*   *   *

Chapter 11

The buzz of the motor waxed and waned. My father steered his faded red International tractor maneuvering in shrinking concentric rectangles as he cut grass in the pasture. His path didn't waver until he nearly drove upon the rigid heap, the grey skin of the tarp folding awkwardly around the lifeless form. Closer inspection yielded a stagnant hoof or a glimpse of the black and white horsehide.

We lazed on the front porch steps drinking icy lemonade. Mom had the best recipe for lemonade, soaking peels in sugar overnight and then dumping them into the fresh squeezed juice. But that extra tartness was tasteless on our tongues today. Benzler's funk continued through the morning, and all of us seemed subdued, sapped of strength from this morning's outburst.

The whine of the mower recurred, the pitch rising as my father returned in our direction. Only when he neared us did the noise of the machine truly overpower the constant hum of the locusts. Actually, that hum came from cicada, but everyone called them locusts. Whatever the name, they were synonymous with the hot, humid midwestern summer, the air thick with ragweed pollen.

Benzler barely touched his lemonade. His head sagged, his straight hair hanging lower than his down turned mouth. His long skinny legs sprawled spiderlike on the porch floor, covered in snug fitting Levis. We all wore bluejeans despite the heat because shorts were for sissies. Benzler's overgrown feet, like a puppy whose paws belied their eventual size, bore untied Chuck Taylor sneakers.

"So what do you guys want to do?" I asked, trying to make something happen. "We can swim, fish, or go over to the golf course." Number three green of King's Mill Golf Course nestled up against the woods across the river behind our house. Because of a blind approach shot, the local hackers couldn't see us as we periodically played tricks on them. Sometimes we'd steal their balls, other times we'd place the ball in the hole to give the unsuspecting golfer a surprise hole-in-one. One time we placed live crawdads right into the hole hoping to see a pinch, but those dads never stayed in the holes and ended up crawling harmlessly around on the green.

My offer elicited little response except a shrug or two, and nothing from Benzler. I decided to lead the group on over in the direction of the course anyway. Benzler tagged along tamely, still quiet, head down. The heat began to melt the pavement, and we made footprints in the grayblack gum.

An old iron suspension bridge a quarter mile down the road provided the only dry way across the river to the course. The bridge spanned the Olentangy River, 150 feet across. The top of the bridge

arched over, 20 feet above the road surface. From there it dropped

another 20 feet or so to the water.

We paused in the center of the bridge and gazed down into the

water. The seasons of the changeling river. In winter, the top froze

solid, all the while the dormant river still breathed below the icy surface.

I'd witnessed the ice breakup and colossal floes that moved downstream,

awesome and powerful. I'd seen spring floods where water rose to the

bridge level. If the floods came early and coincided with the ice floes, it

completely wiped out bridges like these.

Now summer returned, the water level lowered, and the heat and

draught drained the life as the river shrank into a mere fraction of itself.

The water looked clear but still brown colored. Weeds and high reeds

struggled to strangle one another on the riverbanks. A few transient

islands dotted the shoreline. Cattails, with their brown caterpillar tips,

waved skyward in the faint breeze.

We lugged a small arsenal of stones up here and competed for

targets both live and dead. Fish swam in the soft current, mostly carp,

some bluegill. Occasionally you could spot a turtle, the soft-shelled with

the spines and pointy snout, the familiar box turtle, or even the dreaded snapper. You had to be on the lookout for snappers when swimming if you wanted to keep all your toes.

Snakes lived in abundance in these parts too, though most weren't poisonous. Common black water snakes looked nasty with their thick dark bodies, but generally they existed peaceably. Water moccasins provided the only true threat.

Heimer pointed out a target. "See that rock out there?" None of us did. He fired his stone and it plopped next to an exposed rock in the river. "I hit it!"

"You weren't even aiming at that you liar," I said.

"Was too."

"Whatever you say Heimer," I conceded, not wanting to fight again. I looked over at Les and rolled my eyes.

We soon ran out of ammo, so Heimer hocked a big loogie at the river. Spit made a decent weapon when waging war on each other –I'd much rather be hit with a rock than spit- but it had little influence on nature.

Meanwhile, I noticed that Benzler had disappeared. "Where the hell did Benzler go?' I asked generally.

Heimer shrugged, "Beats me."

"Les?" He nodded his head no.

Looking up, I saw that Benzler had climbed atop the arch of the bridge, and stood directly above me. Seeing Benzler up there delighted rather than angered me. We'd climbed up there many times before because my Dad forbade it.

"Alright Benzler, finally joining the living," I yelled out. "Guys, look at Benzler!" The three of us stared up at our friend standing carelessly above us.

Heimer cried "Don't fall wussy!" in a falsetto voice feigning concern. But Benzler's gaunt face didn't waver, no smile, just his hard flat olive drab gaze.

I sensed what he intended to do at the last moment. "No," I yelled, but it didn't stop him. He leapt outward, down and off of the bridge.

"The water's not deep enough!" I warned. But it was too late, Benzler pierced the shallow water creating a dull splash and then a thud as he struck the river bottom.

A hideous snap wrenched my gut. He was dead, he was fucking dead I knew it. The shallow water where he landed ran maybe three feet tops over a solid rock bottom.

"Les," I hollered at my brother. He stood motionless staring in disbelief at Benzler.

"Les. Go get Dad. Now. Run!" The plea finally registered, and he took off. I could still hear the tractor motor from here, so at least Dad should be easy to find.

Heimer and I scrambled to the end of the bridge and crashed down the slippery heavily weeded embankment to the water's edge. We plowed splashing through the murky water to get to Benzler.

Barely keeping his head above the water surface, Benzler moaned in pain.

"Benzler, what the fuck was that?" I yelled. We made it to him, brown turbid water flowing around me just below the waist level. We each grabbed an arm and began dragging him to shore. His moan instantly turned into a shriek.

"Whoa, whoa. Hold on," I said to Heimer. I wondered aloud, "Maybe we shouldn't move him."

Heimer looked back at me saying, "We've got to get him out of this water at least."

"Right, right," I agreed.

We pulled him once again, and again he screamed.

"Can't you get his leg to float or something?" Heimer asked.

"Yeah. Good idea. Let's switch sides," I responded.

Doing that seemed to help and we got him to the shore. On shore Benzler laid quietly if just for the moment.

Unsure of what to do, I pulled up the leg of his jeans to take a look at the injury. The lower left leg bone had broken leaving a giant lump, which pressed tight against the skin. The swelling and discoloration had started immediately. Heimer looked at this and faints.

Benzler stopped making any kind of sound, and lied on the riverbank, completely waterlogged. He risked losing consciousness altogether. I tried to remember anything I could about first aid. What was that about going into shock?

"Benzler, come on man, stay awake," I shook him by the shoulders. "Heimer, c'mon. Get up and help me. I can't carry him by myself?" I stated this in futility as Heimer laid out cold on the bank. The blue fuzz of panic enveloped me.

Dad pulled up in the family station wagon, a Ford LTD "Country Squire." He lumbered down the hillside with Les directly behind him. His calm presence immediately eased me.

Les had told Dad about Benzler, then seeing Heimer, Dad asked, "What's the matter with him?"

"He passed out when he saw Benzler's leg," I tattled.

"For Pete's sake," Dad said. "Les, splash water on him." Les did as Dad said, splashing water onto Heimer's face to revive him. He awakened but looked sickly pale and gray. We turned our attention to Benzler. Dad and I grabbed him under his arms and began to pull him up the hill. The intensity of the pain revived Benzler, and he resumed screaming.

We stopped and my Dad tried to calm him, "Relax son, it's all gonna be OK."

Dad asked me, "What the hell happened here Donny?"

"I don't know. He just climbed up on the bridge and fell off."

"I've told you a hundred times to keep off of there," Dad screamed at me.

"I know, I know."

Dad shook his head and paced back and forth assessing what we should do. "We've got to get him to the hospital," he said. "So we've gotta figure out how to move him up the hill."

Dad tore the leg of Benzler's jeans into strips. He sent me to search for something to make a splint. I found a couple of suitable sticks, and he prepared a makeshift splint for the broken leg. Benzler screamed intensely while Dad tightened it over the wound.

We made a chair by grasping one another's arms, and with Heimer and Les' help we carried Benzler up to the car.

Benzler's moans had decreased somewhat and we drove him to the emergency room at the hospital in Marion.

*　　*　　*

Chapter 12

I rode shotgun holding three comic books in my lap, gifts for Benzler during his recovery. I brought him his favorites: a "Sad Sack", a "Swamp Thing", and a "Mad Magazine."

Dad took me to the hospital to visit for the first time since the accident. He drove us into the hospital in our station wagon that Les and I called "the Squire." Maroon colored with wooden panels running along each side, "the Squire" drove like a tank. Though only a couple of years old, rust already began to bubble on the quarter panels. The damn salt they used on the icy roads in the winter does that.

Dad pulled his Winston toward his mouth and drew in deeply. He blew the smoke out his partially open window. He kept the window down even though it had begun to rain. He drove and smoked without speaking. The lines of his forehead creased as he squinted into the windshield. Tar from the two packs per day yellowed his fingernails.

Benzler had survived his fall, suffering only a displaced fracture of his left tibia. Only? When we took him to the emergency room that day, he needed surgery on his leg to put screws in. As horrible as it seemed at the time, apparently he would indeed recover. He'd been in the hospital now for a few days right through the 4th of July.

As always, Dad tuned the AM radio to WMRN, 1490 Marion, the only radio station in town. We listened to the news with an announcer updating the world about Watergate. Boring politics slop.

"Dad?" I interrupted something about President Nixon's impeachment.

"Yeah Donny?" he replied. He flicked his cigarette butt out onto the street, and then rolled up his window. He stole a quick glimpse at me before diverting his attention back to the road.

"Why do you suppose Benzler jumped off the bridge?" I asked, squirming with discomfort.

"Jumped off? I thought he fell." Silence again. My Dad shook his head. "I'll be damned. That's one foolhardy son of a gun. What? Was he showing off or something? Acting tough?"

"No, I don't think so," I stuttered. Pausing for a few seconds, Dad lit up another cigarette. I continued, "He seemed so sad." I stopped again, sort of afraid to say what I wanted to say. "I think he meant to hurt himself."

Dad choked and coughed. "Hurt himself? What the dickens for?"

"I think he felt bad about Gypsy and all."

"What the devil'd that old horse have to do with it?" he challenged. I told him why I thought Benzler felt responsible for the horse's death.

Dad kept driving, and I waited patiently for his opinion. "Maybe. But it was your horse son. That boy wasn't attached." He resumed, "Besides, he's been hunting and fishing all his life. He should be used to killing animals. It doesn't make a whole lotta sense to me." Dad made a good point. I'd seen Benzler kill many a critter just for sport. I'd witnessed him drop a brick on a live toad and laugh. Down on the farm, boys grew up with death. You grew attached to animals you raised, then led them to slaughter. After awhile you got used to it.

136

"But horses are like dogs Dad. They're pets. You don't eat them. I think that matters," I rebutted.

"I agree with you Donny. But I'm still surprised that crazy kid cares about any damned animal," Dad responded.

We pulled into the hospital parking lot. Dad found a spot between a white Dodge van and a rusted pale blue Volkswagen bug. The rain had cooled things down quite a bit, and the wind still kicked, though the storm had passed.

Marion General Hospital stood three-stories, a brick building with white columns at the entrance. I was born here at MGH. The hospital lay on the southern edge of town next to a Memorial Park dedicated after World War I. A bronze doughboy statue stood tall on the corner of the main thoroughfare, Delaware Avenue. I didn't get why they called it the doughboy. It always made me think of the fat Pillsbury doughboy. Not very flattering for a soldier. Across Delaware Avenue they built the Harding Memorial, for President Warren G. Harding who once lived here, and started the town newspaper about a hundred years ago.

Dad and I moved briskly across the hospital parking lot toward the shelter of the entrance. The wind whipped against my windbreaker, and I protected the comics by carrying them under my jacket.

Dad said, "You know, I bet Marshall tried to kill himself." We paused again as we entered through the front double glass doors. "But it wasn't that damned horse."

"What do you mean Dad?" I asked as we cross the front lobby.

"Well, he's been through a lot. His Dad shootin' himself," he answered. "Heck, the kid finds his father like that. Mess you up for sure. I bet he's having a hard time with it."

"What can I do about it?"

Dad didn't reply right away as he approached the receptionist desk and checked us in.

"We're looking for Benzler, B- E- N- Z-L- E- R," my Dad told the receptionist.

"Room 207. Visiting hours are until 8 PM sir."

"OK. Thank you." We proceeded down the hall and found the elevators. My Dad pushed the "UP" arrow, which lit up.

The bell rang when the elevator arrived, and the door slid open. We entered the compartment, and the door closed behind us. Facing forward, we stared at the illuminated floor indicator in awkward silence.

"Actually Donny, I've been meaning to talk to you about that.....I think you ought to steer clear of Marshall for awhile," Dad finally responded.

What? I didn't know what to say to Dad after that bombshell. Abandon my friend? Now? That didn't seem right.

We stepped off and walked down the sterile hallway, the smell of ammonia nearly gagging me. White ceiling, stark white walls, only the black and white floor tiles broke up the pattern. The lack of windows on this wing created a need for more light. We found Benzler's room, number 207. Knocking lightly, we pushed open the door, and I followed my Dad into the room.

"G'afternoon Marshall," my Dad said, greeting Benzler.

Benzler lay on an electric adjustable hospital bed with his broken leg elevated. He'd propped himself up to watch TV. Bob Barker offered up another deal on "The Price is Right." Just as drab as the hallway, at least Benzler had a window. I looked outside at the windblown trees.

Benzler looked up at us, with his hair messed up, but clean, and his glasses cocked crookedly. His face was devoid of expression, but in particular his eyes looked dull and glassy. He returned his gaze to Bob Barker.

I thought of the usual smart-assed comment to say to him, like calling him Evel Knievel, but decided against it, and merely muttered "Hi Benzler."

He looked back at us, but didn't speak. I inched toward him as if afraid to arouse him.

"So how are you feeling?" I asked.

He spent a few seconds focusing, then replied, "What do you think? I feel like shit." He looked back at the TV.

"I brought you some comic books," I mentioned, extending them to him. He didn't move to take them so I put them on the nightstand. "You can look at them later," I mumbled.

"Lots of pain?" my Dad queried.

"No." He didn't explain, he just continued to watch the tube.

"When they gonna let you out?"

"Don't know." He spoke slowly and deliberately. During the interchange his lazy eyes rested on me unblinking. He didn't glare, he just lacked any animation at all. I struggled through these miserable few moments of stilted conversation. More excruciating silence passed.

"What'd the doctor say about the leg? I asked.

"It's broken."

"I know that. But are you going to be the same? When can you walk?"

"Well I'll never be the same," he asserted placidly. "Who knows about my leg? I don't really care."

I plopped down in a black vinyl hospital chair next to the bed. My Dad remained standing, observing us but not saying anything.

I went on with my questioning, "Has your Mom been in to see you?" He casted me an irritable glance.

"Ha. Not much," he replied flatly. "She keeps crying. Says I'm trying to hurt her."

"Are you?" I probed.

"Look man, I really don't want to talk about this right now." A slight edge grew in his voice.

I pushed on, "Are you trying to hurt your Mom?"

"No," he responded abruptly, louder, short. "It's just always all about her." He stopped speaking and reverted back to Bob Barker. We watched disinterested for a minute or two as someone guessed the price of a new car at $3300.

"Look, are you here to cheer me up or make me feel worse?" Benzler spoke again, his voice escalating.

"Why'd ya jump off the bridge?" I blurted out.

"Boys, boys. Calm down," Dad jumped in uncomfortably. Dad wanted to smooth everything over, but I felt anything but calm. And it was out there now, and I couldn't take it back. The unsaid said. Silence once again descended like the hum of locusts. I could hear with amazing acuity, my Dad's work boots creaked as he shifted his weight.

"I don't know," Benzler eventually said, shaking his head. "Can't you just leave it alone?" He dipped his head, and his arms layed limply at his sides. It seemed as if all the air flowed out of the room like a deflating balloon.

Disappointed, I told Benzler we needed to go. We left him without any further hubbub. Midway down the hallway I stopped, turned back and headed toward Benzler's room.

"Dad, I'll be right back." I stranded him wondering in the hall.

I burst back into Benzler's room, and he looked up at me with those glazed eyes.

"Were you or were you not trying to kill yourself?" I asked him point blank.

He looked down and admitted, "Yes."

"Yes what?" I pressed.

He looked me right in the eyes and carefully enunciated each word. "Yes, I was trying to kill myself."

I stood back, shocked. "Why?"

"I told you before, that one day at your house," he explained. "I can't do anything right. I can't even kill myself right." He stopped, and rubbed his eyes for a moment. He opened them, beginning again, "Everything I touch turns to shit. Everyone hates me. And I can't take it anymore." He stated this with his face drawn blankly, without any emotion. The contrast between the content of the words and his expression seemed so inappropriate that it had more impact on me.

"Do you still want to?" I asked.

"No. I guess not," he confided.

"That's good," I concluded. "Hopefully you're telling me the truth."

"Man, right now I'm just so tired," he added, heaving out a sigh.

"OK. I'll go, and let you rest. Take care of yourself. I'll come back to see you again later."

With that, I walked out of the room for the final time. I found my Dad down in the lobby gift shop looking at paperbacks.

"You through now?" he expressed, exasperated chewing on a piece of Wrigley's Spearmint. Whenever he couldn't smoke he chewed gum.

"Yeah, let's go."

We trudged back to the car. The sun had reappeared in a completely clear sky though the wind still blows. Typical Ohio weather.

Back in the car, I talked with Dad. "Benzler looks horrible."

"What did you expect? He's doped up. He could barely talk for Pete's sake," Dad said.

"What do you mean?" I asked, not completely understanding.

"Yeah, they must have him on painkillers or something. Maybe more. You saw him. Glazed look in his eyes, slow speech."

"Yeah, now that you mention it. I guess that's why he was acting so weird." I thought about Benzler's lifeless gray eyes. "Dad, I don't know what to do. What did you mean before about steering clear of him?"

Dad cleared his throat and explained, "Donny, I know this is hard for you. But you have to understand your mother and I are looking out for your best interest." He didn't look at me, seemingly ashamed of his decision. "He might be a bad influence."

"But Dad, he needs a friend now more than ever," I argued.

"I don't think now's the time to discuss it," he stated firmly, ending the discussion.

Dad drove us home south on route 423, neither of us speaking the rest of the way.

*　　*　　*

144

Chapter 13

Benzler observed a girl looking at him from across the room. She wore a soft blue sundress, light, alluring. As he made eye contact with her she spoke to him, but he couldn't hear. What was she saying? Wake up honey? What does that mean? He awoke from the dream to someone calling his name, and a firm touch on his shoulder.

"Marshall, wake up honey." He recognized the smell of his mother before he opened his leaden lids to view her blurry image. What a weird dream. He licked his dry lips, still noting that metallic medicine aftertaste. Yuck. As his vision cleared, he saw that his mother looked horrible. Her skin looked boiled and gray. Black, deep circles surrounded each eye. His Mom, never a beauty, used to be healthy, robust, and full of vitality, your stereotypical hearty German stock. Since his Dad's death, she had spiraled downward. Benzler's jump knocked her over a narrow edge.

A tall, gaunt man stood directly behind her. Mr. Abernathy, his roommate? An older gentleman with a broken hip, the hospital placed Mr. Abernathy into Benzler's room two days ago. He rarely spoke and had few visitors.

But no, as the man with his mother stepped closer, Benzler recognized the stubbly gray and black beard. Oh, it was just his psychiatrist Dr. Stevenson, whom Benzler had been seeing as an outpatient the past couple of months. Those biweekly visits hadn't been all that productive. More or less ambivalent to the doctor, Benzler didn't find him personally engaging. Doctor Stevenson never fully gained Benzler's trust making progress unlikely. Since the jumping episode a few days prior, Benzler hadn't spoken with him. In Benzler's reality, the doctor had such little impact on him that he hadn't even thought of the doctor.

At the hospital another nameless staff doctor prescribed him medication. Thorazine. Thorazine, an anti-psychotic, put him on his ass and made him drool. In any case, Benzler liked the meds because they took the pain away. He hated them because they took everything else away too.

Doctor Stevenson sidled over and eased down onto an edge of the bed. Benzler's mother distanced herself in the corner of the room. A curtain divided the room, affording some measure of privacy. Benzler's eyelids drooped and he struggled to keep them open. He couldn't wait for them to just leave him alone.

After some small talk, Doctor Stevenson began, "Marshall, do you want to tell me what happened with this bridge incident?" Benzler shook his head in the negative. He layed flat on his back, staring at the white drop ceiling of his hospital room. Through the window, he noticed the fading light. Hunger pangs pulled at his stomach, and thirst scratched at his throat.

The doctor proceeded speaking softly, "Alright Marshall. Your friends and mother have convinced me that you purposefully jumped off that bridge with the intent of harming yourself. Can you confirm that?" Benzler decided at that moment to break off his connection with the doctor. Screw him. He silently demonstrated this defiance with a fierce glare at the ceiling.

Dr. Stevenson rose and approached Mrs. Benzler in the corner.

"He looks to be in pretty bad shape," he whispered, not wanting Marshall to overhear.

She asked him too loudly, "What do you suggest we do?"

Still keeping his voice low, the doctor declared, "As we discussed before, our goal is to protect Marshall from hurting himself further. It's standard practice in cases of attempted suicide to prescribe full time care. The circumstances surrounding your husband's death add more validity to my recommendation. By full time care I'm speaking of a psychiatric hospital of course."

Mrs. Benzler gasped, discernibly shaken. "Where? For how long?"

"I recommend the hospital we talked about called Wilson. It's in Colulmbus, so it's close by. It's extremely well regarded, and has a special emphasis on children," the doctor assured her.

"I don't know. I just don't know what I should do," she whined, her voice cracking, lip quivering. Faint tears pooled in the bags beneath her glossy eyes.

"Look, I know you're thinking of mindless, babbling zombies," he continued. "Straight jackets, electric shock. It's not like that anymore. Psychiatry has progressed dramatically the past few years. Besides, we're not talking about a permanent stay. It'll just be for a few months. In fact, I'm certain it will be beneficial. I think it's time we talk to Marshall about it."

She acquiesced.

The doctor pulled Mrs. Benzler back toward the troubled boy.

Dr. Stevenson began, "Marshall, I recommend...."

"I could hear everything you said," Benzler said, interrupting him. The doctor and Mrs. Benzler glanced at one another. Mrs.

Benzler's eyebrows raised, and the doctor gently placed his hand on her arm.

He then proceeded, "OK then. I feel that admission to a psychiatric hospital for further observation will give you some time to get yourself together."

Benzler again cut him off, "I'm not going to any nuthouse."

Dr. Stevenson picked up where he left off, "You will have excellent treatment there. I'll keep in touch with your progress. It's for the best."

"I'm not going. Aren't you listening?" Benzler stated, voice rising.

Dr. Stevenson looked over at Mrs. Benzler, then back. "Marshall, your mother has already agreed." With that Dr. Stevenson stood, gestured to Mrs. Benzler, and then exited.

Alone now with her son, Mrs. Benzler peered into the approaching headlights. Her eyes shined, her mouth was taut under furrowed brows. Sensing her vulnerability, Benzler cast an intimidating stare at her.

"I'm sorry," she blubbered.

"Shut up," he commanded.

"Marshall…" she plead.

149

"I said shut up," he interrupted again with more emphasis.

Mr. Abernathy began to furiously press his call button.

He stepped up his attack, "Why don't you just get the fuck out of here?"

Mrs. Benzler's sobs turned to helpless heaves.

Callously Benzler spewed, "Too late for tears now Mom." She crept out the door, broken. As she shut the door behind her, he yelled out "I hate you!" His voice rattled the windows. She winced and with her fragile head lowered, she stepped down the hall.

A nurse came in abruptly both responding to Mr. Abernathy and hearing Benzler's voice at the nurse's station, "Marshall, you'll need to keep quiet. You're disturbing Mr. Abernathy and other patients." His anger at his mother vented, Benzler relapsed to his uncommunicative stoic stare at the ceiling.

"Marshall, acknowledge me," the nurse demanded. Still nothing. "Marshall?"

"OK," he obeyed, just to get her to stop. "Please leave me alone."

She abandoned him, and Benzler descended from bad to worse.

*   *   *

Chapter 14

Benzler's muted fury persisted during the two weeks building up to his scheduled admission to Wilson. Adding to his bad temper, his thirteenth birthday passed uncelebrated. On D-day his Mom transported him, driving the straight shot due south on US23. He slumped in the front passenger seat of their Chevy Suburban not uttering a word the entire trip. His Mom tried to speak to him initially, but he remained aloof. He hadn't spoken a solitary word to her since their clash at the hospital.

With no air conditioning in the car, Benzler rolled his window all the way down. That fruitless effort didn't help much with the extreme furnace like August weather. He shoved his face out the opening, and the wind's force pressed against his numbed skin. That would surely wreak havoc with his allergies later.

Benzler observed as they passed cornfields, fields of soybeans, and fallow untended fields overcome by volunteer alfalfa and ragweed. As they cruised by red and white barns and grain silos, he mentally identified tractors, combines, and other farm equipment. Benzler knew every model of tractor, John Deere his favorite. He recited them as soon as he spotted them. "There goes a JD thirty-twenty," he'd say. Not today though. To his Mom he voiced nothing.

Columbus boasted the title of Ohio state capital, and maintained the status as one of the Midwest's fastest growing cities. As they approached the city, the fields and woods gave way to suburbia. Housing tracts, strip malls, and traffic. The smell of exhaust supplanted the fresh country air, and their pace slowed.

Wilson was a private psychiatric hospital about an hour south of his house, located in the Columbus suburb of Worthington. Established in 1947 by a prominent local doctor, the hospital treated patients with a broad spectrum of mental illness. However, most serious cases went to the state hospital nearby. Wilson was reserved for treatment of milder illnesses or families of wealth.

Around noon, they turned into the long drive, and wound between white buildings and verdant grounds. Benzler thought the place looked pleasant enough. Peaceful. With slightly lifted hopes, Benzler and his Mom marched up the entrance walkway through the door marked "Admissions." Benzler needed crutches, but effortlessly kept up with his Mom.

Inside, they found a small foyer with a sofa along each wall, a coffee table cluttered with magazines, and a gray-haired nurse behind a slotted window, like an old-time bank teller. The room smelled musty, like the pages of an old book.

The nurse continued working as the pair drew near.

"Yes?" she snapped without looking up. Benzler looked down at his feet sourly. His left was covered by an already dirty cast, a constant and visible reminder of why he now stood here.

His Mom stated, "I'm here to admit my son."

"Name?" the nurse asked, still without looking up.

"Mine or my son's?" Benzler's Mom countered.

"Your son's," the nurse clarified, continuing to focus her attention downward on her paperwork.

"Marshall Benzler," his Mom answered, agitated by the nurse's rude behavior.

Finally the nurse looked up and handing Benzler's Mom a folder directed, "Fill out these forms, and bring them back up here when you're finished."

They took a seat, filled out the forms, and waited. Benzler flipped nervously through one magazine after another. Since kicking his

Mom out of his hospital room, disinterest has balanced his anger. Now he felt a wisp of fear drifting in. Fear of the unknown, fear of himself.

Benzler kept a close eye on the wall clock. At one-thirty, two burly gentlemen appeared in the doorway, his escorts presumably. Wilson employed these gentlemen as psychiatric technicians to handle a variety of crisis situations. They dressed normally, not in white coats or anything like that. The hospital recruited mostly college students at Ohio State or nearby Otterbein University as well as a couple of others. Generally speaking they selected clean-cut gentlemen, who made good role models for the kids.

He turned toward his now crying mother, and again felt the surge of anger rise over the fear. He had the sudden realization of abandonment.

One of his escorts barked in a deep bass voice, "OK Marshall, it's time to come along with us." An enormous man in his twenties, this tech wore a crew cut and had a square face. One of his thick hands gently coaxed Benzler's elbow, and the boy didn't resist.

Without a word to his mother, he turned away, and maneuvered his crutches through the doorway and into the main building. He didn't look back as the door lock clicked shut behind him. A young nurse joined them on the other side of the door, approaching from down the narrow hallway. She attracted Benzler instantly, despite the circumstances. He noted her wavy shoulder length black hair, and he had a strange urge to feel it.

"Welcome Marshall, my name is Nurse Kincaid and I'm a registered psychiatric nurse. We're going to start you off in a place that we call 'Special Care.'" She spoke to him with an angelic voice, "All of our new patients start there. It's a safe place to be, just until you get yourself oriented." Her soft voice calmed him momentarily.

Benzler began the three-legged march with a tech on either side of him, and Nurse K. leading. Benzler's eyes darted from side to side, searching their faces.

Sensing his apprehension, she continued, "Marshall, you're in a safe place now. We're all here to help you."

Despite the nurse's assurance, Benzler trembled, and his eyes widened. His body recoiled as Nurse Kincaid brushed his shoulder. In his tension Benzler stopped walking. He jerked his head around feeling surrounded, smelling acrid sweat mixed with cologne.

Two more young men arrived, raising Benzler's angst. The newly arrived techs kept some distance, but nervously eyed Benzler.

The nurse tried again, "These gentlemen are psych techs and are here for your safety. They won't harm you." An anxious stalemate passed.

"Marshall, if you'll just walk with us, we'll take it nice, slow, and easy. Everything is going to be fine."

Benzler, stopped, fear in his eyes stuttered, "OK. I'll come easily. But tell them to back off." He nodded his brow toward the growing assembly.

"Marshall, as I said they're here for your safety. They won't harm you. They won't even touch you unless necessary." The new technicians moved in closer, sensing a potential problem, as Benzler hesitated.

Claustrophobic panic exploded in Benzler, the fear rising like soda over ice, and overflowing. He tried to run, but with his broken leg and crutches, he went nowhere. The first huge technician grabbed his arm, and Benzler whirled around striking him with the crutch. That feeble attempt made no impact and the tech forced him to the ground. His glasses went flying and his face hit the floor. Benzler tasted the salt of blood on his lip. The mob of others joined in pinning him down.

Benzler screamed, "Aaaah, let me go," along with a torrent of obscenities. Squirming and writhing, amazingly he could still move under the human mass.

Amid the bedlam, the techs shouted at one another, "Grab his leg. You, get his head!" Chaos ruled for the time being.

Nurse Kincaid stood in the background warning the techs, "Be careful, mind his leg." Despite the melee, Benzler noticed her, and her caring act touched him.

The technicians rolled him in a heavy blanket, trapping his arms and legs. They hoisted and conveyed him down the hall like a human sausage roll to the place the nurse had called "Special Care." Benzler struggled and screamed, and he tried to bite a hand that got too near his mouth. That action resulted in a towel being shoved over his face.

Roughly 10 feet by 10 feet four walls painted pale blue, Special Care contained only an iron padded bed in its center. The techs strapped Benzler down onto the bed binding his wrists, ankles, and waist to the' ponderous bed with leather restraints. His straw hair wet with sweat, veins bulging out of his neck and forehead, eyes wild, Benzler never stopped fighting.

Nurse Kincaid entered with an injection, and that accomplished, the entire staff filed out of the room, and bolted the door. Again Benzler heard that crisp, cold metallic click. Locked tight.

Benzler twisted and turned until the leather straps cut into his flesh. He bellowed though his voice hoarsened. A sensation overcame him like someone pulling down a shade in his brain, and immediately he stopped moving. In a stupor he gazed at the whirring ceiling fan until he drifted into sleep.

*   *   *

Chapter 15

"Hendrick drives the ball into left center. That one's gonna drop in. Gamble rounds third and he'll score." Herb Score blathered, his familiar voice crackling over Dad's transistor radio. I liked Oscar Gamble because he looked cool with his giant afro sticking out from under his batting helmet. Dad didn't like him for the same reason.

"Donny, pass up the wire strippers," he called down to me a second time, snapping my focus on the radio. His muffled voice came from above where he worked on some wiring in the basement ceiling

158

gap. He stood on the top step of a ladder, and I couldn't even see his head.

Score announced games for the hapless Cleveland Indians. Usually this late in the season they'd already been out of the pennant race for a month. This year had been special, however. Pitcher Gaylord Perry won fifteen consecutive starts at one point. In first place as late as July, over the last month they swooned as usual, and had fallen all the way to fourth. Disappointing but not surprising.

I searched for the tool and also for the right moment to ask Dad something. I wanted to go see Benzler, as I hadn't seen him since we visited at Marion General. Not since he transferred to Wilson, about a month ago. Our last discussion about it seemed final.

"Is this it?" I found the yellow handled tool easily. Loaded with a ton of tools, Dad organized everything in his workshop. So for this job, I had a specific portable toolbox with all of the necessary components.

"Yeah, that's right," Dad confirmed. He reached down and I passed up the tool.

This old farmhouse constantly needed something fixed. Having grown up during the Great Depression, Dad thought it was wasteful and lazy not to do things yourself. He wouldn't even think of hiring anyone to help him despite Mom's complaints about him taking too long. Sometimes he let me help him. Like today, I helped him with some electrical work in the basement. Built 150 years ago before electricity, my Dad put in all of the electrical work himself.

I waited below for further direction as Charlie Spikes struck out, another Tribe rally came up short. Regardless of the continual disappointment, Dad listened to the Tribe religiously. He raised me to love his teams too, but I wasn't the fan that he was. Even I couldn't entirely understand his devotion to this team that perennially finished near the bottom of the standings. Being a sports fan carried a lot of pain. At the end of the season only one team won.

During the commercial break I finally blurted out, "Dad, can you take me to see Benzler today?"

"Ask your mother." Dad's standard evasive reply.

"I already did. She said to ask you," I countered. Of course, I already asked her first. I hoped she'd take me. She actually liked Benzler.

Dad labored silently for a few moments, as I stared up from the foot of the ladder. Smoke curled up from a cigarette left burning in an ashtray, the only odor that cut through the basement's musty smell.

Hundreds of river stones stacked on top of one another made up the walls of our unfinished basement. Cobwebs and soot from our coal-burning furnace covered the stones. We poured the black coal through a chute into the basement during winter. Coal dust and rubble scattered in the corner, unused.

Finally, Dad climbed down, his worn leather work boots stepping with care. He wiped a cobweb off of his head, his eyes showing concern.

"It's a long drive down there Donny. Why can't you just write him a letter?" I explained that I had written a couple letters.

"And?" he asked still not satisfied.

"Benzler's not the kind of guy that writes letters. I just want to go down and see him."

"Well, you know that's a long way down there, just like that."

"Maybe we can go next week," I said continuing my pursuit. "It's not that far."

"I don't think it's a good idea," Dad replied looking right at me. He placed his hand on my shoulder, and pressed hard with his thumb.

"Why not?" I pled.

161

He released me and turned away. "Donny, I told you before that your mother and I feel that you shouldn't see Marshall anymore." I could tell that this embarrassed him.

"What? But why?" I crowed in protest. "I don't understand. He's my best friend." But I knew why without asking. And now Benzler had actually been deemed crazy.

"Donny, be careful," he warned. Dad generally didn't tolerate any sass. "You know darn well why." I crossed my arms and frowned. Ending the discussion, he climbed back up the ladder, head disappearing into the ceiling.

"Didn't you ever have any friends?" I asked with sarcasm. I hit a nerve because Dad drops down more quickly this time. Talking back wasn't going to work.

"Donald, you're trying my patience," he said, red-faced. "Your mother and I have given this a lot of thought. We think it's best right now to give this situation some time, so knock it off." His anger died down as he spoke. He took a deep breath, and reached for his cigarette. "Besides, you saw him at the regular hospital. End of story."

"But Dad!"

"Goddam it, that's enough! We're not going anywhere! You're not seeing that crazy kid!"

I realized I pushed him too far because he rarely swore. I once heard him say the "F" word, but that was during last year's Ohio State-Michigan football game. To him "Goddam it" was just as bad. He glared at me expecting a full retreat, vein bulging in his forehead. I stood as a statue, frozen. Should I give up? I mean he was really pissed. Not to mention that he was probably right.

I decided to persist. "But Dad, Benzler's my best friend. He needs my help right now. Please."

"No," he said slamming his fist down on his workbench. "For the last time, NO!"

I turned and walked to the wooden basement stairs and began ascending. I mumbled under my breath, "You don't know what the hell you're talking about."

He yelled, "What did you say?"

"Nothing," I mumbled and kept walking.

"Go on. Get up to your room," he said, getting the last word.

I flashed past my Mom in the hall. She asked, "What's the matter honey?"

I ignored her and ran up to my room.

*   *   *

Chapter 16

Benzler woke from a fitful sleep to the sound of a key turning in the door lock. Normally a belly sleeper, being strapped in restraints splayed on his back inhibited sleep. His body ached from last night's struggle. His broken leg throbbed, and his head hammered like a sledge. He squinted his eyes as the technician flipped on the blinding ceiling light.

The tech knelt down beside the bed. "Good morning Marshall, I'm Mr. Turner. How're you feeling?" Mr. Turner's given name was Steve. But on this children's unit the technicians all went by "Mister" or "Miss," and the nurses and doctors by their titles. Supposedly this reinforced the roles of patient and staff.

Benzler studied Turner's ruddy face, and concluded that he wasn't one of the techs that tackled him. Though Benzler was irritable and defensive, Turner's easy smile and low soothing voice disarmed him.

Benzler licked his cracked lips. "I'm real thirsty. Can I get some water?"

"Sure. I'll be right back." Mr. Turner stood, stretching his lanky form. He stepped out of the room, and locked the door behind him.

Returning a moment later, he unlocked the door bringing a small paper cup of water. He gently tilted the cup so Benzler could drink the cool, refreshing water.

"You locked the door," Benzler observed.

Mr. Turner nodded and smiled.

"Man, I'm tied up here, where am I gonna go?"

Mr. Turner chuckled. "That's right, but I have to follow the hospital protocol."

"Can I get out of these?" Benzler asked, referring to the restraints.

"That's up to the doctor," Mr. Turner replied.

"You mean I might have to stay in 'em?" Benzler asked, raising his voice slightly.

"I really can't say. But I do know that if you're not calm and controlled, you definitely will."

"When does the doctor get here?" Benzler probed pointedly.

"Most of the doctors arrive around eight o'clock," Turner responded. "I suggest you try to relax and keep calm."

In fact the doctor didn't show up until after nine. Mr. Turner escorted him into Benzler's cell. The tech lingered in the background as the doctor addressed Benzler.

"Good morning Marshall, I'm Dr. West." Dr. Reid West started his career at Wilson eight years ago, and the community recognized him as a solid, highly respected psychiatrist. With no striking features, only his hair stood out. He combed his gray-brown hair laterally, flattening it to cover his balding head.

"You're late," Benzler responded.

Ignoring the jab, the doctor continued, "These are not the best circumstances for introductions so I'll save the formalities for later. I'm certain you're eager to get out of these restraints. So, let me ask you a couple of questions, and we'll see if we can get you right out. First, do you understand why you're in the restraints?"

"Yeah. To keep me from kicking those goon's asses."

Dr. West stared at Benzler from behind his wire-rimmed spectacles, not amused. "I'll give you one more shot at it."

"I was upset and out of control."

"And you know that we use the restraints for your own safety, and of course the safety of others?" the doctor asked.

"Yeah sure." Benzler looked past the doctor at the bare sky blue wall.

"Marshall, I'm willing to sign the order to let you out of these things, but you have to commit to me that you'll keep calm and control yourself."

"OK."

"And you'll need to talk with the staff. Can you make that commitment to me?"

"Yes," Benzler replied.

Dr. West continued, "You'll have to stay in Special Care a few days...."

Benzler interrupted, "No way, man. You gotta let me outta this cage."

"I'm sorry but that's not possible," Dr. West responded. "We need to maintain a safe environment on the unit. You need to demonstrate consistent control."

Frustrated, Benzler slammed his head back on the hard mattress, arched his back and shouted, "I am demonstrating control."

Dr. West shook his head, motioned to Mr. Turner and said to Benzler, "All right. With this outburst I have no choice but to leave you in restraints. I'll be back to check on you later."

Dr. West and Mr. Turner exited, again securing the door behind them. Benzler howled and flailed uselessly with his bonds. The leather straps chafed his already raw wrists. Mr. Turner reappeared with a nurse and two other technicians to administer another dose of Thorazine.

Otherwise, the hospital staff did nothing else. They simply let Benzler wail like a two year old. He kept it up for a few minutes, until he fell asleep, spent and drugged. He slept for several hours.

Dr. West revisited him about 6 pm accompanied by a different technician this time. The doctor repeated his role from the morning almost verbatim, but this time Benzler changed his tune. After making his promise, Benzler didn't throw another tantrum. Anything to be free from these restraints.

Dr. West gave the high sign, and the technician stepped forward with a needle-like skeleton key. One by one the tech released Benzler's arms, legs, and torso.

Emancipated, Benzler rose and asked, "Do I have to stay in this room?"

Dr. West rubbed his combover, smoothing it flat across his head. "Yes. As I indicated this morning, it's standard for all patients to get oriented here." Benzler frowned, and didn't hear the rest of the doctor's comments. "The restraints of course are not always necessary. As you earn our trust, we'll gradually grant you more privilege."

After the doctor left, the technician spoke in staccato, "Hi Marshall, my name is Mr. Sharpe. How are you doing? OK? Well, I need for you to change clothes and get cleaned up. You hungry? I'll bring you in some dinner." Fat and freckled with wavy red hair, and a bushy moustache, Mr. Sharpe was a generally trusting and likable man. In his arms he carried clothing, sundries, and Benzler's crutches.

Sharpe let Benzler into the bathroom to shower and change his clothes.

"Can I get some privacy here?" Benzler asked as the tech follows him in.

"Sorry, man. I have to be in here. It's the rules."

Benzler donned the regulation denim shorts and jersey, no underwear.

He asked, "I have to freeball it in here?" Mr. Sharpe laughed a high pitched giggle.

Sharpe brought in some food, and sat Indian style in the corner while Benzler wolfed it down. Sharpe talked non-stop through the meal.

Cleaned up and well fed, Sharpe bade him goodnight.

"Can't you leave the crutches in here?" asked Benzler.

"Nope. You might use them as a weapon. Sorry."

"More rules," mumbled Benzler.

Once again Benzler spent the night in Special Care, but at least he was free from the restraints.

*   *   *

For the next three complete days, Benzler endured being locked in Special Care. Three identical, monotonous days.

In Special Care, his regimen commenced with a 7 am wakeup call by a technician. Relieved to be out of restraints, Benzler slept soundly, though the residual effect of the Thorazine left him groggy.

Every fifteen minutes, every hour, all day a tech's face appeared in the window to check on him. The tech updated Benzler's chart with a notation on his behavior each time. Benzler knocked on the door if he needed to use the restroom or something. A tech brought in his three squares, and sat with him while he ate. Some of the techs would chat awhile. Otherwise, he slept mostly, bored and depressed. Confused and still angry, he wanted no part of this place, the people, and definitely no part of the treatment.

His primary nurse turned out to be Nurse Kincaid, whom he met upon admission. On his first day out of restraints, she carried a small stool into the Special care area to meet with him. A tech shadowed her, but she waved him off. Benzler saw him fall back, but he waited just around the corner.

"Hi Marshall, how's it going?" Small, brunette, and pretty, she had a surplus of enthusiasm and energy. She seemed caring, and genuinely interested in him. Staunch in his resolve to resist treatment a minute ago, here came this pretty little nurse who seemed so nice and sweet. His outlook swung immediately, and now he wanted to open up and tell her everything.

"Hi. Better today." Benzler forced a smile. He didn't want to go back in restraints, and he needed out of this cramped rubber room.

"Well that's good. You look better too. I'm Nurse Kincaid."

"I know. I remember you from last night," he replied.

"I hope you don't hold that against me," she said playfully. "We just try to keep everyone safe. Dr. West spoke with you about that, so you understand why we do that. It's necessary for us to talk, to break the ice so we can begin the therapeutic process."

"I want to get started too," he blurted out self-consciously.

"Let's start fresh then." She extended her right hand in greeting. "Welcome to 6B."

He took her hand. "6B? What's that?"

She explained, "That's the name of this particular ward. 'The Sixes' are the units at the hospital designated for children. The B distinguishes it from 6A, which is right next door. 6B is for kids under fifteen. 6A is for kids fifteen to eighteen."

They continued their chat, friendly, superficially. Benzler watched her talk, the way she gestured with her graceful hands. He basked in her scent of lilac, the lilting quality of her voice. Benzler strove to play along despite his numbed head and disturbed thoughts. Between them they set the goal of getting him the hell out of this room.

The three days passed.

*   *   *

Dr. West finally permitted Benzler to come out onto the main floor area twice daily for half hour stints. Mr. Turner retrieved him for his first time out. Benzler put on a robe over the scratchy denim clothing, and slippers for his feet. His restriction required him to stay in the center of the unit, a place called "The Atrium."

As they emerged, Turner said, "Let me give you the grand tour of your new home." Benzler followed him sheepishly, like the ground hog checking the weather. He decided Mr. Turner was his favorite tech. Turner had an easy manner and made Benzler laugh.

"This is the Atrium." Turner swept his hand in an arc. Central to the building, segregated residence sections surround half of it. Several round dining tables and metal folding chairs made up the floor furnishings. "It's not the Ritz, but it works."

Mr. Turner guided Benzler to the south end of the Atrium. "Over here is the kitchen."

"It's pretty small," said Benzler.

"Yeah. But we don't cook anything here. The cafeteria delivers all the meals." A counter separated the kitchen from the Atrium. The small kitchen accommodated only a refrigerator and a few locked cupboards which held snack items.

Walking to the direct opposite end of the Atrium, Turner stated, "This is the nurse's station." Another long white counter divided this section as well. He pointed to blue lines on the floor tile. "Just so you know, patients aren't allowed past these lines." He checked Benzler's face to ensure he got it.

"I'd like to introduce you to Mr. Spach." Mr. Spach, also a technician, perched along the counter, reigning over the unit, a vantage point with visibility to all sections. He looked up from the sports page of

173

the Columbus Citizen's Journal. "You'll see him as he makes checks on you during his shift."

Benzler said, "They never stop do they?"

"You're telling me," Turner responded. "The checks are hourly for most patients. Every fifteen minutes for special care."

"I know," Benzler confirmed.

Mr. Turner proceeded to show Benzler the housing areas, the recreation room, and the doctor's and administrative offices.

Though Turner didn't call attention to them, there were four doors on the unit, always locked. Most of the ingress and egress occured at the main entrance. Deliveries occurred at the back door in the kitchen. A third door led to the doctor's and admin offices downstairs. The final door, located in the rec room, led out to a courtyard. That door was rarely used.

The tour occupied most of his allotted free "out" time, but it satisfied his building curiosity about the place. Afterwards, he joined Mr. Turner and a Nurse Marder at one of the white Atrium tables. Turner engaged Benzler in light, upbeat conversation.

"I bet it's great to be out of 'Old Blue,'" Turner said, referring to special care.

Benzler sluggishly replied, "Yeah, it is. But I know I'm going back shortly."

Nurse Marder chimed in, "You'll be out for good before you know it." Her thick midwestern accent sounded more like Wisconsin than Ohio. Nurse Marder was a young nurse in her twenties, pale, chunky with dark hair and full cheeks.

"I hope so. I'm going crazy back there."

Turner and Marder laughed. Turner patted Benzler on the shoulder saying, "We don't really use that term around here."

"What? Crazy, oh I get it." They looked at each other awkwardly. Benzler asked, "I thought there were a lot of other kids here. Where is everybody?"

"Well you know, everybody's at an activity right now," Marder said.

The unit currently had seventeen other kids. Benzler made it an even nine boys and nine girls. They ranged in age from eleven to fifteen.

"When can I meet some of them?" he asked anxiously. He suffered from the same stereotypes about crazy people as most of us.

"In time," she responded. "Give it some time."

"What are they like?"

"I suppose you'll find them to be like most other kids for the most part." Turner noticed Benzler's anxiety. "Don't worry about it. You'll make some friends, and be in the groove before you know it."

A few minutes later he returned to Special Care.

After the next week, Benzler's progress got him out of special care all day long. They assigned him a single bedroom in the designated boys' housing area. No roommate. Though given incremental levels of freedom, his restriction didn't allow him in his room. He needed to stay in the Atrium area, where he had no privacy and was ever visible to the nurses and technicians. And at night he continued to sleep in Special Care. So over a period of a month, Benzler acclimated to the unit.

He maintained his reserve with the staff; the techs, nurses, and doctors. He participated just enough to keep moving forward. His broken leg kept him from doing anything physical. He spent the month keeping a low profile, depressed, withdrawn, and feeling alone.

*   *   *

Chapter 17

"Donny, the bus is coming," my Mom hollered up to me. I snatched my backpack, and bounded down the stairs and out the front, screen door banging behind me. I heard a neighbor's rooster crow, as the school bus approached.

I climbed aboard the bus, and looked automatically to the rear. The driver closed the door, and released the airbrakes with a whoosh. The past two years, Benzler and I ruled the back of the elementary bus, but the cool older kids would harass us now. Besides, Benzler wouldn't be on the bus anyway. He was still at Wilson. I ended up slipping into the first open seat. I glided across the cool plastic to the window.

Autumn arrived in Central Ohio. The days fought to hold onto the heat, but they lost. The quickening nights cooled off, and the crisp air brought sweatshirts out of the closet. The smell too, it smelled like football to me. The days shrank, and the leaves turned.

With fall came the first day of school. A seventh grader this year, the bus carried me toward River Valley Junior High School. It was a bit of a longer ride than last year's trip to Waldo Elementary. Positioned amid cornfields at the crossroads of State Routes 98 and 309,

177

RV was about seven miles north of our house. A decade ago, four local township schools amalgamated into one. In addition to Waldo, Claridon, Caledonia, and Martel joined to create RV. They built adjacent Junior and Senior High schools, and the buildings mirrored one another, two stories, both made of brick.

I disembarked at school, and entered the front of the Junior High. I took a left down the first hallway, and shuffled across freshly polished green tiled floors. The babble of a hundred voices filled the crowded corridor. Metallic lockers slammed shut.

The students all gathered in the gymnasium awaiting our class assignments. At Waldo we had only two sixth grade classes, with the same teacher and kids all day, every day. The difference in Junior High, though the classmates stayed the same, the kids moved from subject to subject with different teachers. Eight total periods made up the day.

I took a seat on the wooden bleachers next to Billy Essenheimer. After some banter, he asked me about Benzler.

"Haven't heard from him," I said.

"Where is he?" Heimer asked.

Most of the other kids at school didn't even know Benzler. Many from Waldo asked me what happened to him. I didn't know what to say, but to date I hadn't told anyone the facts. But I thought it'd be OK to tell Heimer. We could count on him to be a good friend.

"He's at a hospital called Wilson. It's in Columbus."

"What for?" he asked.

"Well, he has to stay there for awhile. You know, because of all the problems he's having."

"How long do you think he'll have to stay?"

"I wish I knew. I penned Benzler another letter last week, but he probably won't write back. He hasn't yet, but you know him. I predicted that."

Principal Schecter welcomed us with a big smile and a little speech. A tall man, about 6'2", thin, with a long, drawn face he walked with a limp from some old World War II injury. Following that the parsing began, and we all separated into our new class sections.

After over two hours, ultimately, we began our classes with fourth period. As luck would have it, Benzler wound up on the same homeroom roster as me, section 7-4.

"Benzler." Our new English teacher Mrs. Gimbut assigned the class seats as we all loitered in the back of her classroom. "Benzler. Is Benzler here?"

I stepped up and said, "No m'aam. Benzler's not here today."

"Eidegger," she called a moment later.

"That would be me." I walked over to the seat I'd just been assigned.

Since almost all the teachers started off with alphabetical seating charts, undoubtedly I'd sit behind Benzler's empty chair in each of my classes. In grade school, teachers always started off that way, but they'd separate us soon, same thing year in year out. Apparently not this year though, not now.

After seating the entire class, Mrs. Gimbut opened by going over the synopsis. I considered her name. Gimbut, Mrs. Gim- butt. Ha ha ha. What kind of a name was that? Benzler would have had a field day with a name like that. I looked around for someone to share my mirth with.

Most of my other friends got different sections. Heimer was in 7-3. I barely recognized anyone in here except for Kevin Holtz, a fairy, and Todd Hettwer, a geek. I guess I was all alone now. I couldn't imagine being friends with any of these strangers. I was really going to miss having Benzler around.

While enrolled here at RV, Benzler attended school at Wilson. I guessed they did schooling in there. I never did visit him, but found out they didn't allow visitors anyway. I'd locked horns with my Dad for nothing.

The ringing bell startled me, and the period came to a close. I hustled out of class to my locker to prepare for the next one.

Lockers lined the hallways end to end, a chocolate tunnel standing as high as me. I tested my new combination, 8-30-00. I could forget about that because I jammed a penny in the bottom to disable the lock. Sure, I ran the risk of a stacked locker, but what the heck.

I shared my locker with a kid in my class named Jimmy Kirche. He seemed like a nice kid, shy, littler even than me. He dressed in poor farmer clothes, high-water overalls, hand-me-downs. He must've done his morning chores in his school clothes too. And they must've kept hogs. Other kids made fun of him. "Jimmy, waitin' for a flood?" Floods were definitely not cool.

Appearing without warning from around the corner John Rustin surprised me, a shit-eating grin on his face. His fleshy lips peeled back exposing over-sized perfect white teeth. Well, I'd sure liked to knock a couple of them out. A long time adversary of Benzler, he tracked me down just to talk about him.

"Hey Eidegger, where's Benzler been?" he called out, seething with arrogance. I cringed at the sound of his voice.

Rustin looked at Kirche and said, "What're you looking at?" He rudely shoved the skinny little boy, and Kirche tucked tail and scurried away.

My back to Rustin I muttered, "Aw, c'mon Rustin, leave him alone."

Refocusing on me he said loudly, "I heard Benzler's in the loony bin."

"Who told you that crap?" I turned and faced him. He stood, chest puffed out wearing an RV Vike club football t-shirt. He must've gotten that from his older brother.

"Your buddy Essenheimer, who else?"

"Well, he's in a hospital, not a loony bin," I tried to explain.

"What's the difference? I always knew that asshole was crazy."

I stiffened, glaring at Rustin a moment, sizing him up. Not taller than me, Rustin was just built like a fireplug. Presuming he'd be a tough customer, I quelled my urge to whack him one. I decided to reason with him.

"Look, Benzler's had some tough times lately. He doesn't need any more. Can't you just keep it quiet, and cut him a break?" I pleaded.

182

"You gotta be friggin' kiddin' me. Fuck that. I'm smearin' that asshole." He walked away adding, "He'd do the same to me." I stared at the back of his head as if it was a bull's eye, but let him strut off.

As good as his word, soon Rustin blabbered his warped scuttlebutt to the entire school.

Later that day I caught up with Essenheimer.

I yelled after him, "Heimer, wait up." He turned and I could see his face tighten.

"Digger, where you been?"

"Lookin' for you." I drilled into him. "Did you tell people about Benzler?"

"Now wait a minute, man, I just told a coupla the guys."

"You told that ratfink Rustin."

"Well yeah, he was there. What's the big deal?" Heimer said on the defensive. "Everyone knows anyway."

"I can't believe you'd do that. Benzler's your friend." I stuck my face close to his, and he looked away.

I left him speechless, and he chased after me. "C'mon man, everyone was gonna find out anyway. What's the big deal?" I kept on walking. "Screw you man," he said waving me off, having the last word.

Benzler was going to have a great reputation when he returned.

And it was all my fault.

*   *   *

Chapter 18

Benzler laid on his back in restraints. He tested each of them one by one, but they didn't budge. Out of the corner of his eye, he caught a glimpse of someone at the Special Care window.

"Come back," he tried to yell, but no sound came out. He felt a heavy invisible weight press down on him. The door seemed distant, the window tiny as if he looked through a tunnel. Had he imagined someone out there? Then the lock turned, a deep echoing click. The chamber door crawled open, an endless action. His father entered, appearing as he did a year ago. He peered down at his son.

"What are you doing down there boy?" he asked sternly, apparently disappointed. His frown broke into an odd smile, grew into a

184

chuckle, which then transformed into an all out guffaw. Terrified and confused, Benzler frantically attempted to bring his mind to order.

His father's laugh mutated to a chorus, and he realized that the room has filled with people he knew, all laughing at him. Where had they come from? A trickle of blood leaked out of his father's mouth and down to his chin. It bubbled as he spoke.

"Mr. Benzler can you join us?" One of the students next to him poked him. More laughter. He lifted his head out of a puddle of drool.

The teacher, Mr. Hatterfield said, "No sleeping in class Marshall." Hatterfield swept his shoulder length hair back. Benzler's face reddened as his classmates sniggered.

Benzler's term at the hospital now had reached a month. The initiation had been rugged, the learning curve steep. He adapted to the rhythm as quickly as possible, and he kepts out of trouble.

School made up the bulk of his daily schedule during the week. Fifty-six students attended the certified school located right on the hospital grounds. Two thirds of the students came from the two "Sixes" units, 6A and 6B. Outpatients comprised the rest, most former full time patients who earned back their freedom. The hospital maintained ideal class size with only a half dozen kids per classroom.

Benzler took the same subjects he would have in 7th grade at River Valley: English, Science, Math, etc. He also needed some remediation, since his grades dipped at the end of last year. Thankfully, he didn't have to repeat sixth grade after all.

Finally coherent, Benzler responded to the teacher, "Sorry. I think my meds make me tired."

"That's OK. Just do your best to stay awake. The rest of you," Mr. Hatterfield said, pausing until he has some attention. "No laughing. We all have issues here."

"What are your issues?" asked one of the students. More laughter.

"Ha ha," said the teacher, and then carried on with class. Patience and tolerance topped the list of requisites for teachers at this school.

School let out at two fifteen daily. Monday through Friday every patient attended planned after school activities. Benzler had a two-thirty activity, Creative Arts, and a three forty-five, Log Sawing. The program called these activities Adjunctive Therapy or simply AT.

Adjunctive Therapy took place in a completely separate complex from all other hospital activities. A building had studios for art, sound, and a gymnasium. They had indoor classrooms and outdoor areas containing a sizable garden. They held logsawing outside.

Miss Stanton, a stocky middle-aged woman with long, black hair and bangs led Creative Arts. The doctor prescribed this therapy to get Benzler to express himself, something he hadn't done since his arrival. Benzler started off here working on a collage. Now he painted with watercolors like a genuine artist, and he actually enjoyed it.

After art class, Benzler went to logsawing. The staff assigned this to burn off energy and aggression. Because of his leg, he couldn't execute any of the heavy sawing. But he used a handsaw on more suitable timber, and got to dispense some frustration that way.

Today, Benzler didn't make much headway on his assignment. He worked alone, but had a tech, Mr. Spach tailing him. Spach accompanied Benzler, but he didn't say a word. Of all the techs, Benzler liked Spach the least. Spach was tall and thin with an acne scarred face. Benzler thought he was an arrogant prick with a mean streak.

Mr. Donaldson, a swarthy, dark-haired man with a week-old beard ran logsawing. He approached "Hey Marshall, what's happening? Hey Mr. Spach."

Benzler stopped sawing mid-stroke. "Hi Mr. D." Mr. Spach just nodded, with a smug smirk on his face. Donaldson stood akimbo in front of them as a dozen saws sliced vigorously behind them.

"You're moving kind of slow today," he barked. He could usually be heard bellowing some order or another with his direct style.

"I'm tired. I think it's my meds," Benzler explained. Spach shrugged behind him, rolling his eyes.

"That may be. Nevertheless, you need to get your work done here."

Benzler sighed, and he resumed his cut, but his saw snagged on the limb. He reset the blade and picked up where he left off.

Donaldson continued less harshly. "Tell you what. I'm not the doc, so I can't do anything about the meds. But I can mention it in my report to the council. Maybe they'll take it into consideration. All right? For now, get back to work." Benzler labored through the remaining half hour.

After AT activities, Benzler joined the rest of the patients returning to the dorm unit shortly after five. They had a little free time before dinner at 6. Benzler received a letter from Digger. It contained the same old stuff about all the assholes back home. Only two people

188

had written him, Digger and his Mom. He didn't write either of them back.

Each evening at seven, staff scheduled a variety of regular campus activities. On Mondays and Thursdays, the Phys. Ed. AT staff staged group sports events. On Tuesdays, the units alternated hosting Social night, which required interaction with the other units. Fridays had musical activities at the sound studio, and on Saturday they sponsored a teen night over at the gym. Sundays offered a non-denominational church service.

Initially, Benzler couldn't participate in any of the evening activities due to his Special Care restrictions. Now he participated as much as he could, just for something to do. With his broken leg on the mend, he didn't get to play much in sports, though sometimes he could spectate.

At first, Benzler attended church service out of desperation. He quit though, because it provided no escape.

Card playing was one of the most popular non-structured activities. Of course, the hospital didn't permit gambling or gambling oriented games. Most people played the four-person team game called euchre. A common and popular midwestern game, Benzler's family had played the game, so he already knew how to play. This enabled him to adapt quickly.

Evening snack time was at eight-thirty. At nine everyone performed a chore from the rotating check list. Having grown up on the farm, the chores seemed simple to Benzler. He laughed at the kids who complained about such cinchy tasks. Try shoveling cow shit or baling hay all day.

At ten, everyone had to wind down and be in his or her dorm area. Ten-thirty, lights out. Currently, Benzler struggled to even stay awake until curfew. Lately, he completed his chore at nine, and then went straight to bed. All in all, they kept everyone extremely busy around here, and isolated from the world outside.

The next day at the doctor's council meeting, they discussed the progress of all patients. The team met downstairs in a conference room, and consisted of Dr. West, the nurses including Nurse Kincaid, a tech representative, the unit social worker Mrs. Masterson, and school and Adjunctive Therapy staff as necessary.

"Next," said Dr. West as they finished discussion of one patient and prepared to move on.

"That would be Marshall Benzler," piped up Nurse Kincaid who sat at the table directly to West's right. She straightened her notes, "He's been doing OK. General good behavior, talking during our 1:1s. He hadn't been a hundred percent engaged with staff, and he hadn't formed any relationships with other patients. Nurse Kincaid sat up straight with both palms down on the table as she spoke. "He's been complaining about being tired all the time. He blames it on his meds, and I tend to agree with him. He tries, but just doesn't have much emotional affect. He's a bit of a zombie," she concluded.

Both Mr. Hatterfield and Donaldson related their interactions of the previous day. Other staff added supporting anecdotes.

Dr. West contemplated the options, smoothing his hair. "He's on Thorazine right?" Nurse Kincaid nodded. "I have to admit that during our therapy sessions, he's, what did you call him, a zombie? Yeah, I think that's apt." He paused and leaned back in his chair. "He hasn't had any acting out since the first day. No history of psychosis. Maybe we should cut it out altogether. See what happens."

The staff unanimously agreed that Benzler needed something, and elimination of his medication seemed a likely place to start.

*   *   *

Chapter 19

"How's it feel to be off the meds?" Dr. West asked, kicking off their next therapy session. Benzler had begun formal psychotherapy after his first week at Wilson. He met with Dr. West for an hour twice a week, Mondays at ten and Thursdays at two.

"Better," Benzler replied. "I thought restraints were bad."

"What do you mean?"

"The meds are like restraints on your brain," Benzler explained.

Dr. West chuckled. "That's an interesting observation. I haven't heard anyone describe it quite like that before." He rubbed his chin thoughtfully, a faint smile on his face.

"Besides, I was tired all the time."

"Well, that might be the depression some too," Dr. West countered. "Regardless, under the circumstances, I think elimination of that particular medication was for the best."

Dr. West held therapy in his office downstairs. The sizable office contained a giant dark cherry desk with a throne like chair. But for one on ones, he joined Benzler on a pair of Eaton Square chairs separated by a small round accent table. The doctor eased the boy in slowly, breaking down the wall. Benzler had a tough time engaging with anyone.

After his statement, Dr. West sat still. The afternoon sun shined into the office, leaving four bright parallelograms on the carpet. They could see a row of golden maple trees just outside the window. October in Ohio had to be the prettiest month.

The extended silence made Benzler squirm.

"Anything in particular you'd like to share today?" West offered, letting him off the hook, if only for the moment.

"Nope," Benzler said, not biting. He slouched in his chair, chin down, and arms crossed. Dr. West permitted the silence to build again until Benzler came up with something, anything.

"Well, I had a weird dream about my Dad," Benzler finally confessed.

"What was weird about it?"

"He was alive," Benzler stated bluntly.

"OK. So what happened?"

"Nothing really."

Dr. West took off his glasses. "Marshall, that's the first time you brought up your Dad at all, which is good. I suspect that the trauma surrounding the tragedy of his death is at the core of your issues." He talked using his glasses like a pointer for emphasis. "I must say that without addressing this, you'll never improve. I know you'll tell me in due time." He allowed his comments to sink in. "How about we start today? Huh?"

Benzler constricted, his muscles clenched, as his anxiety level exploded internally. Outside, he didn't move.

"I don't want to talk about it." He forced the words out of his mouth, like sausage out of a grinder. Benzler's eyes sank, and he appeared much smaller to Dr. West.

"I understand," Dr. West said calmly, with empathy. He put his glasses back on, and waited until Benzler regained his composure. Benzler looked back up at the doctor, eyes red, but no tears. He brushed his stringy blonde hair out of his face.

"Why don't you tell me some more about the dream," the doctor probed, dwelling on the rare opening that Benzler provided.

With herky-jerky hand gestures he said, "Well, he was just like before. You know. He seemed mad at me."

"Why do you say that?"

"The way he looked at me." Benzler knees bounced rapidly with nervous energy.

"Was he often mad at you?"

"I don't think so. He left that to my Mom," he responded tersely, irritated. "But then he started laughing at me."

"Do you know why?"

"No. That's when I woke up. I fell asleep in class, and everyone laughed at me."

"Oh I see. That sounds like 'dream incorporation.' That's when real events around you infiltrate the dream. It's usually auditory, happens when the sound wakes up the dreamer. It's quite common."

Benzler clammed up once more, and searched for escape in the wall clock. Dr. West scrutinized him, leaning forward, elbows on his knees, and his fingertips touching.

"Look Marshall. When are you going to start your treatment?" Benzler's eyes widened slightly, but he said nothing. "You're just going through the motions here," Dr. West added.

"But…"

Dr. West stood up and interrupted him, "But what? Let's talk about your father, right now." Benzler repeated that he couldn't, and the doctor said, "We're going nowhere. You seem to be more interested in the clock than disclosing anything. Why don't we cut our losses. Go back upstairs."

Shocked, Benzler exclaimed, "But we have over a half hour left." Dr. West simply waved him off.

Angry and unsettled, Benzler climbed the single flight of stairs, and re-entered the unit. He maneuvered easily now that he was off crutches. Unnoticed at first, soon Benzler's disturbed energy crashed over the Atrium like a rogue wave. He marched straight across the floor, and into his room.

Up in the Nurse's Station, Nurse Marder observed Marshall blow by. She recognized a potential situation, and called the two techs in to prepare for an intervention. She thought to herself, the doctors always did this; they stirred up problems during therapy, and then unleashed ticking time bombs back on the unit without warning. She always had to clean up the mess.

Marder heard one loud bang behind Benzler's closed door. She braced herself, and went after him.

She stopped outside of his door, and listened first. Hearing nothing further, she rapped lightly. No answer. She tapped one more time, and then gently opened the door.

"Marshall. You OK?" The boy lay face down on the bed, head buried in his arms.

"Uh huh," he said, muffled in his sweatshirt.

"Do you want to talk?"

"Uh uhn," still muffled.

196

Nurse Marder hesitated, listening. Nothing else.

"OK then," she concluded. "Please let me know if you change your mind." She began to shut the door.

"Nurse Marder?" Benzler said.

"Ya?"

"Can you tell Nurse Kincaid I want to talk with her when she gets in?

"Ya, OK." She closed the door. She gave the "whew" sign to the techs who were standing by.

*   *   *

Benzler didn't leave his room, he didn't even move from his prone position much for the next two hours. Dr. West touched a nerve by challenging him. He'd buried his father and his feelings deep. He realized that Dr. West was right. But it was like lancing a boil. Especially without the meds to deaden his pain.

Mr. Turner knocked on his door to see if he'd attend logsawing at 345. Benzler refused, which normally would get him into trouble. But the staff unexpectedly gave him a free pass today.

Not long after she arrived for her swing shift, Nurse Kincaid came a calling.

"Marshall, you wish to talk?"

He jumped up immediately at the sound of her voice.

"Yes." They convened on a couch in the open dorm area. They had privacy since the unit was deserted due to activities.

"Nurse Marder tells me you're having a hard time today. What's going on?"

Benzler frownsed, and then complained, "Dr. West kicked me out of his office today. That's so unfair."

"He kicked you out?" She leaned forward with her elbows on her knees.

"Yeah. And I didn't do anything."

"OK, slow down, and tell me what happened." She raised her hands in a stop motion. "First though you know I'm not going to take sides. Dr. West is a very smart man, and he knows what he's doing." Even in his agitated state, her light, flowery perfume distracted him. "Why don't you tell me the details, starting at the top."

Benzler leaned back with his hands apart. His mouth formed a pout, and he squinted his eyes. "I went down for my usual two o'clock with West. It started pretty good. I told him about a dream I had with my dad in it."

She stopped him. "You know I don't like that tone. Sit up straight and tell me. No whining. You've got to face this."

He started again, "Dr. West just started criticizing me. What an asshole."

"Marshall. If you don't stop that I'm not going to sit here and listen to you."

"Sorry," he said, and took a deep breath. "He yelled at me because I can't talk that much about my Dad yet." He needed to stop, holding back his tears, bile rising in his throat.

Torn because she empathized with him, Nurse Kincaid didn't want to reward him for not talking. She pushed him, "Go on."

"That's it."

"That's it?" Benzler nodded. "OK," she responded. "What would you like me to do about it?"

"I don't know," he said flatly. He doubted he'd ever be able to dredge up the pain.

"Look," Nurse Kincaid said. "Dr. West is absolutely right. We're here to support you, whenever you're ready. But please, you have to talk about this stuff. You can take baby steps if you want. Maybe talking about the dream is just a beginning."

Benzler dropped his head in his hands, and the tears finally flowed. His anger dissipated, but the tears represented his sense of hopelessness, and the futility of his predicament.

Nurse Kincaid scooted over next to him, and put her arm on his back. They stayed like that for a long ten minutes. Benzler let her go finally, and retreated to his room for the rest of the evening.

*   *   *

Chapter 20

During that sleepless night Benzler stewed in anger at Dr. West, at everything until he determined that he absolutely must get out of there. He resolved to run away, to escape. But how? The total unit lockdown made for a bleak predicament. And his leg limited his mobility, so he couldn't just run off. He scoured his brain for ideas until he dozed off.

Waking with a start, it occurred to him that his broken leg, always seen as an impediment, may actually be the solution. Each

Friday a single tech accompanied him off campus for physical therapy. No locked doors. Since today was Friday, he hatched his plan for that very afternoon.

The scheme preoccupied him all morning. Butterflies killed his appetite as he anxiously awaited the schedule posting to find out which tech would escort him. Yes! Mr. Sharpe got the job. He liked Sharpe a lot, and didn't want to get him in trouble. But Sharpe's girth would hinder any pursuit. Moreover, Sharpe's trusting nature should curb any suspicion.

When the time came, Mr. Sharpe transported them in the hospital car, a blue four-door sedan. On the drive, Benzler mulled over his plot. Mr. Sharpe attempted to interest Benzler in polite conversation.

"Hey buddy, I didn't know you were a Browns fan," Sharpe said with his rapid fire speech.

"What?" Benzler said, confused.

"Your jersey." Benzler looked down at the #44 Cleveland Browns jersey he wore.

"Oh yeah," Benzler responded minimally.

"You like LeRoy Kelly, huh?" Kelly wore number 44 for the Browns for ten years.

"Yeah, but he doesn't play for 'em anymore." Benzler sat in the front seat next to Sharpe and didn't look at him.

"Oh that's right. He jumped to the World Football League," Sharpe remarked, but Benzler didn't say anymore.

"So how's your leg doing?" Sharpe continued.

"OK."

"How're these PT sessions going so far?" Mr. Sharpe asked.

"Obviously they hurt," Benzler replied bluntly.

"Oh yeah? What do they have you do?" Mr. Sharpe persisted through the resistance. Benzler gave his best effort to act normally, meanwhile his anxiety skyrocketed.

"Well, they make me do leg exercises, and it hurts like hell."

"How long 'til you stop this jazz?"

"I don't know," Benzler said, showing slight irritability. "A few more weeks I guess."

"How'd you bust it anyway?"

Benzler didn't respond for a few moments. The car radio distracted him blaring "Magic" by Pilot. "Oh oh oh it's magic, ya know."

He finally said, "You know, I don't really want to talk about it." That killed the line of questioning.

Undeterred, Sharpe directed the conversation to something less controversial, the weather. It was a beautiful fall day, sunny with billowing white clouds floating on a blue background.

Sharpe closed with, "Can you believe it's supposed to rain tonight? Look at this," he gestured toward the sky with his free hand.

They arrived at their destination, a single story brick building on North High Street in Worthington. Several medical offices consolidated to form this complex. Once parked, the tech ushered Benzler into the office and checked him in. After a short wait, they called Benzler in for his appointment. Benzler's heart and breath rate quickened. The unsuspecting Sharpe took a seat in the waiting room. With Sharpe's guard down, Benzler thought he had the perfect opportunity here.

As the assistant, a squat Asian woman guided him into the examination room he asked her if he could use the restroom. She pointed him down the hall, so he proceeded that direction. He entered the bathroom, took a leak, and then stared at his reflection in the mirror. He removed his glasses, and splashed cold water on his face. He ran his damp fingers through his stringy blonde hair.

"C'mon, you can do it," he encouraged himself. He paced, cursing his cowardice. "Have some balls." He slowly opened the door, and peered into the empty hallway. Freedom beckoned just through the back door at the end of the hall.

Benzler snuck out of the bathroom, hobbled down the hall on his walking cast, and stepped out the back. He embarked on his journey across the parking lot to High Street.

His heart nearly leapt out of his chest as he drove his legs as fast as he could. *Walk fast. Don't look back. Walk fast.* He stopped at the intersection, and waited for the light to change. Cars raced down High, but he barely noticed the blaring horns, and the fumes spewing from exhausts. Benzler felt that everyone looked at him, and they all knew his secret.

High Street spanned the entire metropolitan Columbus, north to south. When the light turned red, Benzler booked across the four lanes. He set off south on High, but before long comprehended that he'd be noticed "missing" sooner or later. And a lone teen runaway with a heavy limp could be easily spotted on the main drag. If Sharpe woke up, he'd look here first as well.

Therefore after a few blocks he cut down a side street, and found a parallel avenue to continue southward. When he felt he had traveled a safe range from the therapist's, he unleashed a celebratory whoop.

"Wahoo," he cried and pumped his fist in the air. "Screw you Dr. West." Benzler peeled off his Brown's jersey and the sweatshirt he had on underneath. Standing there shirtless, he felt the warm sun bake the skin on his shoulders, and at the same time a stiff breeze chilled his face. As a thin disguise he quickly put on the jersey, then the plain sweatshirt on top of it. *Thanks for the reminder Mr. Sharpe.*

He resumed his trek, a Jack-o-lantern grin spread across his face. He looked up at the blue sky and breathed deeply. He spied a single jet with its trailing twin lines of false white clouds, and wished he was aboard right now. No matter, he was free. He cried out again, "Yes."

Benzler's plan didn't have much depth, simply to be "out" of the hospital. He hoped that by the time they realized the mistake, he'd be amid the bustle of The Ohio State University, so they wouldn't find him.

Ohio State University, "THE" Ohio State University to Ohioans, abutted High Street a handful of miles south of the therapist's office. He had been to campus before, so he did possess some vague familiarity with the location.

Other than that, his escape plan fell flat. Money posed one concern. Patients collected an allowance of only two dollars per week. Since he hadn't exactly mapped this out in advance, he'd only gotten the two bucks. He didn't know anyone, and had neither kith nor kin in this

205

vicinity. And he had a healing broken leg. Oh well, he'd take his chances. None of this dampened his spirit to start.

Back at the physical therapist, the busy office gradually emptied as they completed a number of late Friday afternoon appointments. Benzler's PT ran behind, and hustled to catch up. When he discovered Benzler's empty room, he inquired with the assistant.

She peeked into one vacant patient room after another. Puzzled, she located Mr. Sharpe, scanning a Sports Illustrated in the waiting room.

Sharpe's freckled face beamed through his red moustache. "I'm waiting for Marshall Benzler. He had a four o'clock appointment. Do you know how much longer?"

He saw her eyes widen, and finally suspicious, he stood up.

"I saw him when he came in, but not since. I don't think he's still here," she replied.

"What?" cried Mr. Sharpe. "How can that be?"

"I don't know. He asked to use the bathroom."

The tech rushed to check the bathroom in a panic. He frantically checked all the patient rooms. He looked down the hall and observed the exit door. "Is that door locked?" he asked hesitantly, pointing.

"No," she replied. "It's a fire exit."

"Where does it go?" Sharpe asked, his voice pitch rising.

206

"Just to the rear parking lot," she said. "I'm so sorry."

The technician darted to the door and raced to the car. "Shit. I'm gonna be in so much trouble." He jumped in the car, and decided to search the surrounding neighborhood on his own. "That little sonuvabitch. I'm toast." He pounded on the steering wheel.

Mr. Sharpe hunted for Benzler about thirty minutes down High Street and around the Worthington area. Eventually he gave up, and returned to inform the hospital authorities that his patient has eloped. At this point, the hospital dispatched several other techs as a search party. And of course they contacted the local police.

By now, even with his awkward gait, Benzler had traveled all the way to the Whetstone Park of Roses, about halfway to campus. He cut into the park to avoid the main street. He appeared to be a regular teen walking home from school. He chose one of the numerous footpaths, and passed a basketball court where boys his age argued over a foul call. He passed a playground with mothers trailing small children at play. He observed one small child eating a whole red apple. The apple looked enormous in contrast to the toddler's hand.

His stomach growled and for the first time today he thought of food. With nightfall, he felt the chill in the late autumn air.

Underdressed, he wore only blue jeans and the sweatshirt over the jersey. But he would have looked odd wearing a big parka earlier.

Soon he exited the park, and wandered through an adjacent neighborhood. Turn of the century Victorian houses lined each side. Maple trees towered overhead, and showered gold and red leaves, which twisted and turned as they fell to the ground. The street ran lower than the houses, and short stairways pierced the hills before each home.

As the sun set, the clear day turned gloomy, and shadows faded into mist. His exhilaration over his getaway waned. He contemplated quietly while he walked, turning over and over what to do with his life. And more germane, what to do now? He thought regretfully of Nurse Kincaid, knowing he was letting her down. Fear and depression crept in once again.

Benzler returned to High Street when he arrived at campus well after dark. One of the largest universities in the United States, Ohio State boasted a student population of over 50,000. A lot of people crowded around this area, especially on weekends during football season. Tonight, hundreds of students cruised up and down High Street. A long haired boy, wearing a tie dyed tee-shirt and blue jeans, bumped into him.

"Watch it man."

"Sorry," Benzler replied. He felt overwhelmed by the throngs.

But at least here nobody stood out. Not even a young boy with a limp. Benzler assumed that hospital staff, and probably the cops too would look for him. But he intended to lay low, blend in, and therefore be difficult to find.

High Street, from Dodridge all the way to the Short North district was lined with shops, restaurants, but mainly bars. Unfortunately, because of his age Benzler couldn't duck into a bar to keep warm or hide, but he could go into restaurants. His growing hunger pangs reminded him that he hadn't eaten all day. With the meager $2.00 to his name, he entered a McDonald's on High and approached the service counter. The warmth of the establishment felt good, and the smell of fries brightened his mood.

"May I help you?" asked a McDonald's cashier. His nametag indicated the name James. He wore a red and gold pointed hat.

Benzler examined the menu board behind the counter. "I'll try one of them all-new Egg McMuffins."

"They're only available at breakfast," James said.

"I didn't have any breakfast."

"It's dinnertime. Pick something else."

"Oh," Benzler replied. He took another minute to look at the menu, while James stared at him, and rapped his fingers on the counter.

"I'll take a cheeseburger then, with small fries, and a Coke," Benzler said, his voice cracking.

"That'll be a dollar five."

Benzler produced two crumpled dollar bills, and surrendered them, still balled up to the clerk.

The cashier sneered at Benzler, smoothed the bills in an exaggerated motion, and made change. Benzler collected the coins, and gazed at the 95 cents in his palm. He knew full well their limitation. He stuffed them into his front jeans pocket, and grabbed his tray.

Benzler found a seat near the back by the restroom. He freed the burger from the paper wrapper and devoured it. Delicious. He tore open a ketchup packet, and squirted the contents onto the wrapper. He dunked his fries and enjoyed the salty sweet combination. He washed the food down with his cool soda pop, and savored the burn as it went down. All of these were forbidden fruit at the hospital.

The other fast food diners paid him no attention. He isolated quietly and warmly, alone in the back. Now what? With a full belly, his thoughts reverted to shelter for the night. By now his elation over his freedom had dissipated almost entirely.

Through the window he observed the forbidding cold, dark night. It was now about 9 pm, and rain began to splatter. It gradually sank in that his escape idea may not have been that great. For now he decided to stay at McDonald's as long as he could.

Then two Columbus police officers strode through the front door. Benzler slid lower in his chair. He had no way of knowing if these particular officers received the report about his escape. Maybe they just wanted a mid-shift snack. In any case, his resultant paranoia altered his strategy lickety-split.

He slipped out of his seat, and crouching low he slunk into the men's room. Inside, he entered a stall and locked the latch. He climbed up on a black toilet seat, pulled up his legs and waited.

The bathroom door swung open and someone entered. Benzler's heart leapt as his breath rushed out. He kept still. Whoever entered the room pulled on the stall door where Benzler hid.

"Anyone there?" the person asked.

Benzler froze, his temples pounding. After a prolonged pause he mumbled, "I'm in here."

"Sorry dude," a student said. Whew! It wasn't one of the cops. When the intruder left, Benzler poked his head out of the bathroom, and scampered out of the back door of the restaurant undetected.

As he exited, a gust of wind blew sleet sideways into his face. Hands in his pockets, he hunched down like a turtle. Getting back on the side streets, he continued south, not lost, but not dead on sure of his surroundings. Despite the rain, a bonfire raged outside the Sigma Alpha Epsilon fraternity house on his left. Many people drank by the fire, and created a ruckus. The smell of smoke permeated the block.

Benzler glanced at them as he walked past. He questioned himself and his predicament in contrast to the apparent celebration. He had run away from the hospital because he was angry and dissatisfied. But now, wet, cold, and tired, his anger had vanished, and the hospital didn't seem so bad.

He played out his minimal options. Go back to the hospital voluntarily. Nope, unacceptable. Back there he'd go into Special Care for sure, probably forever. That was guaranteed after a runaway. He hated S.C. No way would he go back there if he could help it. The thoughts of S.C. rekindled his anger and his resolve to stay free.

He trudged on, but later even that resolve lagged. *What else is there? Mom? If I calls Mom now, she'll just take me right back to the hospital. Friends? None of them can even drive yet, and they live an hour from here. I've got nobody.*

Benzler found that he had stopped while crossing a bridge. He looked down into a ravine, and he absently wondered if a drop from here would be fatal. *What are you thinking about?*

He suppressed the negative thoughts, decided he better just keep moving, and find some place to sleep. It got colder, and the drizzle kept falling. He picked a random apartment building and tried the door. It was locked. He tried another, then another, and all of them were locked. He checked some parked cars, but they were locked too. Someone came out of a nearby apartment, so he ducked down. His sense of desperation grew.

As he rambled further south, the buildings and neighborhoods appeared more rundown and blighted. Finally he found an open apartment building off of 7th Avenue. He entered the off-white, stucco, three story building. He staggered down the first floor hallway, his walking cast a mess, soaking wet. After inspecting all three floors, he settled for a small alcove off the first floor hallway by the laundry and the garbage. He dropped to the linoleum, pulled his knees to his chest, and hugged them tightly. Despite his shivering on the bitter, hard surface, he managed to fall asleep.

He dreamt of a warm, sunny day, and he stood outside of a barn. His father materialized in the doorway, smiling broadly. Wind swept across the hay in an adjacent field, bringing it to life. His father beckoned him to follow, and the boy did so noticing that he had no leg cast. He followed until his father turned back on him. His father's face soured, and again blood drooled out of his open mouth. His father lunged forward and pushed him.

Benzler awakened to an actual shove on the shoulder, and someone yelling at him. Fully roused, he became aware that it was not his father, but two policemen standing over him.

"Wake up son," one of them growled. A flashlight blinded him in the dark. "Do you understand me?" The policeman paused for a second as Benzler nodded. "Are you Marshall Benzler?" Again Benzler nodded. "We know who you are, playtime's over. Get up." Then more loudly, "Now."

Benzler didn't budge, so the gruff cop jerked him up by his left arm, and pulled him to his feet. The other cop still illuminated Benzler with the bright flashlight.

"Ouch man, watch the leg," Benzler griped.

The policeman stuck an unsympathetic finger into Benzler's face, "Don't you raise your voice to me young man. You're the one in trouble here. You better watch yourself." Benzler thought he resembles Bluto from the Popeye cartoon. The other one who wielded the flashlight seems gentler, much taller and thinner than Bluto.

Benzler felt the urge to complain some more, but fear muzzled

him. He resigned himself to the capture. *Wow it's the cops. What'll*

happen now?

"Am I goin' to jail?" he asked aloud.

Without a response, Bluto yanked the same arm with a tight grip.

Flashlight tugged on his other arm. They slapped handcuffs on him with

his arms behind his back. They steered Benzler over to the squad car,

and forced him into the back seat. Benzler stumbled face first into the

back seat. He maneuvered into as comfortable a position as possible,

which wasn't easy with his arms behind his back.

The car lights flashed red, white, and blue, while the officers

proceeded, business as usual in the front, ignoring their catch. Bluto

drove and Flashlight picked up his mike, and told the dispatcher that

they'd apprehended the fugitive.

After he replaced the transmitter, Benzler heard him say, "What

a waste of time."

They pulled out of the parking lot behind the dingy tenement,

and the gravel crunched under the tires. Benzler guessed that they head

north, and in about thirty minutes he recognized the hospital

surroundings. The strange combination of dread and relief peaked. He knew he'd soon be back in Special Care, but at least he'd be warm. He wondered what Dr. West and Nurse K. would say.

The squad car parked at the loading dock directly behind unit 6B. Half dozen technicians crammed the back corridor waiting to escort Benzler. They primed for any possible confrontation.

The squad car halted, and both cruiser doors opened simultaneously. Benzler watched the officers through the diamond barred window that separated the back seat from the front. He leaned forward awkwardly, hands still cuffed behind his back.

Flashlight rounded the car to the driver's side, while Bluto opened the door and drawled, "Get on out."

Benzler slid laterally in his seat, and as he swung his legs out, Bluto grabbed his sweatshirt, helping him out. Both cops assisted him up the few back stairs.

One of the techs opened the rear door, and the cops, one at each of Benzler's shoulders, brought him through the door.

"Here's your boy. Where do you want him?" Bluto asked the gang of techs.

They stood in awe of the policemen. Finally, one of the techs led the way to Special Care, to the blue room again. Once back there, the cops removed Benzler's handcuffs.

"You think you guys can handle it from here?" Bluto asked in a condescending tone. Then they withdrew abruptly, job completed. Benzler didn't resist at all.

After the officers departed, the technicians milled about noisily outside of Special Care until dismissed. Mr. Bennett, the nightshift tech, attended to Benzler. Bennett got him to change into the denim clothing. Bennett had always been decent to Marshall, but they have had little interaction because of his shift.

A nurse whom Benzler didn't know, substituted on the late shift that night, and she came into S.C. to talk with him. Dejected, Benzler sat on the floor in the corner of the room, his knees up, arms wrapped around them just like he did in the apartment.

She knelt down beside him and asked, "Are you OK?"

His forehead on his knees, he only said, "I'm cold." Mr. Bennett removed the thick blanket from the iron bed, and draped it over the boy's back. The nurse asked him some more questions. Basically she felt him out to see if he needed restraints or not. She also gauged any possible drug or alcohol abuse, and concluded that he was OK. Then they left Benzler alone.

He stared at the blue ceiling, listening to the fan whirr. His lifeless eyes misted and a single tear rolled down his cheek.

As if amazed, he spoke aloud, "Maybe I did try to kill myself."

Perhaps it dawned on him for the first time. "I deserve to be in this

nuthouse. I must be crazy." He tightened the blanket over himself like a

cocoon, and put his head back down on his knees.

He rocked gently while he sat numbly on the floor. He had an

epiphany, realizing that the only way to get out of here was to take

responsibility and get himself straightened out. Only then did he drift off

to sleep.

*   *   *

Chapter 21

Benzler's Dad stood outside the door of the family barn back

home. He always wore the same thing; his flannel jacket and deer

hunting cap. That was what he had on when he died. He waved for his

son to follow, then disappeared inside. Marshall trembled with

foreboding, then hastened across the barnyard. He felt like he sunk in quicksand, so he broke into a sluggish run. He entered the pitch dark building, and a swallowing, smothering dread overwhelmed him. As he adjusted to the shadows, he beheld his father sprawled at his desk, and he sensed something has gone terribly wrong.

Benzler woke up back in Special Care, sweaty and startled. *Man that dream bugs me. Why do I keep dreaming about my friggin' Dad?* His head cleared and he recognized his surroundings. Good ol' Special Care. He stayed in the same cell as last time, the blue room. Old blue. Benzler guessed he'd probably spend about a week in here. There was nothing to do in here but sit and think. No dodging the issues. No distractions. But that'd be the point now wouldn't it?

He swung his legs over to sit upright on the bed. A tech peeked through the window, and opened up the door when he perceived the occupant awake.

"How goes it Marshall?" Mr. Turner greeted with his genial grin.

"What time is it?" Benzler asked. He rubbed both eyes hard with his knuckles.

"Four," Mr. Turner answered. Benzler had slept for fourteen hours. "You need anything?"

"I have to piss."

That done, Turner asked, "Are you hungry?"

"Nah." The door latched with a metallic click as Turner exited. The all too familiar routine commenced.

Benzler lay back on his iron bunk, hands clasped behind his head. *What the hell am I doing here? Goddam it. Fuck Mom. Fuck Dr. West. I can keep on fighting, but where will that ultimately get me? Back in here. Back in this shithole every time. And certainly not out of this hospital. Damn, damn, damn.* He rose again, and he paced within the small chamber. He went over this, over and over in his head. *Resist, end up back here. Get along, try and work things out, who knows what'll happen?*

Finally after a couple of hours deliberating, he concluded that he should play by the rules. He made up his mind to once again work with Nurse Kincaid and Dr. West to get better.

At dinnertime, Mr. Turner brought Benzler a plate of food. Turner joined him in the Special Care room, and sat cross-legged on the floor by the door while Benzler ate. Benzler picked at some roast beef, but found he still didn't have much of an appetite. The smell of the dry brown meat nauseated him.

"Is Nurse Kincaid working tonight?" he asked the tech.

"As a matter of fact she is." Turner bobbed his head up and down.

"Can you please tell her that I'd like to speak with her?"

"Will do," Turner replied, head still bobbing.

Benzler tried the baked potato, but it was already cold, the skin tough. "So what's going on out there?" he asked with a head nod toward the open door.

"Nothing much," Turner said. He stretched his legs out straight in front of him. "A bunch of the kids are watching the series."

"Aw man," Benzler exclaimed. As much as he loved sports, Benzler had completely forgotten that the World Series started today. "Is there any way I can watch?" he pled.

"Sorry man, not in here you can't," Mr. Turner stated bluntly.

"At least tell me who's winning then?"

"The A's were up 2-1 a minute ago."

"Who's on the mound tonight?"

"Let's see." Turner looked up at the ceiling. "Holtzman versus Messersmith I think," he responded, looking back at the boy. Benzler toyed with his succotash, then gave up and pushed the tray away. He chugged down a carton of whole milk, stopped, and looked at Turner.

"Wait a minute, today's Saturday isn't it? I must be out of my mind. Did my Buckeyes win?" He tossed the empty carton onto the food tray.

Turner stood up, and talked excitedly. "Yep. They beat Wisconsin 52 to 7."

"All right. At least that's some good news."

"How'd Archie do?"

"He got his hundred."

"Cool." Benzler smiled. He remembered listening to the ballgames on the radio with his dad last year. His mood faded as the memory sank in.

Later, Nurse Kincaid visited for a one on one per his request. He jumped up when she knocked. He was happy to see her, but concerned about her reaction to his elopement.

She wore a knee length white dress, and leaned against the doorframe with her legs crossed and her left arm clutching her right elbow. "How are you Marshall?" she began, without expression.

"I slept great," he smirked. "I had a long night you know." He hid behind his false cockiness.

"Stop that," she scolded. "Pride in resistance is not going to help you. I know you wanted to come back here."

Taken aback by her insight, he shocked himself at how quickly he balked at his own resolve. He had committed himself toward a renewed compliance no more than an hour ago.

She lectured, pointing with her index finger, "If you are to get better, you need to demonstrate commitment. If to nothing else then at least to yourself. I can't help you, Dr. West can't help you. We're only facilitators. I know it sounds trite, but in order to get well, you have to help yourself." She turned to shut the door, and her voice trailed, "Let me know when you're really ready to talk to me." Benzler started to yell for her to wait, but didn't. She walked off abruptly, and he listened to the click of her heels recede down the corridor.

"Nice going," he muttered. He brooded over the faulty exchange for a while longer, and realized that he needed to try that over.

The next time that Mr. Turner poked his head in the window, Benzler flagged him down, and once again begged to see Nurse Kincaid. She kept him waiting this time, but she did make it back to see him before her shift ended.

Contrite, he avoided eye contact, and looked downward, arms crossed. "OK. OK. I'm sorry. I want to get better. What do I need to do?" he grumbled, his face flushed.

She looked at him dourly, "You can start by telling me what really happened yesterday."

"I ran away, so what?" Benzler said still flippant. She began to walk away again.

"Wait, wait," he called after her. "I'm sorry."

She returned, and raised her voice in response, "You know so what. That's the most obvious form of resistance. You were making progress too." She pled with him to be open. "So why?"

Frustrated Benzler mumbles, "I just feel all cooped up in here."

"No, you feel cooped up inside here." She pointed at her left temple. "You'll never know what kind of freedom you'll get until you open up. C'mon, talk to me. Please."

Benzler fumed silently. Despite his resolution, he couldn't get past the simple fact that he was angry.

She nudged him harder. "Marshall. Come on. Talk. Tell me about it. Have some courage."

He jerked his head up. "Courage?" he boomed, eyes piercing. "Courage? You don't know what it's like. It's easy for you to sit there and judge me. It's easy to criticize me. You don't know. I don't WANT to talk about finding my Dad with his head blown off." He whirled away from her. He lowered his voice again, and spat out, "And

224

you don't want to hear about it." They left the smoke from his outburst wafting in the air for a moment.

Nurse Kincaid spoke softly, "Marshall." She touched her hand on his back. "That's where you're wrong. I do want to hear. I know that must have really hurt. But you can't keep it in. You have to let it out or it'll eat at you like cancer." He spun around. His fiery eyes glared at her, and his rage melted into tears. He reached out to hug her.

"Why did he do that?"

She said gently, "I can't answer that."

She calmed the boy until he recovered. "You know you can talk to me when you're ready." With that she retreated and left him in his solitude.

He simmered with his anger for a while. He genuinely wanted to get better, but he just glimpsed how hard it would be. One quick query, one simple challenge from Nurse Kincaid, and he tumbled. The jagged edge of his emotions was just too fragile. But again, he determined to persist on the path toward getting better.

*   *   *

Sunday evening Benzler booked time to meet with Nurse Kincaid. When she eventually got free, she rejoined him in Special Care.

225

This time she brought in one of the Atrium chairs, while Benzler sat Indian-style on his bed. She left the heavy Special Care door open, and Benzler could hear activity on the unit.

"Are you ready?" she asked. He nodded in agreement. He chose his words for a minute, and then he began to tell the story.

"Mom and Dad had been fighting for weeks. They never told me what it was about; they always fought after us kids went to bed. I couldn't ever hear any specifics, just them yelling at each other." He wrung his hands while he talked rapidly.

"Anyway, this went on and on and I didn't think that much about it. It bothered me, but I just thought all parents argue." Nurse Kincaid paid close attention, careful not to disturb the setting.

"On that day, Mom took David and Nancy to the plaza shopping and left Dad and me at home. I helped him most of the morning fixin' one of our tractors out in the barn. He was real quiet while we worked. Not sad or anything, just busy with the work. He was like that sometimes. Most times he was full of life, you know. Once in awhile though, he'd just be different. Like he wasn't even there.

"Finally, he let me go in and watch TV. I was watching an episode of 'The Little Rascals,' the one where Spanky is little and all the kids are at the orphanage. The kids put plaster in the milk, and they all keep saying 'don't drink the milk.'" Benzler feigned a whisper. "And

then the others'd say 'Why not?' 'It's spoiled.' The headmaster finally

comes in and says, 'You kids put that milk on your mush and eat it.'"

Benzler imitated a craggy, old man voice.

Nurse Kincaid interrupted his tangent, "I don't really want to

hear about the Little Rascals, Marshall."

"Oh yeah. I'm sorry. I love that one," he apologized. "Anyway,

that's what I remember was going on when I heard it." He paused, and

Nurse Kincaid looked at him with "What?" on her face without actually

asking it.

"Definitely I heard a sound like a big 'pop.' It must've been the

gunshot. It came from outside by the barn. I didn't think that much of it

at the time. Something strange though made me worry, but I just ignored

it." Benzler stopped for a second and took a deep breath. Nurse Kincaid

waited patiently for him to continue.

His speech rate slowed discernibly. "An hour or so later Mom

comes home. She asked me where Dad was so I told her he's out in the

barn. Wasn't 'til suppertime that any of us thought about him again.

That's when Mom asked me to run out and fetch 'im. I don't know why

but I didn't want to, and I said have Davey do it. She just yelled at me to

go on. I felt a funny feeling walking out to the barn. It was already dark out, and cold. I noticed right off there wasn't any lights on. That freaked me out 'cause Dad wouldn't be sitting out there in the dark. So I opened the big sliding barn door, and hollered out for Dad, but got no answer. Just the wind and some wood creaking. You ever been in a barn at night?"

"No," she replied.

"Well..., it's creepy. I found the light panel and switched them all on. The tractor we worked on was still sitting there only nobody was working on it." Benzler slowed again and shut up. Goosebumps rose up on his arms. He wiped his eyes, and his nose. Nurse Kincaid reached over and patted his arm to reassure him.

He looked up at her, sniffled, then resumed, "I stood in the door and called out once more for my Dad. His office was dark, and the door was closed. I could hear something scurry up in the hayloft, and even though I knew it was probably a mouse, it still made me jump. I guess I just knew all along that something was dead wrong. The air was thick with it.

"I tiptoed across the floor over to where my Dad's office was. I pushed open the door with one hand, and I felt for the light switch, up and down the wall 'til I found it and flipped it on." Benzler quit again.

He broke down in shudders. Sympathetic, Nurse Kincaid rubbed his back until he pulled himself together.

"And then Marshall?" she asked.

He forced out, "I turned on the light." He waited a second. "I saw him." Another pause. "There was blood all over the place."

Each pause got longer. Nurse Kincaid stepped into the bathroom and retrieved some tissue for him.

Benzler blew his nose and again carried on. "I stood frozen just staring at him for awhile. I didn't even check him. I just knew. Finally I ran back into the house to tell Mom. I don't know what was worse, finding my Dad or running to tell Mom." He stopped again.

She leaned forward in her chair. "How did you feel then?"

"I don't know, just bad." Benzler leaned back and closed his eyes. "I couldn't help feeling like it was all my fault."

"Do you still feel that way?" Nurse Kincaid prodded.

He nodded his head affirmatively, "But it's not the same."

"What do you mean by 'not the same?'"

He rubbed his face with both hands. "Then I was scared, worried, and sad. Now more than anything I'm just mad." His face hardened, and he set his jaw.

"Marshall, I've been involved with many survivors of suicides. What you're feeling is normal. Everyone goes through certain stages toward recovery," the nurse counseled him.

"Yeah, none of that matters though." He laughed dryly.

"What do you mean?" she asked.

"My whole life is fucked." Benzler stated this knowingly with a steely gaze. "There's no way outta this. There's nothing you or anyone else can do to help me."

Nurse Kincaid paused, and sat motionless. Then she offered, "That's where you're mostly right. I'm committed to helping you. We're all committed to helping you. But any help we can give hinges on you. You have to change your mind about your own life."

Benzler put his head down, and shook it back and forth, back and forth.

The nurse continued, "I want to thank you for telling me about your father. It's heart wrenching, and I'd give almost anything to not have you go through it. You're very brave to tell it. It's a very important step, but it is only the first step in a long process. Now we have to pick up the pieces and go on."

Benzler continued to shake his head.

"Marshall, are you OK?" He looked up at her red-faced, eyes blank.

"I think the next step is to talk about this with Dr. West." She waited for his response, but she got none. She went on, "Do you think you could do that?"

Benzler remained unresponsive. Nurse Kincaid finally said, "I'm worried about you. I know this must be extremely difficult. But you're in a safe place here in Special Care." She stayed with him, watching over him for about five more minutes. "I need to go now. Let me know if you'd like to talk further later. You'll be OK."

She exited the room, and pushed the massive door closed behind her. Benzler clenched and unclenched his fists repeatedly.

He grunted aloud, "Why?" He repeated it, and began to pound on the mattress. "Why, why, why, why, why?" He collapsed onto the bed in exhaustion.

*   *   *

Chapter 22

A month later, Benzler and a small group crossed the hospital grounds as they returned to the unit from afternoon activities. Benzler's hooded head bobbed above the motley gaggle as they walk. His gait had improved markedly as his leg mended.

The sky darkened prematurely, and the hidden sun set behind thick gloom. Benzler enjoyed the cool mist as it wet his face. He took a deep breath.

Autumn delivered ample contrast to Ohio. Following a vibrant, colorful October, November turned bleak and brown with oppressive gray skies. One good thing about the annual transition of fall to winter was that ragweed too lay dormant; therefore Benzler's allergic response cleared up for the winter.

Benzler's personal November had been a contrast as well. Sufficiently recovered from the drama of October, Benzler put all his efforts into his treatment. He maintained focus and drive to get better. He relied on Nurse Kincaid as his primary support, and she came through for him every time. She encouraged him to work hard with Dr. West, in school, and in Adjunctive Therapy, and she coached him through the changes.

He built stronger relationships with the staff, though he still kept his distance with other patients. He rapidly earned more trust, and subsequently more privilege and standing on the unit. He opened up with Dr. West, and coincidentally the dreams of his father had stopped.

The overcast evening insulated the pack of patients like a damp blanket as their escort, Mr. Spach led them back to their locked dorm. As soon as they breached the entry, shrieks from Special Care shattered the secure illusion. The clamor served as a conspicuous reminder to Benzler of where he was and why.

"What the hell is that?" Benzler asked aloud with a grimace on his face.

"New kid," replied another patient, a know-it-all girl whom he didn't like.

"Fresh meat," Benzler stated nonchalantly.

Spach gave him a stern look. "Take fifteen."

Benzler regarded the tech. "I was going there anyway." He peeled off his raincoat, and escaped to his room for some peace and quiet.

Since Benzler's arrival in August, six of his fellow campers had been discharged. Some had gotten better, the rest were released for other various reasons. With every exodus, the hospital admitted a replacement. This newbie was named Johnny Jarvis.

An hour later, Benzler played euchre with Mr. Sharpe and a couple of others in the Atrium. Shortly after his capture and return to custody, Benzler had apologized to Sharpe. Since Sharpe hadn't gotten in any hot water, it made their reconciliation easier.

While the unit's latest addition kept up the disturbance, Benzler again complained, "What the hell is the matter with that kid?"

The jovial technician ripped off his high pitched staccato laugh.

"What's so funny?" Benzler glanced at Sharpe with one eyebrow askew. He shuffled the partial deck of cards.

Sharpe smirked. "You came in the same way, howling, biting. Don't you remember that buddy?"

Benzler dealt the next hand, and emitted a belligerent "No."

"Well you did. Think about it." Sharpe chuckled some more.

"Well, can't you give him some meds or something?"

With a final giggle, Sharpe shook his head, "C'mon and play cards."

After a few days, Jarvis adjusted to his new home; at least he had stopped the bellowing. With his incremental improvement, staff allowed Jarvis time out of Special Care to interact with others on the unit. Though he was a year older than Benzler, Jarvis stood the same height. He had olive skin, green eyes, and coffee colored hair. He came from a small town in southeast Ohio near the West Virginia border.

Brimming with energy, he talked nearly non-stop as soon as he showed up on the Atrium's white tile floor. He lacked many conventional manners, even saying please, thank you, and excuse me. And, he quickly displayed negativity along with the excess volume.

Benzler mostly avoided the newcomer, like an older dog that ignored the pestering overtures of a puppy. He watched the emergence, and noted that it did bear similarity to his own, not that long ago.

One evening at snack time, Benzler placidly spread some Cheez Whiz on Ritz crackers at a table near the kitchen. Jarvis plopped down with a thud in a metal chair next to him.

"So you're Marshall, huh?"

"You got that right." Benzler looked at him with condescension. "I see you finally got out of that smelly SC robe."

"What's your deal man?" Jarvis asked with furrowed brow.

"Whaddya mean?" Benzler feigned indifference.

235

Jarvis excitedly explained," I heard all about you. Running off, causing trouble, and shit."

"So?" Benzler replied, still unaffected.

"So now you just sit around here like a lump a cowshit." Jarvis crammed a stack of Saltines into his mouth. He managed to say, "What are y'all some kind of goodie two shoes all of a sudden?"

The remark visibly irritated Benzler, who bit back with some anger, "No. I'm just keeping out of trouble. I wanna get out of this place someday." He stopped eating, and sat upright on the edge of his chair.

Jarvis stared right back at him. "That a'int no fun."

"Spinning your wheels in S.C. isn't much fun either," Benzler responded defensively. His volume raised just enough to cause others to quiet down and take notice. Mr. Spach reclined at the Nurse's Station, and cast a menacing glare toward them.

Jarvis tried to calm the situation down. "Peace man. I just thought you might be cool's all." He moved his plate to an adjacent table.

During Benzler's next one on one with Nurse Kincaid, he confided to her, "I don't like that Jarvis guy."

236

They met in the quiet room, one that many of the staff used for private discussions. Benzler rested on a short, cinnamon colored couch, and Nurse Kincaid directly faced him in a matching chair. She had her hair pulled back in a tight ponytail, and had her notepad and pencil in her lap. Glass walled the room on all sides with a thick panel to the outside. The warmth of the unit inside starkly contrasted the dark, chilly night.

"Why not?" Nurse Kincaid responded. In the confined space, Benzler always thought how nice she smelled, with just a touch of lavender.

"He's cocky. He just bugs me," Benzler justified.

"Well, you have to understand that he's here for a reason, just like you." She crossed her legs, and delicately made tiny circles with her raised foot. "Maybe you should try to be a little more empathetic and tolerant of his situation," she counseled.

Benzler looked down at his hands, and picked at a hangnail. "Yeah. I suppose so. But he's the one who's calling me out."

Nurse Kincaid pressed him, "What do you mean, specifically?"

Benzler recounted his previous encounter with Jarvis.

"I see," she said when he finished. She looked at him with a kind, gentle expression. "Marshall, do you remember when you first arrived?"

"What? How can I forget? But what does that have to do with him?"

"Bear with me a moment." She scratched at the back of her neck beneath her ponytail. "Describe the way you felt to me."

"OK," Benzler said, then paused. "Um. I guess I was a little leery of everyone."

"How about very leery? I'd say you were scared."

"I suppose so."

"Do you remember how resistant you were?"

"Yeah, that's the same thing Mr. Sharpe said."

"Well, John has to go through the same sort of thing."

"I guess."

"I'm trying to draw a parallel between the two of you, because I'd like to ask you a favor."

"Shoot."

"I'd like you to try and make friends with John." She pointed with her pencil as she spoke. "He needs a mentor, and it would be a good way for you to take more of a leadership role on the unit."

Benzler leaned back in his chair, rolled his eyes, and sighed.

"You know we've talked about how you haven't established any good relationships with your peers."

He wiped perspiration from his forehead, but still didn't answer.

"It would look very good with the council when we do your next progress review."

In the end, she finally convinced him to give it a try.

*   *   *

The two boys more or less kept clear of each other the rest of the week. Benzler passively observed Jarvis' misconduct in school, on the unit, and in activities. He acknowledged some similarities between himself and Jarvis.

With Nurse Kincaid's prodding, Benzler began to assert himself in an attempt to find some common ground. First of all, as both boys enjoyed sports, they bonded discussing the minutiae of Buckeye football. Since Jarvis turned out to be a Pittsburgh Steelers fan, they playfully argued over the rivalry with Benzler's Browns. Second, Benzler discovered that Jarvis loved rock music, and listened to Aerosmith, one of his favorite bands as well. Over the next couple of weeks they spent time together listening to music and playing pool. The past few months on the unit had enabled Benzler to polish his billiards skills. He casually taught the novice Jarvis a few pointers.

A couple of days later, the two of them shot eight-ball together in the rec room. The unit's only hi fi stereo was located there. They played quietly, and listened to the Aerosmith eight track that Jarvis owned. The affable Mr. Turner oversaw them, while he lounged in a chair.

The lanky Jarvis lined up a gimme, drew his stick back, and struck the white cue ball hard. It cracked against several other balls as it caromed around the table.

He missed, and yelled, "Damn."

"Only a fool shoots hard pool," Benzler admonished.

"Fuck off."

"Watch your mouth," said Mr. Turner, but not too severely. He didn't even sit up in his chair.

Jarvis responded with a cocky laugh, and an insincere, "Sorry man." The attitude pushed Turner's threshold of tolerance, but the tech let him go.

Benzler applied blue chalk to the end of his cue. "Why are you always acting like that?"

"What? That?" Jarvis extended his hands out in innocence. I'm just having fun, man."

"Yeah, but in the long run you're only hurting yourself." Benzler knocked in the ten ball, and set himself up for the next shot.

"You think you're one of the techs or something?" Jarvis spouted back at Benzler.

"No." Benzler sank the nine ball, corner pocket. "But, man do you wanna stay in here?" While Benzler took his turn, Jarvis stood erect spinning his pool stick in his hands.

"It's not so bad. Three squares a day, nobody really hassling you." He mimicked playing guitar with his pool cue with fake strums to *Dream On*. "Not like over at TICO," he added.

Benzler looked up from the table in disbelief at the mention of TICO, short for the Training Institute of Central Ohio. "You were in juvee?" He looked to Turner. "Did you know that?" Turner confirmed the true statement with a nod.

"You better believe it," Jarvis said, chest puffed out.

"What'd you do to get stuck in there?"

"You name it." Jarvis smiled proudly.

Now Benzler rolled his eyes. He caught Mr. Turner looking askance as well.

"What? Did you kill somebody or something?" Benzler joked. Jarvis raised his index finger to his lips, and nodded secretly toward Turner.

"C'mon. Get serious." Benzler shook his head, and again focused on his next shot. "Really, what was it like?" Jarvis went on to brag about his various escapades. Benzler rightly suspected some embellishment, still, the talk of Juvenile Detention interested, even impressed him. Meanwhile, Benzler ran the table so that only the eight ball remained.

"If it doesn't work out here, won't they send you back there?" Benzler asked.

"I don't know, maybe." The point caused Jarvis to lose a bit of his swagger.

"And what about after that? Prison?" Benzler questioned Jarvis with an edge that cut right through the facade, challenging his warped life strategy.

"Nah, I ain't goin' to no prison." Jarvis shrugged. "I ain't that bad. It'll work out."

"Yeah. But don't you think the best way to make it work out is to make progress here." He smacked the eight ball into the corner pocket.

Jarvis said, "You win. Again. Wanna rack 'em?" He pulled balls out of the pockets, and rolled them back onto the table.

"Nah, I've had enough." Benzler placed his stick flat on the soft felt table, and started out of the rec room. Jarvis popped out his eight-track tape, and joined him.

Once the boys got out of Turner's earshot, Jarvis grabbed Benzler by his shoulder, and looked at him squarely. He posed a question, speaking low.

"Do you really think these people care about you?"

Uncomfortable, Benzler backed away. "Yes, I do. Most of 'em are cool. Nurse Kincaid has helped me a lot."

"OK, maybe a couple of 'ems alright." Jarvis crossed his arms and leaned forward. "What about Spach? Most of 'ems assholes. Do you really think when they're at home that any of 'em give a rat's ass about us? No way. They're not your friends, they're not family. When push comes to shove, they don't care squat about you. So I ain't falling for any of their mumbo jumbo." He waved both hands in front of him.

Benzler didn't react as he reflected on what Jarvis said. Some of it definitely rang true.

"You may be right about all that stuff, but right now this is my best bet."

*   *   *

Chapter 23

"I have to say I'm genuinely impressed with your progress," Nurse Kincaid said as she initiated another one on one two weeks later. They assumed their normal spots in the quiet room. A cardboard decoration of a turkey dressed up as a pilgrim still remained on the window, though Thanksgiving had already passed.

On the opposite side of the dense, transparent wall, a pitch black night consumed all light. A single floor lamp, giving off little more than a nightlight, threw a dim yellow upon them. However, adjacency to the fluorescent Atrium ensured more than sufficient light.

Benzler blushed and looked away. He definitely struggled with receiving positive feedback, and couldn't help questioning the praise. Nevertheless, she made him feel giddy, and he laughed bashfully. "Come on. You don't mean that."

"No really I'm serious. Since your elopement, you've completely turned it around. I'm proud of you." She pushed the compliment with a smile. But Benzler detected an uncommon nervous energy from her.

"Thanks. You helped." He pulled his stringy, shoulder length hair out of his eyes. He hadn't cut his hair since before his admission in August.

"No, you've done all the hard work. You must keep focusing on that," she emphasized.

The past two weeks had gone smoothly. He advanced in all phases of his treatment. He began work with a designated social worker, Mrs. Masterson. Together they confronted the iceberg that was the fractured relationship with his family. Even after all this time, he still hadn't been allowed to see his Mom since he arrived. In any case, he sowed the seeds for success, and for the first time he envisioned the possibility of a promising future on the outside. Everything seemed to travel in the right direction.

Still, therapy proved to be truly difficult. Nurse Kincaid steadily guided him when he got discouraged, and she brought him down to earth when he flew too high in the clouds.

She continued lauding his progress. "I'm also impressed with how you've taken John under your wing."

"Yeah. Turns out we got a lot in common."

Despite his initial misgivings about Jarvis, they had become friends. He offset Jarvis' persistent negative challenges with his own will to succeed in treatment. He actually bought into some of Jarvis' cynicism, but overall they agreed to disagree.

"I think both of you are benefiting from the relationship. It's good for you to be a role model."

He reminded her, "That was your idea you know."

The nurse and her ward moved on with their customary appointment for about an hour. He talked with her about many things, but in general he just told her how he felt better about himself.

Then his world crashed down on him.

As they wrapped up she stopped, sat upright, and closed her notebook. She pushed her pencil into the notebook rings, and then clapped her hands together. "I have some good news to tell you." She reached out and touched him on the forearm.

He sensed her excitement, but there was something else too. He pressed her, "What is it?"

She clasped her hands back together. "My husband got this great new job opportunity. It's a big promotion that he's really been working toward."

He squeaked out, "Congratulations." All the while he wondered where this was going.

"The only thing is, well, it's in Boston." Her eyes searched his face for a read on his reaction.

"What does that mean?" Benzler squinted and narrowed his eyebrows.

She took a breath. "We've thought about it a lot. And we've decided we're going to move." Benzler paled as the blood rushed to his feet. He felt lightheaded, and his limbs turned to lead.

She observed him turn white. "Marshall? Are you OK?"

He couldn't move. He heard himself mutter, "Sure, I'm OK," but he sounded to himself like he was under water. He mumbled another, "Congratulations," but it echoed hollow and heartless. He glanced outside into the darkness, and caught their silhouette reflected on the glass.

She went on, "Well, I just wanted to let you know as soon as possible, to give us plenty of transition time." She stood, which signaled the end of the discussion.

He looked down at her white leather shoes. Typical nurse's shoes. Comfortable, practical.

He uttered, "When do you leave?"

"In two weeks. Like I said we should have plenty of time to close."

Benzler stared at her shoes some more.

"Marshall, are you gonna be alright?" She rubbed his shoulder softly, and he recoiled.

He spat out, "I guess I'm just stunned."

She nodded her head, "Yes I understand. It came up suddenly." They waited, inert and tense for a minute, shackled by propriety. She wanted to flee, while he felt like screaming.

"Well, I have to get back to work. We can talk about it more tomorrow." She exited and left him alone.

He stared at the same spot where her shoes just stood. Eventually he trudged to his bedroom, and lied on his back on his bed. One by one he counted the holes on his ceiling tiles. He felt like he was falling, like a crutch had been ripped from beneath him.

Twenty –five, twenty-six.... Jarvis was right. Ha. I can't believe I stood up for her. Twenty-seven, twenty-eight.... What a fool. She doesn't friggin' care. Twenty-nine, thirty....You opened up to her; you

let yourself get attached to her, only to be trashed again. Damn. Thirty-
one, thirty-two....

What did you expect? That's right, deep down you suspected it
all along. He kept on counting. He thought about his Dad. Betrayal.
He thought about his Mom. Betrayal. His friends. *Where are they now?*
Huh? A coupla stupid letters, that's all. And now her.

How can she do this? How could I let her? What am I gonna do
now?

*   *   *

Chapter 24

Benzler perceived the rap at his bedroom door seconds before
the hinge creaked as it opens. On the edge of his bunk, Benzler held his
head in his hands. His long, straw-like hair draped between his fingers.
Without a glance Benzler groused, "Jeez, these checks are never-
ending."

Only 8 by 8 feet square, the bare, musty room consisted of a twin bed, a plain wooden dresser, and a closet by the door. He didn't decorate as he never intended to stay long. No posters, flags, or pennants like some of the other kids. The only light came from sun that shined through his threadbare off-white curtain.

A technician poked his head in. "Sorry to bother you Marshall, just doing rounds." Benzler recognized Mr. Turner's distinctive baritone, and his gaze chased the voice. Turner encroached further into the doorway with his clipboard in hand. Benzler's angry face stared back at him. He couldn't conceal his bloodshot eyes with dark bags beneath them. An alarming sight on such a young boy.

It was Saturday morning after Nurse K's last day. He'd suffered through a rough couple of weeks. He closed with her, but remained aloof mostly. He hadn't communicated much to any of the staff since her announcement. Instead, he festered in his room, withdrawn and irritable. When he had emerged from isolation during the week, he banded with other cynical patients, particularly Jarvis. The positive balance they recently shared had shifted precipitously toward the negative. Each night this week, they had managed to magnify some kind of petty trouble into punishment, ranging from timeouts to work details.

"What's going on Marshall, you don't look so good?" Mr. Turner observed.

Benzler barked, "Don't bother me now." Regretful, he softened his expression as he sought some sympathy. "OK?"

"All right. But you need to get out of bed. Let me know if you want to talk later." Turner ducked back out, and he closed the door behind him.

Benzler returned his head to his hands, and rubbed his forehead with his palms. His head ached, his heart yearned. He couldn't shake this sense of betrayal.

He tried to recall the dream that woke him up. *What the hell was that?* He had found himself in his father's workshop again. His Dad had lain face down on the desk. In the dim light the blood appeared black. His Dad had jerked upward suddenly, and turned to the right, where Nurse Kincaid stood in the corner. *What on earth was she doing there?* That was when he awoke. He sighed heavily. It occurred to him that he hadn't dreamt of his Dad in a month.

Eventually he heeded Turner's advice, and lumbered out to the Atrium for breakfast, though he wasn't hungry. He found Jarvis, who dug into a plate of eggs and toast.

"Look what the cat drug in." Jarvis talked with his mouth full as usual. Benzler didn't reply. The rain drops that began to fall on the glass door drew his attention. He took a seat across from Jarvis.

"What's the matter with you? You look like shit."

Surly, Benzler replied, "This fucking place. I wanna get outta here so damn bad."

"No shit. What's new about that?" Jarvis asked.

"Nothing," Benzler grunted. "It's just really getting to me right now."

Jarvis devoured his breakfast, and chattered throughout. Benzler moped, oblivious to the rant until two other boys joined them, Jamie Wells and Mike Taylor. Short with long reddish blond hair, Wells always wore a Cincinnati Reds baseball cap. Since unit rules prohibited hats inside, this provided a constant chafing point with the staff. Taller and thicker, the dim-witted Taylor tailed Wells around wherever he went. And both of them shadowed Jarvis, and revered his shenanigans.

Wells said in his high-pitched voice, "Benzler, you look like hell."

"Yeah, what happened to you?" Taylor chimed in with an insipid grin.

A testy Benzler snapped, "Duh, do you think so? Ever have any original ideas between the two of you?"

"Chill out Benzler," Jarvis defended his toadies.

"Yeah man, what'd we do?" squeaked Wells.

Benzler shook his head and looked down at the stark white table in front of him. He placed his palms flat, pushed himself up, and escaped back into his room. *Morons.*

He quarantined himself until the next hourly room check. This time Spach burst in without warning.

"Christ, don't you ever knock?"

"Marshall, you need to get out of bed, and out of your room." The turtleneck sweater Spach wore made his neck look even longer.

Benzler bit his lip. "All right. I'm coming."

"You need to take a shower too. It stinks in here." Spach couldn't say anything without a tone of condescension.

"Man, you don't have to get personal."

"You know the rules about hygiene. Get cleaned up."

Benzler reluctantly did as he was told. He and Spach had feuded even during Benzler's so called good phases. Benzler considered him simply mean. He didn't care for Spach at all, so since the onset, he had made it his best practice to avoid him.

After a quick shower, he threw on the same flannel shirt and a jean jacket, and joined a group outside in the courtyard. Still sluggish, he located a solitary spot under some cover on the steps. The others played a rowdy game of kickball despite the steady sprinkles.

Jarvis soon spied him and approached. "Hey farmer, sorry we got under your skin this morning. Didn't mean anything by it."

Benzler forced a smile. "Don't worry about it, hillbilly. I shouldn't let this place get to me."

The two friends talked about his anger over Nurse K's leaving. Ultimately, he confided, "I guess you were right. These guys don't give a crap about me really. I'm just passing through, one more patient."

"That's what I been talking about," said Jarvis. "That cute little nurse sure had you fooled. But in the end it all becomes clear."

Benzler agreed in principal, but as Jarvis spoke he still felt defensive about Nurse Kincaid. But he held back his anger, kept quiet, and just nodded his head. *Fuck her anyway, the traitor.*

The storm brought harder rain, because the air was too warm for snow. The techs called the game, and escorted everyone back inside.

That evening, as Benzler once again found solitude in his room, Jarvis rescued him to play some eight-ball. But upon entry into the rec room, Benzler saw Spach in there.

"Spach?" he asked Jarvis as he stopped short outside the door.

"C'mon man. He's the only one available." Jarvis rolled his eyes.

"I hate that pit face."

"I know. Just be cool."

The rec room stereo blared loudly, Aerosmith, "Train Kept Arollin." Three of the girls from the unit relaxed in the rec room also. Mr. Spach spoke with one of the girls, and ignored the two pool players.

Benzler unwound some, and tried to get into the game. Unable to concentrate, he played poorly and lost the first two games. During the third, frustrated he botched another easy shot and muttered, "Fuck it," under his breath.

Surprisingly, Mr. Spach heard him. "That's enough Marshall. Take fifteen."

"You heard that? Aw, c'mon man, I'm sorry. It slipped," pled Benzler.

"I said take fifteen," Spach repeated firmly.

"Man, you must have rabbit ears," Benzler complained.

"Make it thirty," Spach upped the ante. He showed his typical zero tolerance, and his penchant for power struggles.

Benzler glared at Spach. "What? You don't have to be like that. I said I was sorry."

"Make it forty-five, Marshall. Keep it going." Spach rolled his hand over in a circular motion.

"Fine. I want to stay in my room anyway." He tossed his pool stick onto the table. He grumbled, "Idgit," as he made his way to the door.

"All right, that's it. You're going to open door." Spach referred to open door special care. Staff sometimes used open door to defuse conflicts.

Benzler stopped in his tracks. "No way. I'm not going in there, asshole."

Spach rose, turned off the stereo, and the room fell silent. "C'mon we're going."

"Fuck you man. You can't do that." Benzler's face was stone cold.

"Watch me." At that point Spach strode past Benzler to the rec room door, and called for assistance from the tech who manned the Nurse's Station.

A jubilant Jarvis spurred Benzler on with a slap on the shoulder. "I'm with you man," he whispered. "Let's stir up some shit. Let's go down swingin' together." He rubbed his hands together excitedly.

Spach pointed at Jarvis, and then made a thumb jerk motion toward the door. "John. You. Out." He added, "Everyone else out of the rec room. C'mon everyone. Out."

Benzler set his jaw and told Jarvis, "Go get some of the guys."

Jarvis' eyes brightened. "Good idea." He rushed out along with the trio of girls, and he recruited the two boys from earlier, Wells and Taylor.

Two other evening shift techs, new staff on the Sixes came into the rec room with Nurse Marder, who attempted to take control of the situation.

Benzler reached down and picked his pool cue back up from the table. He had not previously viewed it as a weapon. *No turning back now. I'm not going down easy, not tonight. I might have to fight my way out of this.*

The nurse said, "Marshall, we need to deescalate this. I need for you to communicate with me."

"He started it." Benzler's eyes drew a bead on Mr. Spach. "I admit that I screwed up. But I said I was sorry, and even then he

257

couldn't cut me any slack. And he's the one who made a big deal out of it. The prick." Benzler glowered at Spach, even after he finished. Finally he reverted his eyes back to Nurse Marder.

She resumed, "Nevertheless, I need you to calm down, put down that stick ya got there, and talk with me."

"I am fucking talking to you," Benzler responded, his voice raised. At this moment as if by design, Jarvis and his rogues physically pushed by Mr. Spach and the others into the rec room.

"Hey," Spach shouted. He reached for the back of Well's shirt as he scooted past, but he missed. "You guys get out of here."

Jarvis whooped, "Fuck off man. We're sticking with Benzler, dickhead." All three boys lined up with Benzler. They squared off behind the billiard table, which acted as a buffer between the patients and staff.

The two novice techs had never handled this kind of firsthand, united threat, and their apprehension showed. On the other hand, the seasoned Spach bristled with anger not fear. Only Nurse Marder maintains her composure so far.

Benzler still absently gripped the one-piece pine pool cue. Jarvis watched this, grabbed one for himself, and then armed the other two boys as well. Benzler looked down at the slender rod in his hands and rolled it

258

back and forth. He felt the smooth yet solid wood. The boys had definitely passed the point of no return.

Reinforcements arrived from other units across campus. The boys could easily view their numbers grow through the glass rec room windows as the mass gathered around the unit's Christmas tree. As the boys stared, the never used locked door in the back of the rec room opened. An oblivious technician, who thought he was taking a short cut, wandered in right behind the boys. He stopped and grasped the situation. He smiled with an "Oops" look on his face.

Immediately, Jarvis took a swing and slammed his pool cue across the tech's arm. The cheaply made stick snapped in half, and the broken shard flung into the corner. The tech dropped to his knees, and cried out in agony.

Nurse Marder's hands flew to her face, and she gasped, "Oh my gosh."

Spach and the two other techs stepped up to help their injured comrade, but the boys held them at bay with their improvised weapons. Jarvis brandished his shattered cue, and threatened them, "Back off." To the injured victim behind him, he turned and spewed, "Go on! Git!" The tech turned tail, and scurried out the way he came.

Additional techs kept coming as the condition intensified. An enormous tech entered the room, and whispered something to Nurse Marder. Benzler recognized his square face and barrel chest from his first day at Wilson. The techs all called this one "the Enforcer." Three techs now stood in behind Mr. Spach and Nurse Marder in the rec room, with more assembled in the Atrium.

Nurse Marder spoke again, "Boys, please put down those sticks. What do ya expect to get out of this? What are ya going to do now?"

"No, no no!" Benzler yelled over her. "What are YOU going to do now? None of you know what the hell you're doing." He waved his pool cue toward the staff. Jarvis wore an evil grin behind him, while Wells and Taylor appeared almost as shaken as the staff. Unsure what they'd gotten themselves into; they couldn't back down now without losing face. They lingered in the background behind the raging Benzler and the impish Jarvis.

Nurse Marder tried again, "Oh my Marshall. You know we do the best we can here."

"Shut up," he screamed at her, spittle spraying. "Just shut the fuck up!"

Marder now appeared frazzled, speechless. "But..." she stuttered.

"I said shut the fuck up!" Benzler interrupted, and she stopped. The vein on his forehead popped out. Benzler looked at the group of staff members, who stared at him, mouths agape. He feigned a lunge forward toward them with his pool cue. They all jerked back in concert as if choreographed. He again pointed the stick at them. "You guys get out of here now. All of you." None of them moved. Benzler waves the stick at them again. "I said now. Leave us alone."

Nurse Marder nodded and waved the techs out of the room. By now the Atrium area teemed with bodies, probably every available staff member on duty.

When everyone filed out, the four boys remained alone in the rec room. Benzler collapsed onto the green felt covered chair, still with the pool cue. He rolled it back and forth in his hands.

Jarvis cranked up the stereo, and the other two boys celebrated, with high fives and laughs as they relished their short-term triumph. Benzler didn't participate with them, as he second guessed the futility of their predicament. His outrage died down, and he seemed to search for answers within the grains of his wooden cue.

Jarvis noted his behavior. "Whattsa matter with you?"

Bile rose in Benzler's throat. "What the hell are we doing? We can't win this."

Jarvis hollered over the loud music, "What? We're on a roll man. We can't quit now." He threw his arms up in the air.

Benzler thought on it awhile longer, and then set his weapon down. He said, "This is hopeless. We're gonna end up in juvee."

Jarvis responded, "I don't care. Go ahead and give up." Energized, Jarvis paced back and forth, eyes wild. "But one of these dumbasses is goin' down."

"But Spach's the only asshole," Benzler argued. "The others are OK."

"You kiddin' me?" Jarvis shouted back. "We came in here 'cause we got your back. And now you're pussin' out?" He looked at Wells and Taylor, who again hung back. "What about you two? You pussin' out too?" They looked at one another and nodded their heads no, though their eyes told a different story.

As Benzler stepped down as the leader, Wells and Taylor looked to Jarvis to fill the void. They began to powwow on next steps when the Atrium erupted with commotion. The boys halted and looked toward the rec room door. The mass of techs outside suddenly split, and a handful of policemen blitzed in wearing full riot gear. Another pair gained entry simultaneously through the back door, the same door the injured tech came through earlier. The officers took down all four boys swiftly and

262

forcefully. They knocked each of them onto their bellies, and they wrenched their arms behind their backs to handcuff them. Only Jarvis resisted. Benzler took it all in serenely, up to the point that the cops tackled him. He sustained only a slight rug burn on his cheek from the carpet. The cops subdued the boys in less than five minutes.

The police hustled the four through the crowded Atrium to squad cars out back. They shoved Benzler and Jarvis into the back seat of one squad car, Wells and Taylor another. Jarvis scowled at Benzler. Benzler said, "Looks like you'll be headed back to TICO after all." He never uttered another word to Jarvis. Ever.

Jarvis redirected his ire toward the cops up front with a barrage of questions, but they didn't even acknowledge him. Finally one of them said, "Just you quiet down back there sonny boy. You'll find out soon enough."

They rode off into the night without control of their immediate fate. Benzler viewed the string of taillights in front of them as they cruised down the highway. He could spot houses already lit up with Christmas lights, and wondered where he'd spend Christmas this year. But right now his personal destination was unknown.

*　　　*　　　*

Chapter 25

As soon as he spied Dr. West's face in the Special Care window, Benzler leapt out of his bunk like a terrier after a fox. He put his own desperate face in the opposite side of the same window, and cried, "Doctor West!"

The technician with the doctor deeply commanded, "Step away from the door," and Benzler complied. The tech unlocked the door to let the doctor in, and Benzler saw "The Enforcer." *What's he doing here?* His massive frame dwarfed Benzler's skinny teen body. Benzler cowered in trepidation, though only for a moment.

The tech withdrew, and left the doctor. "I'm glad to see you Dr. West. Where have you been?"

"Hello there Marshall." Dr. West greeted Benzler somewhat distantly. "How are you faring?" The doctor remained in the open doorway, and carried a large green three-ring binder, Benzler's medical chart.

Benzler forced a polite response. "I'm doing OK. I hate Special Care though, when can I get out?"

Dr. West chuckled, and rubbed his forehead. "You do get right to the point, don't you?"

Benzler had spent one sleepless night in an isolated cell at the local sheriff station. Early this morning, he and two of the other boys were returned to Wilson. Jarvis wasn't with them. Because of the assault on the technician, he would likely be remitted to a juvenile detention center. In any case, he didn't return to the hospital.

In conjunction with the police, the hospital authorities had elected not to press charges on the other three, including Benzler. Of course they placed all of them directly into locked Special Care.

"When do I get to come back?" Benzler begged the doctor. Upon return this morning, they had not placed Benzler on his own unit, but on Unit 1. He didn't know any of the staff here, though he did recognize some of them from various hospital activities. Initially, he assumed they stuck him here only because of logistics. Wells and Taylor obviously must have occupied the only two Special Care rooms on 6B.

However, Benzler began to wonder when none of the staff from 6B came to check on him. As evening set in, Dr. West finally showed up. That's when he found out.

Dr. West answered, "Well, to be honest with you it's a bit different this time." He shifted his feet. "You won't be coming back to the Sixes."

"What?" exclaimed Benzler. He brushed his hair out of his eyes, as if that would help him understand.

Dr. West continued, "Yes, it's fairly complex. But I'll try to explain it." He paused and stroked his comb over. "All this time you've been a voluntary patient."

"Voluntary?" Benzler's eyebrows raised.

"Well, not you personally. You're mother placed you here. But it wasn't any kind of court ordered commission." Dr. West stopped to see if Benzler understood. "Wilson is a private hospital and expensive. Up to now, your bills have paid by your family's insurance." Benzler nodded his head. "Insurance companies regularly review cases like yours, and in your review this morning they decided not to cover your stay here any longer."

The doctor stopped again, and then stated deliberately, "Apparently it has to do with your lack of progress. Last night's antics I'm sure put the nail in the coffin, so to speak."

"What does that mean?" Benzler asked, doubly confused. He looked intently at the doctor to provide clarification.

Dr. West stared right back, and twisted at the corner of his moustache. "It means that we'll keep you up here only until we can close your relocation issues."

"What happens to me?"

"Well, I do know that you'll be leaving the hospital shortly."

"When?" Benzler's intensity rose with each nugget of information.

"In the next week or so. As soon as we establish where you will go from here."

"Where? You mean I ain't going home?" Benzler experienced ambivalent emotions; excitement over getting out, mixed with fear over the uncertainty of where.

Dr. West explained, "Not necessarily. We're looking at the options in order to evaluate which opportunity would be best for you and your family."

Benzler plopped back down on the iron bed. Dr. West stepped entirely into the chamber, and he leaned his back against the wall. He wore an olive sweater vest, and tie.

"Why can't I just go home?"

Dr. West replied, "Well Marshall, you came from a troubled environment, and you haven't made significant progress here. That leads us to the logical conclusion that more than likely you'll arrive at the same outcome."

This frank reproach shocked Benzler like a slap. And despite preliminary discussions on the topic, the idea of going somewhere other than home still took him by surprise.

After a moment of reticence Benzler asked, "So what happens now?"

Dr. West blew out an exhale. "I'm going to let you out of here first. You don't appear to be any immediate threat to yourself or anyone else. No sense in being locked in here if you're going to be discharged soon." Dr. West jotted down a note in Benzler's chart. "Most of the next couple of weeks you'll spend transitioning. Your Social Worker, Mrs. Masterson will come by to see you as soon as she can."

"So when can I get out of SC, and these silly things?" He tugged at his denim pajamas.

"In just a few minutes. I only need to sign the order, and then this gentleman can help you get checked out. I'll take care of that right now. Hang in there, Marshall."

"Will I meet with you anymore?" Benzler asked as the doctor began to leave.

Dr. West predicted, "The future is not yet established. Long term? That's doubtful. In the next week, I'll see you if possible." Dr. West vacated, and his Ferragamo shoes clacked on the tile, echoing like the inside of a tunnel.

Benzler's sense of awe faded, and the enthusiasm about going home built. *At least I'll be out of this hell hole.*

"The Enforcer" came back a few minutes later, and assisted Benzler's exit.

"Hello Marshall, I'm Sam Grayford." The tech's square smile matched his large angular head.

Grayford's calm manner relieved Benzler's fear. "I've seen you around. I just found out I'm going home. So that's good."

"Excellent," the tech replied. "So I've heard. Well, welcome to unit one."

Benzler changed into his street clothes and followed the technician to his temporary room on the new unit. Everything seemed like it would work out just fine.

*　　*　　*

Two days later he met with his social worker to get an update on his placement situation. Benzler bounded into her office eager to

269

discover any news. He could barely contain himself while he waited for Mrs. Masterson to finish clacking away on her Underwood typewriter. She greeted him cordially, and bade him to sit down. Benzler grunted impatiently.

She was unmarried, in her mid 40s, and obese, with long, frizzy gray-red hair. The giant, frumpy, purple pant suit she wore reminded Benzler of Grimace, the McDonald's character. Despite being employed here for 11 years, her sparse office décor amazed Benzler. Overstuffed bookcases, filing cabinets, and just this drab furniture. Nothing for Christmas at all. The office smelled like Pinesol, covering up mildew.

"Marshall, it looks like you're going home after all." She spoke with a patient, maternal demeanor.

"Yes!" he interrupted her with a cry of approval. He clenched his right fist.

"We've looked at all of the options and determined that's the best choice," she added.

"What options?" he asked.

"There weren't very many, that's true," she admitted. "I investigated halfway houses and foster arrangements. But because you live in such a rural area, other than looking at staying with relatives, there wasn't much. Ultimately, going home is the best option."

"That's good, I think," Benzler said. "When?"

Mrs. Masterson continued, "Next week. On Monday December 23rd."

"Next week?" he exclaimed. "Wow that's fast."

"We figured you could spend Christmas at home. Let me tell you your Mom was very excited to hear that. She'll come and pick you up and take you home. It's as simple as that," Mrs. Masterson concluded. "Well of course, that depends on the weather, hoping a big snowstorm doesn't move in."

Benzler asked, "Will I come back here anymore? You know, to see Dr. West or something?"

"Good question, but the answer is no. Based on the situation with your family, and the distance, meeting with Dr. West regularly would be prohibitive. You'll be scheduled to meet with your local doctor, Dr. Stevenson," Mrs. Masterson explained. "I believe you met with him in the past."

Benzler groaned, "Oh no, not him. He's such a dork." He leaned back in his chair, and crossed his arms. A sneer carved his face.

The social worker's eyes drifted downward, a disappointed expression on her face. She remained closemouthed for a moment, and then stated in slow Midwestern speak, "Marshall, Dr. Stevenson is one of the most respected doctors in Ohio."

He yielded easily. "All right, all right, I'll do it."

"That's the right answer Marshall. I hope you mean it because you don't get a lot of choice here."

"OK," he replied. "So are we done here? I need to start packing." He looked around the room, antsy.

"Marshall," she said and stopped again. She looked at him with his stringy blond hair, and Falstaff beer sweatshirt.

He finally made eye contact. "What? Did I say something wrong?" he asked irritably.

"Not wrong exactly. But I'm troubled by your attitude." She folded her hands in front of her, and rested her heavy elbows on the desk. "I'd say it's unanimous that the staff here doesn't want to send you back home. You leave here with your treatment unfinished, and we're concerned over your chances of success. You don't seem to acknowledge the gravity of the situation or even seem to care."

Benzler watched a row of skeletal maple trees just outside of her window. The wind gusted and the tree branches moved back and forth, and seemed to taunt him. The nearest tree tapped at the glass with a bony finger. The forbidding sky had the look of snow. "I'll be fine. You don't need to worry about me," he said in feeble reassurance.

She breathed heavily. "That's easy to say, but much, much harder to do. Going back to the same environment using the same tactics will likely generate the same results. And you know very well of what I am speaking." She paused, and looked at him with her gentle green eyes. He slumped down in his chair while she talked, and closed his eyes. "Marshall?"

"I'm listening." He raised his lids.

"Have you considered a strategy for your homecoming?"

"Whaddya mean?" He sat back upright.

"A plan. What will you consciously do differently to create a better outcome?"

"I guess I haven't really thought about it," he confessed with a flushed face.

"Well then I suggest that you get in touch with Dr. Stevenson immediately."

"I will, I will. I already said I would," Benzler conceded.

"OK Marshall. I believe you. I guess that's all then. You can go."

He popped up quickly, while she labored to lift her girth out of the chair. "Goodbye and best of luck to you." She offered her hand.

"Oh yeah." Benzler shook it, and then departed from her office. He burst outside, and threw both hands upward in a touchdown gesture.

"All right, I'm going home!" The cold froze the hairs in his nose, and bit at his cheeks. He tucked his neck down into his jean jacket, and hunched over, he hurried back to the warmth of Unit 1.

He thought about her comments, and they bothered him. *Don't pay any attention to her. She doesn't know what she's talking about. Everything will be good, sure it will. And I'm not seeing that jerk Stevenson either.*

*   *   *

Chapter 26

"So the big day is finally here." Mrs. Masterson engaged Benzler in light conversation, while they waited in the social worker's office. He spied a new bowl of hard Christmas candy on her desk. He

274

took a piece, popped it in, and sucked on it. At least it helped his cottonmouth.

Monday December 23rd arrived, and Benzler's worldly belongings lay packed in his lone suitcase and two brown paper grocery sacks, truly bag and baggage.

Benzler rolled the lime candy on his tongue and replied, "Finally." He watched out of her office window, keeping his eye out for any sign of his Mom. She was due any minute now.

What a splendid day it turned out to be, sunny and clear. Patches of snow cover the ground, which sparkled as it melted. The mocking trees had no wind to give them life, so they waited too, harmless.

"I'll bet you're excited to see your Mom," Mrs. Masterson added.

"Yeah, it's been four months."

She stood and tugged downward at her black dress, straightening it over her wide hips. *At least she's not wearing purple again,* he thought.

Benzler's overall stay in the hospital lasted from August up until now, just before Christmas. Now they saw fit to boot him out, and ship him back home. Somewhere in his unconscious he recognized this as another failure.

He ross to his feet because he couldn't sit still. He leaned on the windowsill, and pressed his forehead on the cool glass.

"Well, if you play your cards right, you'll fit right back in," Mrs. Masterson stated in a positive, if cautionary tone. "Remember what I said though. I feel strongly that you should meet with Dr. Stevenson right away." She smiled, and Benzler noticed only her tea stained teeth.

"Don't worry. I remember." He wasn't so sure though. He did remember the boring, clock watching sessions with Dr. Stevenson. Call them anything, but not helpful.

Mrs. Masterson droned on, though he tuned her out. "I know we didn't plan it that way, but actually the timing of your return home during the holidays has advantages. You can focus on integrating back in with your family before school starts back up."

After an anxious pause, Benzler complained, "She's late. Where the heck is she?" A knot the size of his fist tightened in his stomach. The window fogged so he pulled his head back leaving oil smudges from his fingers and forehead.

Steady and calm, Mrs. Masterson reassured him. "Oh she'll be here any minute. I spoke with her this morning on the phone, so she's ready. She's very excited to see you."

He grumbled, "I'll bet." When he saw the social worker frown, he self-corrected, "Yeah, I bet she is. I'm excited to see her too."

His Mom showed fifteen minutes later, and a staff member escorted her to Mrs. M's office. Her outward appearance had improved markedly since he last saw her. Apparently she had made an attempt to help herself while he'd been hospitalized. She looked leaner, dressed up for the occasion, and she got her hair done. Benzler even smelled the scent of perfume. She had certainly gone all out.

She embraced him tightly, while his hold remained tenuous. "My how you've grown!" she declared. Her hands gripped both shoulders, and she looked him over. He wore a half grin, and avoided direct eye contact.

"Yeah. Four inches since I've been here." He giggled uneasily. His mother quickly wiped away a tear from her cheek.

"Look at your hair, it's so long." She swept a lock at his shoulder with one hand. "You know we're just goin' ta have ta cut it." Benzler just smirked. *Hell if we are.*

She stood back to take in the whole picture. "How's your leg sweetie?"

The thin smile he wore disappears. "Better. Time heals all wounds, Ma."

Together the three met for twenty minutes to finalize the essential discharge paperwork. Benzler abided, legs bouncing like pistons, concerned only with getting out of there, and going home. Once they completed the forms, Mrs. M. accompanied them out the door, and bade them goodbye.

The brilliant sun created an unseasonably mild day with a rare winter blue sky. Benzler emerged as if from a cocoon. Arms raised wide, face upward, and eyes closed he absorbed the rays. He felt like the scene from "The Wizard of Oz," where Dorothy stepped out of a black and white world into one of Technicolor. He always loved that scene.

His Mom lent him a hand loading his chattel into the back of their old Chevy Blazer. He climbed in on the passenger side, surprised by the clean and vacuumed truck. They didn't speak as they pulled out of the driveway. The tires crunched on the freshly poured salt. Benzler drank in the hospital grounds one last time. He recollected the steamy August day when he arrived here a few short months ago.

"Man, am I glad to get out of here," he muttered aloud. His Mom didn't respond, but cast him a sidelong glance.

After a minute, she did speak up, "We're all ready for you at home. Your room is just the way you left it." Her voice cracked and her eyes darted back and forth to the various vehicle mirrors. "We're having spaghetti and meatballs for dinner tonight, your favorite."

Benzler disregarded her blatant denial. "Thanks. Great." He snickered again. "I can't wait to see everyone."

She navigated them homeward on US 23 northbound. The car heater blasted, and kept them warm, while the defrost battled to tame the fogging windshield. Benzler observed the transition from suburbia to farmland.

He mused, "It's like we're going back in time."

Her head jerked, and her brow furrowed. "What's that?"

"We're retracing our steps from the drive down in August."

"Uh huh." She looked at him as if he spoke in tongues. He resumed window watching.

Nothing much had changed except for the season. They passed latent fields of snow covered dirt clods, which Benzler imagined as white caps on Lake Erie. The fields were emptied, as farmers stowed the equipment in barns for the winter. Forests of fully needled tall pines boasted next to naked maples and oaks. They flew by Delaware State Park, and Mom Wilson's roadside farm stand. Mom's displayed giant signs every hundred yards or so in the mile approaching the stand. Each red sign shared an item they sold, one word at a time.

"Mom, Wilson's, bacon, ham, corned beef.......U, R, here," Benzler read each one aloud in a monotone like he always had. They drove on past.

He fidgeted with the buttons on the AM radio, and the dial jumped to the preset stations. He found nothing to his liking, but persisted.

"Would you please leave that alone," his Mom finally said.

"I want to hear about the storm." She eyed the darkening sky, and the wind whipped the snow horizontal.

Between stilted but polite conversation, they endured frequent silent gaps. And they avoided any talk about the hospital. Mrs. Benzler subtly suggested, "I told Doc Stevenson you were coming home." He didn't acknowledge her. "I set up an appointment for you."

"Mom, I just got out. Can't it wait," he rebuked. She squelched the urge to lash out; instead she tooea deep breath and said nothing.

Ultimately they reached home, back to the same house; the place where all his problems originated.

They entered through the back porch, where at first Kukla barked at him, her tail high and stiff. "C'mere girl."

When he removed his jackets and boots, he petted the dog, and she licked his face, the tail now wagging. "That'sa good girl."

Inside the kitchen, Grandma greeted him with a smile and a hug.

"Aah, welcome home Marsh." She seemed as small and frail, but much older than before.

Benzler noticed straightaway the strong smell of bleach and pine. His Mom cleaned the house, and she decorated too. A Christmas tree, stockings, the works. All that gave a sense of commonness back. He almost felt normal.

Grandpa approached and extended his work worn hand. "Good to see you son." He grasped his grandson's hand and gripped as firmly as ever.

Benzler's younger brother David waited, instructed to show restraint before the arrival. When permitted, he ran forward and squeezed his big brother around the waist.

"Look at you, you're so big." Benzler rubbed the bristles on his blonde crew cut head. His sister still held back, and her blue eyes stared at him shyly from behind her Mom.

"I think she's scared of your hair," Mom asserted with a chuckle.

"Nan," Benzler called for her. "C'mon out here." When she balked, he grabbed her by the arm, and pulled her into him, hugging both kids together. "You've both grown so." The siblings laughed, delighted to have Marshall home.

After the brief but joyful reunion, he lugged his stuff up to his bedroom, and took ten minutes up there alone. He collapsed into the chair next to the window, and gazed out at the snow. The sparse dusting on the ground gave a mottled appearance. Though not yet enough to cover the yard, the snow started to stick. The frosted glass windowpane felt cold without even a touch. He basked in the comfort of his own house.

How he longed these past few months to be back here. But despite the welcome, right now he felt estranged. From his bedroom window he could see the barn, but he didn't look. No need to stir that up. Not yet anyway. He descended the stairs, and rejoined the family to begin his life anew.

He savored the home cooked meal; he hadn't tasted home cooking since well prior to his hospitalization. He relished the company of his kin. His family seemed happy to have him back, especially his little brother and sister. That first evening concluded a triumph, like a little honeymoon. But all honeymoons must come to an end.

*   *   *

Chapter 27

I waited until the very last second to step out of the house. With the bone-chilling cold again today, I wanted to spend as little time as possible outdoors.

Perched on a cozy bench in our foyer over a heating duct on the floor, I kept toasty while I watched out the window for the bright yellow school bus. The bus coasted down St. James hill and crossed the bridge at the bottom. Yes, that was Benzler's bridge. In the winter, the bald trees provided no camouflage, though every other season the leaves blocked the view. Butterflies stirred in my gut, as I readied for the first day of school after Christmas break.

Now that he was out of the hospital, Benzler would attend River Valley for the first time. I looked forward to having my friend back, but worried for him. The rumors mushroomed the first semester. Kids from Waldo already knew him, so it didn't change their minds much, bad or good. But kids from different elementary schools formed mostly mean opinions. And don't forget about the faculty.

283

After the turn onto my road, RVUSD bus #4 picked me up at 730 sharp. I rushed out, and even in that brief time the wind bit at my nose and cheeks until I climbed aboard. Straightaway, I spotted Benzler about halfway back, sitting alone.

He waved at me. "Hey Digger!" I strolled down the narrow aisle, and glanced to the back. As I predicted, some older teenagers usurped both the title and authority of the back seat.

"Welcome back, man," I said. First thing, I noticed his long hair that spilled out over the neck of his coat, but didn't mention it. We slapped hands like on the sitcom "Good Times." Everyone went around school these days saying "Dyn-o- mite." The duel for cool between Jimmy Walker and The Fonz was on.

I slid in next to him on the sea green seat. I sensed immediately how much his body had grown too. Envy sparked in me because I hadn't grown much at all yet, and now he was at least a full head taller than me.

"First day of school, a brand new year," Benzler stated.

We sat still and quiet on the cold bus. I wore a bulky down parka, big old gloves, and a stocking cap. Benzler had on his Dad's oversized olive drab Army jacket. Even though he was my best friend, I didn't really know what to talk about.

"Jack drove right past me this morning," Benzler eventually said.

"What?" My parka made a whish sound as I moved to look at him.

"Yeah. I was standing out there freezin' my ass off and he goes whizzin' right by," he explained.

"Wait a minute." I shrugged. "How come you're here then?"

"Some Pollyanna hollered at him and he came back." Benzler added, "Dimwit."

"Who? Jack or the Pollyanna?"

"Jack!" he snapped. "I've only been riding his friggin' bus for ten years."

"More like seven."

"Whatever." He stared at me with a frown. "What are you, the Shell Answer Man?"

"You can't blame him," I said in defense of Jack. "You haven't been on the bus all year."

"True," he agreed, and slumped his shoulders.

Jack crept forward through the snow and slush on the slippery river road toward the Junior High School. A kid flagged him down from the roadside, and he pulled to a brake screeching stop. With a bang, the accordion doors flung open, and another student climbed on bringing a burst of cold air with him. One by one the bus filled up.

"You glad to be back?" I mustered. I glanced at my friend's profile, and saw light and fuzzy facial hair beginning to accumulate on his chin. Damn, I wondered when I'd reach puberty.

"That's a dumb question," he responded.

"I know, I know. But how was it?"

"The hospital?" He stiffened, and folded his arms. "It sucked the big one."

"Whaddya mean?" I prodded him, curious.

"You know, like my big dick." He smiled at me with only one side of his mouth.

I rolled my eyes. "Ha ha. Very funny. I mean why did it suck? Numbnuts."

Right off he said, "Well, they locked us up first of all."

"Like in a prison cell?"

"No. It was more like camp or something. But the doors were always locked," he explained. "And I could never forget that."

I looked down at graffiti written on the back of the seat in front of us. Jenny + Rusty TLA. And a couple of nastigrams. "What else? Were there like drooling, babbling morons running around?" Now that we'd started, the questions poured out of me.

286

"Not really. A few were kind of like that, but not on the unit I was on. It was mostly just kids like me," he said.

"Did it help being there?" I asked tentatively. I hadn't talked with him in so long, I wasn't sure how sensitive he was about this stuff.

"Man, what's with all the questions?"

I felt the red heat of a blush fill up my face. "I don't know. Sorry."

Benzler paused as he pondered the question. "You know, my first reaction was, 'Hell, no way.'" He stopped again as a kid took the seat in front of us. Jack revved the engine, causing our seat to vibrate, and we lurched forward. "But I liked one of the nurses there. She helped me for awhile. And my doctor was OK. I guess on the whole it did help." A gust of wind caused the bus to shudder. We both watched the trees dance through the window.

I figured he answered, so I decided to keep going. "How do you feel back home with your Mom?"

"Man, can we change the friggin' subject?" He squirmed in his seat.

"Sorry man." I felt like a fool again, and tried to think of something else to talk about. Sports, Benzler always loved to talk about sports. "Hey man, did you watch the Rose Bowl?"

287

He dropped his head backward, and groaned. "Aaaarrrgggh! That's no better." Our beloved Buckeyes lost the championship game to hated Southern Cal by one point on a last second two-point conversion. I didn't bring up any more topics, and neither did he. We just sat tight the rest of the way.

We started back to school on the first Monday in January at 8 am. Benzler needed to check in down at the office first thing, so he didn't join the class until 2nd period. Ohio History class, with Mr. Papadakos. Mr. P. coached the Jr. High basketball team, and looked the part. He was 6'4 with orangutan arms, black hair and eyes. I played guard on his team, so he liked me. He tended to favor athletes, and treated kids he perceived as troublemakers strictly.

Benzler entered class about 9:15, almost two-thirds of the way through. He lumbered in with wide eyes, and interrupted Mr. Papadakos' lecture.

"What do you want?" Mr. P asked Benzler curtly. About twenty-five students made up our class, and all eyes turned toward Benzler. The coach wore a white turtleneck, and a navy blue blazer. Most of the students dressed warmly in sweatshirts or flannels. They keep the classrooms a chilly 65° because of the energy crisis.

"Umm. I'm s'posed to be in this class," Benzler stammered.

288

"Who are you?" Papadakos asked, and ran his left hand from his forehead back through his thick black hair. His right hand clutched a two-foot wooden pointer.

Benzler looked lost, still wearing his army jacket, and holding a small duffel bag. "Marshall Benzler." His voice went up at the end, as if he was unsure.

"Oh yeah. I heard about you. You're late," Mr. Papadakos replied with a smirk on his face. "Come on in."

"I had to take care of some stuff in the office." Benzler looked around at the lack of any empty seats. "Where do you want me to sit?"

"Well, do you think you can stand in the back?" Mr. P gestured with his stick. "We've only got a few more minutes."

The coach turned his back, and Benzler just stared at him. The students kept looking at the strange new spectacle, none of them smiling.

Coach P took off his wire-rimmed glasses and wiped off the lens with his pocket handkerchief. "Now, where was I?"

Holly Bell raised her hand, "You were talking about the Greenville Treaty."

Papadakos realized that Benzler still hadn't moved. "Well?"

"All right." Benzler dragged his stuff to the back.

Glasses in his left hand, pointer still in the right, Mr. P faked a bow, waving both arms out to his sides. "Thank you." He resumed class, continuing to wipe his glasses, "OK. After Mad Anthony Wayne... hey don't sit on that." He raised his voice and pointed the stick at Benzler. A wall heater ran beneath the row of windows along the back wall of the classroom, and made a waist high ledge that Benzler now sat upon. Benzler looked up at him, hazel eyes hardened.

"What's your name again?" Papadakos asked.

Benzler took awhile to respond. "Marshall Benzler."

"Benzler, right. Well Marshall Benzler, do not sit on that heater." The class began to giggle. "I don't want anyone in my class burning their butts." The class roared in laughter.

When it quieted down Benzler complained, "But there's no place else to sit."

"I know and I'm sorry about that," Mr. P stated, but he didn't sound like he meant it. "Nevertheless, we've only got a couple of minutes left, so just stand there." Benzler got off the heater, and his boots hit the tile floor with a thud.

"OK. Back to the Greenville Treaty." As the teacher spoke, Benzler picked his duffel up off of the floor, and steered around the class.

Mr. Papadakos stopped lecturing, mouth open. "Hey, where do you think you're going?" Benzler ignored him and slammed the door on the way out. Mr. P stood dumbstruck in the front of the classroom. I could barely hear him mutter, "Of all the nerve."

The bell rang, and the class jumped up and headed for the halls. Mr. P hurried out of the room among the throng of students, and appeared to make a beeline toward the principal's office.

Confused by Benzler's actions, I too ran out with the crowd. Why didn't he just do what the teacher asks? I checked for him at his locker, but he was nowhere to be found. I decided to go directly to our next class, 3rd period Phys. Ed. He should have already been there since we had the same section.

I made my way through the locker room, a musky cave overgrown with boys in their skivvies. Gangly adolescent bodies changed into gym clothes. I found my gym locker and dressed on the wooden bench that divided two rows of orange metal lockers. Still no sign of Benzler.

I put on my shorts, tee shirt, and stretched white tube sox with blue and gold stripes all the way to my knees. I laced up my Converse tennis shoes, and then I strutted out into the gym.

In 7th grade the boys and girls had separate PE classes. We shared the gym at the same time, but a giant partition split it at half court. Full-size pennants adorned the walls of both sides in the school colors of blue and gold, and each bore the head of our mascot, the Vikings. I passed by a clique of girls on the bleachers, and gave them a nod.

On the boy's side, we chose up teams for basketball, and soon the sound of dribbling balls echoed in the gym. The girls played volleyball with the offbeat thud of bump, set, and spike. Sneakers squeaked on the hardwood. I forgot about Benzler for the time being, distracted by the thrill of the game.

The gym teacher Mr. McAfee paid little attention to us, as he reclined on the bleachers with the sports page. An ex-football star, Mr. McAfee's glory days took place right here in this high school. He hung onto his fleeting fifteen minutes of fame as a coach and PE teacher. Bald with a belly, Mr. Mac still struck an imposing figure with his broad, thickly muscled shoulders and chest. Even in January, he showed them off by wearing tank top t-shirts. He also had a reputation for ogling the girl's class. Pervert.

About twenty minutes into class Benzler slipped in wearing street clothes. I saw him hoist himself up on the corner of the stage at the far end. Nobody else seemed to notice him.

292

"Hey you, what are you doing?" Mr. Mac's shout knifed across the gym. The sound of dribbling dwindled to nothing, and we stopped our game to see what Mr. Mac was going on about. Benzler shriveled up while Mr. Mac stalked over to him.

I could hear Mac's words during the exchange because he spoke with a high pitch and elevated volume. "You have to be dressed in PE and that's that." His finger pumped in Benzler's face with each word. Benzler mumbled something back that I couldn't make out. McAfee blasted, "That's no excuse. Besides, you're late. You need to get down to the office." Benzler once more stomped out of class. Only ten o'clock, and already he was making quite an impression.

Mr. McAfee turned back to us. "All right ladies, show's over. Get back to it."

*   *   *

In the sweaty locker room after class, I overheard someone ask, "Who was that kid Mac was yelling at?"

David Kornberger who always acted and talked as if he knew everything replied, "That was Marty Benzler. He's that kid who's just back from the loony bin." Amid the metallic slam of lockers, a lot of

293

jokes and laughter at Benzler's expense followed. I'm not sure why, but I didn't say anything. I wanted to defend him, but I couldn't bring myself to. My chest tightened, and my face burned. I guess I was ashamed of myself. I dressed in a hurry, and got out of there.

*   *   *

Later, I caught up with Benzler at lunch time down in the cafeteria. He leaned with one foot on the wall behind him like a flamingo, all by himself at the entrance. People gave him a wide berth as they passed.

When I approached he said, "Damn, she's a fox," as he eyeballed a passing girl.

I kicked at his lone foot on the floor to get his attention. He stumbled, and then shoved me. "So what happened down in the office?" I asked.

The vague smell of some kind of meat filled the lunchroom as we got into the line. He launched into a story of his adventure.

"I walk over to the office thinking 'Here we go again, new school, new principal. Last year it was Mr. Steinhauser. I wonder how this guy's gonna be.' I go in the fishbowl they call an office, and I walk up to the bird lady to tell her what's what."

Located at the front of the Junior High building, next to the main entrance, students passing by could see right into the office through the glass lobby.

"Mrs. Joyce?" I asked. I felt more at ease now that I saw he treated this all as a joke.

An Aunt Spiker looking middle-aged woman with graying hair and black horn-rimmed glasses, I heard Mrs. Joyce had worked that desk since the school opened in sixty-three. She ran the office like a Nazi.

"Whatever her name is. Anyway she makes me sit in a chair in the corner forever. Finally, Schecter limps in, looking to me like a mean sombitch."

We progressed through the lunch line. Mystery meatloaf, smashed potatoes, green beans, a peanut butter cookie, and milk. Forty-five cents. We grabbed our trays, and found a place over in the corner of the crowded dining hall.

Benzler continued, "He's got a pretty nice office too. Better'n Salamander's. He had that dumpy office that was that hideous green color." Benzler opened up his milk carton, and took a swig. "Have you seen it?"

"What, Salamander's office?"

"No stupid, Schecter's."

"Nope," I admitted. "I don't find it hard to stay out of trouble."

He shoveled a spoonful of mashed potatoes in his mouth. I watched him shake his head and look at me smugly. Now I began to worry that he didn't take this a little more seriously.

He went on. "Schecter's whole office is dark. His desk, the cabinets, all dark wood, cherry I think. He's got those plaques n' WWII shit on the wall. It's plush. His ashtray's full of butts, and the office smells like smoke. He smoked like a stack the whole time he's lecturing me."

Benzler got up and did an exaggerated limping walk around the table as he mimicked the principal. "Marshall, your reputation proceeds you. I'm going to make myself perfectly clear. I absolutely will not tolerate any problems from you. What are we going to do about this?"

I laughed until milk came out of my nose. Benzler sat back down, and a sad look came over his face. "So what happened then?" I asked.

"Well, he stared me down worse than ole Salamander. And he pulled out a pack of cigarettes and smacked it onto his palm, like this." Again Benzler mimicked the principal, "I'm considering suspending you.

Then just like that he let me off the hook. Turns out he's nothing like old

Sal. He cut me some slack since it's my first day n' all. Imagine that."

I wiped my nose again, drippy from the milk passing through.

"That's good. I mean you didn't really do anything. But you best be

careful around here."

Benzler looked over at a table full of girls next to us. He

winked, but they ignored him. To me he said, "So, you've been here

three months and never been to the principal's office?"

I watched his cocky face chew another spoonful of potatoes. I

cut off a piece of meatloaf and ate it. A dry and hard slab, I might as

well have eaten my boot. I added more ketchup to give some semblance

of flavor.

"You've been here three hours and already have been?" I asked.

"And you're proud of it?" I shrugged my shoulders, and kept eating.

He replied, "It feels good to be wanted." He looked at me

sideways, his eyes slits, still smirking. "You're such a priss Digger.

Face it man, you're just not as cool as me."

That comment set me off. "Yeah. You're real cool, spending all

that time in a psych ward." He stopped and his face changed into a

menacing stare. We didn't speak through the rest of our meal, though we

both snorted and snuffed, and made unnecessary noise with our utensils.

Earlier, I'd felt guilty that I didn't stick up for him in the locker room, but not now. If he acted like a jerk, he wouldn't have any friends. Not me anyway. We walked back to our lockers together, but we still didn't talk.

At our lockers, John Rustin came up behind us. Rustin played on the basketball team with me, and many of the players like him. I wasn't sure why. I hadn't warmed up to him, mostly because of his feud with Benzler.

He slapped Benzler on the shoulder. "I just wanted to welcome you back," he paused and then added, "Asshole."

"It didn't take you long did it?" Benzler slowly turned back toward his locker, head down. But I could see him clench his fist, and set his jaw.

Rustin just stood there legs apart, arms crossed over the goofy leprechaun on his dark green Notre Dame sweatshirt. "That's it? That's all you got for me?"

"Rustin, back off," I stepped in.

"Shut up Eidegger. I thought you had better sense than to stick with this loser."

The bell rang and the three of us remained in a standoff. Finally, Rustin laughed, a stuck up, mean sort of laugh. "Fuck it. I'll catch up to you later Psychoboy."

Benzler lunged toward Rustin, but I held him back at the shoulder. "It's not worth it man. Don't let him get to you."

Rustin sneered, turned his back, and swaggered down the hall.

After Rustin left, Benzler brushed off my hand. "I don't need your kind of help." He left me there, and threw out over his shoulder, "Where were you earlier when I did need it?"

"What was I supposed to do?" But he didn't look back. He was gone.

*   *   *

Chapter 28

A trickle of salty sweat burned my eye, so I wiped my forehead with my light blue sweatband. I dribbled the ball twice rapidly, p*ound,* *pound.* I aligned my hand by the black stripes. I pushed the basketball up, and I watched it roll off my fingertips.

Boing, the ball hit the back of the rim, a brick that caromed off. One of Pleasant Jr. High's forwards grabbed the rebound, and five of us in blue and gold scrambled after the one in black and red. He launched a desperation shot from half court as the buzzer sounded. Our home crowd of about fifty fans, mostly parents and some students, gasped, and we watched the shot barely miss. Whew! That was close. We won 43-42.

Back in the locker room, we savored the victory. The sting of the hot shower replaced the sting of my choke. With a flushed face and a white towel wrapped at his waist, Rustin marched his thick body over to me.

"Way to go, asshole. You almost lost it for us, missing that free throw." I paid him no mind, but I knew full well that he was right. Still, you just didn't say things like that. Not to your teammates. Besides, we won anyway.

Later, my Mom drove a few of us over to the Pizza Chef on Marion-Galion Rd. in our station wagon. A triumph over our archrival deserved some extra celebration. We met several other teammates there for pizza, root beer, and some laughs.

300

Most of the light inside the joint came from the kitchen, separated from us by the ordering counter. At a table in the semi-darkness, Jeff Davis said to me over the din, "I hear you're friends with that Martin Benzler character." Jeff started at forward on the team. Blessed with longer than usual legs, his short torso made him look unbalanced. As awkward as he appeared, he played a solid game of ball.

A peanut sized knot formed in my stomach as soon as Benzler's name came up. "Marshall," I corrected him. A red and gold Hudepohl Beer neon sign flickered behind his head.

"What?" Billy Preston's "Nothing from Nothing" blared from the jukebox, and made it kind of hard to hear.

"His name is Marshall Benzler not Martin, and yes he's my friend."

During the fall semester, while Benzler stayed at the hospital, I made several new friends at RV, Jeff being one of them. It started slowly, as I had few old friends from Waldo in my class. But then sports always seemed to grease the wheels of friendship for me. First, we played football in the fall, and then basketball followed in November. In this new year we had games on Tuesdays and Thursdays after school. Needless to say, that took up quite a bit of my time, and the new friends filled the gap left by Benzler's absence.

Davis took a bite of pizza, and fought with a string of mozzarella. "Isn't he a nutjar? I heard he spent time in a psycho ward."

I picked up my glass mug and sipped my root beer, thinking of the right response. The jukebox switched to the next song, Elton John's "Lucy in the Sky with Diamonds."

"Benzler is a little off the wall, and does some crazy shit. But he's an OK guy."

"Really?" Jeff replied, with a raised left eyebrow. "Didja hear?" He beamed and nudged my arm. "Rustin's nicknamed him 'The Weed.'"

"Don't listen to Rustin. He's a …."

Micheal Walker interrupted, "I'm in that class, Benzler's a friggin' weirdo." Walker backed up Davis at forward. Blonde, tight curls almost formed an afro on top of his head.

I looked at them both, and said directly to Walker, "I'm in your class too, remember? He's not a weirdo. You barely know him, so what makes you say that?"

John Rustin stuck his head between Davis and me, and butted in. "Hey, are you guys talking about 'The Weed'?"

"Why can't you guys just give him a chance?" I pled, and threw my hands up.

Rustin poked his finger at me, blunt jabs into my shoulder blade. "Digger, you know what your problem is? You're friends with that turkey."

I stood up, and took a step back. "You know what? That's not cool. You guys are out of line." I waved both hands at them as a dismissal.

"Hey, it's not just me. We all think so." He swept his arm in a circle, which included the whole table. Everyone stopped what they were doing, and watched us, even my Mom.

Shaking my head, I walked away from him, and joined the next table with some of the other players. Rustin yelled after me, "You need to dump him, man," and then he cackled. I thought of these guys as my friends, but I definitely didn't like the way they acted. I continued on with the evening, and tried not to let it bother me. Mom looked at me puzzled, but she never brought it up.

*   *   *

"Digger." I recognized Benzler's voice rasp over the phone line as soon as I answered. The early Saturday morning call surprised me as we hadn't really spoken since our argument last Monday, his first day back to school.

"Benzler. Hey whaddya doin'?" I stood in the family room in front of a wall length bookcase. The smell of bacon wafted in from the kitchen.

"Nothin', you?" At least he sounded chipper, that was good.

"Nothin'." I traced around the circular number holes on the phone dial with my index finger. "Whaddya want?"

"I wondered if you wanted to come over or something," he asked. He paused, but before I could answer he said, "We can go ice fishing, and then maybe you could stay over."

I thought it over a minute. The grandfather clock ticked evenly, and I could hear my little sister watching "Scooby Doo" in the next room. "Nah. I can't, I'm busy."

"Busy with what?" I detected an obvious tone change in his voice. The pit began again in my stomach.

"I'm already going to the mall with some of the guys from basketball." I glanced out the bay window at the white fields.

The line went quiet. "Hello?" I checked to see if he was still there.

"I'm still here." His voice cracked. He forced out, "Who's goin'?"

"Davis, Walker, some of the others." In the silent gap, I thought about inviting him, but didn't. I knew he was not welcome.

"Oh. Well, I guess I'll talk to you later then."

I hung up the phone slowly as Mom called me for breakfast. My gut told me he was disappointed, and I felt guilty as if I was betraying him somehow.

In the kitchen, Dad asked who was on the phone, and then he grimaced when I told him. The crow's feet around his eyes stood out in the bright kitchen light.

"Look Dad, I'm not even doing anything with him," I took the seat opposite him at the oval table.

"All right." His coffee steamed in front of him to the left, while cigarette smoke spiraled from an ashtray on his right. "For Pete's sake Donny, it's not like you're not allowed to talk to him." He looked at Mom tending the stove. "But your mother and I will be very selective about Okaying any activities." She flopped two over-easy eggs onto my plate, and looked at me with doe's eyes. No longer hungry, I stared at the eggs, and tried to figure out what he meant.

305

Dad said grace, and we ate. He dragged from his Winston which resulted in a coughing fit. When it subsided he said, "Your mother told me about your friends the other night." I poked into an egg and the yellow yoke spilled out over the white. "Look at me when I'm talking to you, boy." I complied. "Maybe you should stick with some of these new friends for awhile."

"OK Dad. I will."

*   *   *

The Southland Mall lay just on the south edge of Marion, located at the spot where Delaware Avenue became Marion-Waldo Road. An open-air mall with several shops setup in an overall rectangle, the entrances to the stores all faced toward the middle. Maple trees lined the pathway with park benches in a central landscaped area. Snow covered everything, and few shoppers walked outside.

The mall's cornerstone stores, JC Penney on the south end, and Sear's to the north, faced one another like a stodgy elderly couple on opposite ends of a long dinner table. Various stores made up the gap in between: House of Fabrics, Gray Drug, Twin Fair, and Musicland. The mall also housed a movie theater now showing "Towering Inferno," an

306

arcade called the Red Baron, and a few places to get a bite to eat.

Outside of the square, you'd find Star Lanes and an A & P grocery.

Eight of the fifteen players on our basketball team showed up.

Davis and Walker were here, but also Essenheimer, Klinefelter, a guy

named Kevin Schenk, Mark Havermeyer, and John Rustin. I didn't

invite him.

We ambled around the mall aimlessly in a gang. We inspected

the stores from the inside, especially on a frozen day out like today. We

didn't shop really, of course we did check out the chicks, and pulled

juvenile pranks. The clerks watched us closely, and customers seemed to

be afraid of us.

We wound up down at the arcade; the sign above the Red

Baron's door had a German WWI fighter plane up against Snoopy atop

his doghouse. We entered the place that had the sweet smell of old

cotton candy, and the sticky floor that went with it. We wasted our

quarters on pinball machines and games. I played my favorite, which

featured a Panzer tank fight, and then Benzler appeared out of nowhere.

He tapped me on the shoulder, and I looked up at him startled. He wore

the same old army jacket, and his glasses were still fogged up from

outside.

"What are you doing here?" I asked between missile shots.

"How about 'Hi, how are you?'" he retorted. He smiled though, so I thought he may be OK.

"I'm in the middle of a game." He folded his arms, and waited, watching over my shoulder until the game ended. I stepped away, and a little kid took my place at the game immediately.

"When I talked with you this morning you didn't say anything about coming here," I stated. Pinball bells rang all around us.

"My Mom needed some stuff, and asked me to join her. Don't think I didn't notice that you didn't invite me though." His face was pale, though the sweat on his forehead wet his bangs.

"It's not like that," I responded, defensive.

He looked around the poorly lit arcade. "Shit, Heimer and Felt are here too? You didn't mention they were coming." His face sagged but when he saw Rustin, his face went completely blank.

"You guys are hanging out with Rustin now?" He looked at me as if I had killed his dog or something. He frowned and walked straight for the door of the arcade. Rustin spotted him, rushed over, and shoved him in the back. Benzler lurched forward out the door, and slipped and fell onto the slushy sidewalk. I hurried over to break up the potential fight. Benzler stood up just as I got there, and pushed me away. He took a swing at Rustin, but missed. His momentum allowed Rustin to get behind him, and wrenched his arm up behind his back.

Rustin yelled into his ear, "You're a fuckin' weed man. You're a worthless loser. Why don't you get the hell out of here?" He let the red-faced Benzler go. Benzler rubbed his shoulder, and brushed the snow off. He didn't even look at Rustin, but instead he directed his venomous eyes at me.

"Fuck all you guys," he said. Without another word, he walked away.

After Benzler left Heimer came over and said, "What was that all about?"

We watched Benzler storm down the mallway. I looked over at Heimer, "Just passing through I guess."

I felt Rustin's meaty paw squeeze my shoulder. "It's all your fault, man. You keep inviting your psycho buddy around."

I swept his hand away. "Knock it off."

"I keep tellin' you, you gotta lose that shithead." Rustin never knew when to quit.

I decided to chase after Benzler, to see if I could help him somehow.

As I left the group at the Red Baron, Rustin shouted after me, "When you find him, tell him I'm gonna kick his skinny ass."

Rustin started to follow too, but Heimer grabbed his shoulder and he backed off. I searched up and down the mall twice, but once again Benzler vanished.

*   *   *

Chapter 29

When the bell sounded, Benzler split from 4th period English class, and entered the second floor corridor with the rest of his classmates. I chased after him, dodging between kids who swarmed the aisle. I spotted his head bob above most of them, and his bright green John Deere ball cap made him easy to track.

I caught up to him downstairs in front of his locker, and grabbed his shoulder from behind. "Hey man, I need to talk to you." My face was flushed, and I breathed heavy from the upstream swim.

He eyed me with a suspicious smirk. "About what? Your new best buddy Rustin?" It was the Monday following the Red Baron incident, and he had successfully avoided me since then. Even on the school bus this morning, he actually got up and moved when I sat down next to him. That embarrassed the heck out of me. Two short weeks out of the hospital, and Benzler was losing it.

He turned away from me, and focused on his lock combination. I started to explain, "Look man, I didn't invite him there on Saturday."

As I spoke, John Rustin blindsided him with a hard push out of nowhere. Benzler banged his forehead on the metal door, and his hat flew to the floor. The blow left a red mark just above his left eye. His anger flashed and he whirled around to see Rustin behind him with legs squared and an evil grin on his face. Rustin wore a large white Ohio State Football sweatshirt, Levis, and cowboy boots. Benzler's face seethed in obvious dislike of his enemy.

"Nice boots," Benzler snapped. "Did you clean the cowshit off'em before school?" Rustin's grin broadened, and he began to repeatedly smack his fist in his hand.

"What do you want?" Benzler snarled. His toothpick arms dangled from his flannel shirt sleeves, rolled up to the elbow.

"I told you," Rustin replied. "You never should have come back, 'Weed.'"

"What's with you? Why can't you leave me alone?"

As Benzler bent over to pick up his hat, Rustin tried another shove. This time Benzler responded in kind, and the two locked arms in an awkward dance. Long and lean, Benzler's head rose several inches over Rustin's even with his boot heels. But Rustin's girth swallowed Benzler.

The shoving match stopped briefly, and the war of words resumed. The energy of the situation rippled up and down the hallways, drawing a crowd. Nearby classmates already started to assemble in a half circle; eager to watch the ever popular school fight.

"Benzler, we don't need looneys around here," Rustin said loud enough for the mob to hear. Sweat dripped from his forehead. "Why don't you go back to the psycho ward where you belong?"

"Well, if they had an asshole ward, that's where you'd be." Benzler successfully picked up his hat, and planted it firmly back onto his head.

"You're the asshole, psycho." Rustin flashed a thick-lipped scowl, which exposed his mammoth choppers.

"You'd better watch it," Benzler threatened. "I'm gonna wipe that stupid smile clean off your face."

Only one possible conclusion remained. The two boys eyeballed one another, and the bystanders hollered catcalls like on Friday night fights. A couple of Rustin backers in the crowd, Schenk and Havermeyer encouraged him. "C'mon Rustin, whaddya waitin' for?" Schenk spouted. Havermeyer threw in, "You're always talking about it. Kick his ass."

Benzler had no one in his court, except me. Many of the kids didn't even know his name. He glared at Rustin, and waggled his fingers in invitation. "Bring it on fatboy."

Probably because of the peer pressure, Rustin made the first move. He lunged hard toward Benzler, and drove his shoulder into Benzler's belly like a football tackling dummy. He forced Benzler's back against the locker, creating a huge metallic thud. The move pinned Benzler, so that he couldn't defend himself.

I leapt in behind Rustin, and pulled on his drenched sweatshirt to try and get him off. His elbow smashed backward into my face, and I saw an explosion of stars. Ouch. I tasted the salt, and brought my hand up to my nose. It came away red with blood, and the drips fell faster onto the floor.

Rustin slammed Benzler once again into his locker, and Benzler's head crashed against the metal. That was when Benzler brought his knee up into Rustin's groin, a solid, soundless thud that sickened all of the male observers.

Rustin stopped immediately, he let Benzler go, and paused for a moment until the familiar delayed onset pain rolled in like a shock wave. He slowly dropped his knees to the floor, rolled onto his side, and cupped his balls with his hands. Benzler stood over him, a look of surprise on his face, while Rustin groaned and rocked back and forth. Some cheers erupted at the result, and more scuffles broke out among the onlookers.

"Make way. Make way." Principal Schecter muscled through the crowd. He jerked Benzler away from Rustin by the elbow, and then knelt down to check Rustin out. Someone brought me some paper towels for my bloody nose.

The school nurse, dressed in white and smelling of Bactine and Bandaids, arrived, and escorted the ashy gray Rustin to the nursing station. With a limp, Mr. Schecter parted the wall of people, and dragged Benzler and me to his office. Everyone stared, and the scuttlebutt started right away.

"Here we go again," Benzler whispered. The principal made us wait outside while he went into his office, and closed the door behind him. He came out a minute later, and beckoned for Benzler to come in, alone.

"Well, well, well, Marshall Benzler. I was wondering how long it would take." He smiled at Benzler like the Cheshire cat. I thought to myself that was an odd expression under the circumstances.

Schecter continued, "In fact, I congratulate you for keeping out of trouble for a whole week. Much better than I expected. Of course that doesn't excuse what happened today." Then he shut the door, cutting off my eaves dropping. I could still hear voices, but muffled.

My nosebleed under control, I settled into a stiff brown chair, one of four wooden ones lined up in wait just outside the principal's office. The overall school office breathed with activity. Mrs. Joyce barked orders to other staff members who jumped to exact them. Busy school faculty darted back and forth on their normal day. The pace didn't help my anxiety any. My legs jumped like pistons in anticipation of my fate. Mom and Dad were gonna kill me.

After some time Benzler came out, so now it was my turn. I entered the principal's office for my first time, head down, hangdog style. I recognized details from Benzler's earlier description, the photos,

315

the furniture, and most obviously the smoke. Mr. Schecter leaned his long, broad torso across the desktop.

"I have zero tolerance for fighting." He looked me squarely in the eyes. My heart stopped as I waited for the other shoe to drop. "However, in your case with your outstanding record, I believe we can make an exception."

He sat back, and put his arms over his head, and clasped his hands behind his neck. I breathed a sigh of relief. Schecter's smile came back. "In fact, I think you were just trying to break things up. Can you tell me what happened?"

I recapped the story as I saw it. He listened carefully, nodding occasionally but when I finished he said, "Donald, I find it hard to believe that John Rustin harassed Marshall Benzler the way you've described. Benzler's the troublemaker here, not Rustin."

"But…" I interrupted.

"No, there're no buts," Schecter said.

"But it wasn't his fault," I cried, defending my friend.

"Frankly, I don't care. He always has an excuse. It appears to me that the common denominator for all his problems is himself. And he needs to be taught a lesson. That's why I'm suspending Mr. Benzler."

With that Schecter dismissed me. Though my personal fear of the firing squad wilted, still it wasn't fair what was happening to my friend.

When I exited the office, Benzler still lingered there with his chin in his hands and a long face. His hat had found its way back onto his head. "What are you doin' here?" I asked.

"Waitin' for my Mom, late as usual." He adjusted his chair, removed his cap, and ran his hand through his hair.

"Your Mom?" I realized I still held on tightly to my bloody rag, so I tossed it into the trashcan.

"Yeah man. I got suspended. She's pickin' me up." He touched gingerly to the welt on his brow.

I took the seat next to him. "I heard. How long?"

"Five friggin' days."

"Five days? Damn. That ain't fair." We waited together in silence. His limbs jerked, searching for a comfortable place. The longer we waited the more disturbed he got.

"You?" he asked.

My face burned, and I felt guilty. "No, nothing for me."

"Figures."

After a couple of minutes I touched back to the topic I originally wanted to talk to him about. "What about me and you?"

317

"What about it?" He looked down at the cap in his hands.

"Are we cool?" I watched him out of the corner of my eye.

"Yeah. We're cool." He looked over at me and winked. "Thanks for sticking up for me." He patted me on the shoulder, and an odd sense of ease came over me.

His mother showed up about an hour later. I waited with him the whole time, missing lunch and the beginning of study hall, though that'd probably land me in detention. She lit into him as soon as she burst into the office.

"Marshall, can't you keep it together? What's the matter with you?" she yelled. Her knee length brown coat bundled her completely, and a scarf wound too tight on her head.

"It wasn't my fault," he appealed, and recoiled from her. He made the "quiet down" gesture with both hands.

"It's never your fault," she screamed back even louder. The bustle of the office deadened, and all parties looked away. Embarrassed for him but not wanting to get hit by any shrapnel, I tried to disappear into my chair.

"Can you explain yourself? Fighting?" He began to make an argument, but she cut him off again, mid-word. "It takes two to fight. How can that not be your fault?"

318

She refused to listen to anything he had to say. So, he finally

gave up, and take it. He sat silently, his glazed eyes peered into the dead

air in front of him.

She steered him by the arm out of the school office, and pushed

through the pupils in the main hall to the front door. Outside she

continued to holler at him all the way to their Blazer. It seemed like the

whole school had paused to watch the train wreck. Once they pulled

away, normal life at RV started again.

*   *   *

Chapter 30

Benzler's Mom scolded him as soon as he came in the door.

"You're getting snow all over the floor. How many times do I have to

tell you? Take your boots off on the porch." He held his tongue, while

he wiped up the melted snow with a rag. She oversaw him, hands on her

wide hips. "Now get up to your room. It's a mess."

It was Monday, the final day of his school suspension, and he had just returned home after helping his Grandpa all morning. He and his mother had worn each other thin this last week together.

Marshall gritted his teeth, brushed past her, and headed upstairs. He mumbled so low she could barely hear, "So's the kitchen. Why don't you get your fat butt in there?"

She squawked immediately. "What? What did you say?" She looked like she was ready to leap out of her skin. "You get your ass upstairs this instant young man." She pointed up the stairway. "And you can stay up there until dinner."

Despite the public blow up over his suspension, Benzler and his Mom had started the week at peace. But a petty argument after supper last Wednesday evening cracked the veneer of the hollow relationship they'd maintained since his homecoming. After that, bit-by-bit, each small irritation grew. Benzler couldn't sneer, his Mom couldn't discipline without fear of triggering something worse. The pot finally boiled over this afternoon in mid-January.

As he climbed the steps two at a time he again muttered under his breath, "Why should I come down for supper? It all tastes like shit anyway."

This time she didn't even hear exactly what he said, but she grasped the tone, and chased after him up the stairs.

"Marshall, Goddam it get up there! Don't you talk back to me." She caught up to him at the top of the stairs. His sweatshirt ripped as she pulled him to her. She smacked him across the face with an open hand. He staggered backward and fell down against the wall. She bent down and swatted him again, and he covered his face with his arms.

"Alright, alright, I'm going," Benzler sniveled. His Mom broke down, turned away and thundered back downstairs, rubbing her sore hand. She had not struck him in any way since he came back. Benzler slowly stood, and reset his glasses. He wiped his stinging lip, and looked at the blood that smeared onto the back of his hand. He marched into his room and slammed the door in a way that rattled the doorframe.

His mother flopped her heavy frame on the living room couch, and stared into the television in a daze. The chaos of Vietnam invaded the screen as the top story once again. She paid no mind. She shuddered and choked back her tears. Benzler's brother and sister cowered, and gave each other wide-eyed looks. They'd traveled this road before.

Benzler's little brother asked, "Mom, can we watch 'Speed Racer?" She didn't acknowledge. He passed in front of her, and switched the knob on the set, and again she didn't seem to notice.

Upstairs, Benzler lay on his back on his bed, with his eyes squeezed shut and jaw set. He punched into his pillow. "Bitch, bitch, bitch. Always fuckin' bitchin'. I can't do anything right for her." He thought back to the hospital, the betrayal that he felt there, and now back here again. "I knew this was gonna happen."

His rage surged and he jumped up, and kicked his desk chair over. He ripped the sweatshirt off, tearing it to pieces. He grabbed a baseball bat from the corner of his room. The feel of the smooth ash handle in his hands reminded him of the pool cue he held that night at the hospital. He yelled out and swung at the lamp next to his bed. It exploded in a pop and a flash. He gawked in disbelief at what he had just done.

"Hi ya!" He spun and tomahawked a model B-17 Bomber his father had helped him with. The plastic plane splintered into a hundred pieces, and the bookcase it rested on split and collapsed.

The crashing noises shocked Benzler's mother out of her stupor, and she rushed back upstairs. Benzler felt the thud of her footfalls, and reached his bedroom door first. He barricaded it with his body, and then he pulled the chair he kicked over and leaned it under the knob.

She tried the handle and then the door with her shoulder. "Open this door," she commanded. He didn't answer, and he definitely didn't open the door. Benzler looked next to his beer can collection stacked on his desk in a massive pyramid. He took aim at the plump brunette wearing an old-fashioned bathing suit displayed on a purple can of Olde Frothingslosh Ale. She vaguely resembled his Mom, though he couldn't remember the last time she put on bathing attire. He let fly again, and knocked down the entire stack. Cans scattered everywhere, and made a horrible clatter. He let out a maniacal laugh, and yelled "That one's outta here!"

His Mom raised her voice, "Marshall Taylor Benzler. You open this door immediately." He answered with another crash, so his mother raced back downstairs in a panic.

Hands shaking, she called her father-in-law next door on the phone, Benzler's Grandpa. A dry scratchy voice answered, "Hullo."

"Cecil, this is Rose."

"Hiya Rose. What…"

She interrupted his greeting. "Marshall's locked himself in his bedroom. He's having a fit." Her white knuckles gripped the black phone tightly.

"Oh my goodness, I'll be right over." Grandpa hung up without hearing any more.

Mrs. Benzler diverted to the television room to check on her younger children. They turned their frightened eyes to her, but she gave them no reassurance. She merely closed the door to shelter them.

She then waited in the kitchen wringing her hands, and emitting tiny squeals with every noise that emanated from above. Grandpa arrived in his light blue full cab Chevy pickup a few minutes later. He ambled in his old man walk across the snowy sidewalk, boots open and unbuckled. He entered and stomped off the wet snow, and he heard a loud crash from upstairs.

He looked up. "Is that.....?" His daughter-in-law just nodded, her fist pressed against her forehead.

"How long's he been in there?"

"Half an hour," she replied. "I called you up after he blocked the door, and started thrashing his room. Can you talk to him?" she asked, eyes pleading.

"I'll see what I can do." Grandpa struggled up the stairs, the arthritis in his back slowing him somewhat. He treaded to his grandson's door with some trepidation. He suspended his wrinkled, thick veined hand an inch away from the knob for a moment. He tests it and found that it wouldn't budge.

He rapped lightly on the door, "Marshall? It's Grandpa." He

waited uneasily, but got no response.

He tried again, "Marshall?"

He discerned a faint, muffled, "Go away."

"Marshall. Are you OK?"

"I said go away!" the boy yelled.

"We're worried about you son."

Another unknown object smashed directly on the door.

Steadying himself with the handrail, Grandpa hurried back

downstairs to his daughter and reported, "He's not comin' outta there

anytime soon."

"What should we do?" Mrs. Benzler asked. They both looked at

the ceiling and listened to some odd pounding, then another crash.

Grandpa Benzler searched in futility at his fingernails for an

answer. He let out a sigh. "Maybe we should call the sheriff." The

kitchen light shone off his balding head.

Not seeing a better solution, she agreed, and quickly walked over

to the phone. She dialed each number, frustrated watching the rotary dial

slowly spin back to zero each time.

A monotone female voice answered, "Marion County Sheriff's

office."

"I need someone right away," Mrs. Benzler panted, out of breath. "My son's gone wild. He's smashing up the house."

"Whoa, slow down, Ma'am," the dispatcher interrupted. She held the receiver away from her ear, with a pained expression. "Slow down and start over. Excuse me Ma'am, who are you?"

"This is Rosemary Benzler and my son's going crazy out here," she blurted out, slower but still frantic.

"Where's here dear?" the dispatcher asked.

Mrs. Benzler had trouble focusing. "Uh. The Benzler farm. South County. Near Waldo."

"Out on Benzler Road?"

"Yes. Send someone out here. Right now. Please."

"OK Ma'am. Calm down. Now tell me what's going on."

"It's my son. He's locked himself in his room. He's smashing everything, and we can't get him to stop."

"OK Ma'am. I'll send someone out right now," the dispatcher assured her, and then hung up.

The sheriff's dispatcher looked over at the deputy, Jack Jameson at a nearby desk. Jameson, a ten-year veteran of the sheriff's department, sipped black coffee from a red thermos. The big boned deputy sported a solid beer gut, and his boyish face had perpetually flushed red cheeks.

"That was Rose Benzler. Says her kid's going wild. Can you go have a look Jack?"

He smelled the coffee, and then took another drink. "Aaah."

"Jack?"

The deputy recalled what happened to the father, a high school classmate, as he had happened to be the first officer to arrive at the scene of the suicide just over a year ago.

"Isn't the boy just back from that mental hospital?" the deputy inquired.

"Yep. I believe so," she confirmed.

"Great," the deputy complained. "Why do I always get the crazy ones?"

The dispatcher regarded him crossly. "Jack...."

"Oh, alright, I'm going." He pushed himself up from his groaning chair. He strapped on his gear, and grabbed his hat and coat. He ventured outside into the cold afternoon. The sky began to darken.

The sheriff's station was located on Marion-Williamsport Road on the other end of the county. Thirty minutes later the deputy showed up in his cruiser at their house. By then, the storm had ended, and

Benzler had calmed down. He hiked across the unshoveled walk, and knocked on the screen door at the side of the house. He wondered why a storm door was never put up, especially with this year's hard winter. Despite the unfortunate circumstances, he knew the family had capable relatives and neighbors nearby to help.

Mrs. Benzler answered the door, and let the deputy in. Though evidently still upset, Mrs. Benzler wasn't crying. Grandpa hovered behind her, a grim look on his face.

"Afternoon Ma'am. Sir." The deputy pulled off his hat, and rubbed his gloved hand over his mussed hair. "May I come in?"

"Of course, of course." Grandpa nodded, and Mrs. Benzler said, "I'm sorry I called you down here. My boy calmed down, so I guess I don't need you now."

"That's good." The deputy nodded his head and smiled. The house had an odd musty smell. He paused a moment to listen. "Well, I come all the way out here. Can I have a look around?"

Mrs. Benzler's mouth opened, and her eyebrows rose. "I said I don't need you anymore." Grandpa touched her arm to rein her in and she jerked his hand away.

The deputy stated crisply, "Yes Ma'am, but I would be negligent in my duties if I didn't at least have a good feeling about things before I left." The twang in his voice betrayed his family's Kentucky roots.

"Well OK," she conceded. "He's upstairs now, second door on the left."

Jameson was disturbed by the quiet. He could hear a television behind that closed door there. He crept up the stairs and the mother and grandfather tailed him to the bottom of the staircase. He thought, "They sure are acting like a coupla squirrels." He tapped gently three times on the door as directed by the mother. Upon receiving no answer, he tried the door which opened easily, no barricade.

"Hello," the deputy called, his deep rich voice resonating in the dark room. He observed that the room had been well trashed. Books, clothes, a busted lamp, beer cans lay all over the floor. Posters ripped off the wall. Bookshelf knocked over, the desktop tipped on its side with all the contents spread all around. The room had the acrid scent of perspiration and teenage funk. The boy lay on his stomach on the bed, his head deep into the pillows. His back rose and fell evenly.

"Hello," the deputy repeated. He stalked into the bedroom, stepping over debris toward the motionless figure. Just as he bent over to

329

tap the still figure on the shoulder, Benzler turned over abruptly, startling both of them.

Red-faced from his spent rage Benzler asked, "Who are you?"

Red-faced by nature the man replied, "I'm Deputy Jack Jameson. From the sheriff's office." Jameson thought the boy looked much different than a year ago, but maybe it was just the hair.

"Why are you here?" Benzler asked curtly. "What do you want?"

"Well, your Mom called me out here. She was frightened by your behavior." He glanced around the room and gestured with his hand. "Look at your room for God's sakes."

"Well….she's an asshole. She bitches at me constantly." He planted his face back into the pillow. "I hate her," wafted out of the cushion.

Jameson didn't quite know what to make of this. He wasn't a guidance counselor or a damned shrink. Of course they trained on how to deal with crisis victims. He leaned down awkwardly to pat Benzler on the back. The boy was drenched in sweat.

"OK, OK now. It's all gonna be all right." The deputy stayed with Benzler until the boy calmed back down. Jameson silently left the room, and carefully pulled the door shut behind him.

330

He tiptoed downstairs to the kitchen, and updated Mrs. Benzler and Grandpa. "Yer boy's gonna be fine I think. I guess he's spent hisself for now." He carried his black officer's hat with both hands in front of him.

"Thank you so much for coming out." She wore a half smile. "Sorry to drag you all the way out here for nothing."

"Don't mention it. Just doin' my job." He dug his foot into the floor like a bashful schoolboy.

"I know but still, thank you." Her hands clasped together as if in prayer.

"You're welcome." He paused for a moment.

"Can I get you something to drink?" she offered.

"No'm. I'm just still trying to piece this together. So what exactly happened?"

"Where do I begin?" Mrs. Benzler sighed, and relieved her girth on a kitchen chair. "Today, when he came home I just told him he needed to clean his room. That ended up with him trashing it."

"Did you try and stop him at all?" the deputy asked.

"That's when he blocked the door, so I couldn't."

"Um huh." The deputy thought a moment, biting his lip. "Does he have any access to alcohol?"

331

"Alcohol?" she asked, her face scrunched up, puzzled.

"I saw beer cans lying everywhere," the deputy clarified.

"Oh no," Mrs. Benzler affirmed. "He collects those stupid cans. They're empty. That's not it."

"That explains the lack of smell." The deputy shifted his feet, and crossed his arms. "Did you strike him at all?" There was a short pause at the awkward question. "I noticed a bruise on his face and a swollen lip." He touched his face to demonstrate.

She stood and pointed her finger, "Don't you tell me how to discipline my boy." Again Grandpa gripped her arm to restrain her.

"Just calm down Mrs. Benzler. I'm not trying to tell you anything." By instinct the deputy's right hand moved to rest on his pistol handle. "You called us remember? I'm obliged to follow up." He noticed the fearful look in both of their eyes, as they watch the weapon. He put his hand flat beside him.

She settled back down onto the rickety chair. "He talked back to me, and I slapped him in the face. That's all." She added, "Don't you have any kids?"

The officer nodded, and rubbed the brim of his hat. "Is he by chance seeing a doctor, you know since he came home from the institution?"

332

"Well no," she responded. "He doesn't like Dr. Stevenson, and I haven't made him go." Her shoulders slumped and her chin drooped. "Maybe I should have."

"Yes. May I suggest that you rethink that in light of this outburst? This time things calmed down. It doesn't always work out like that. Believe me. Just my two cents." He paused and waited for a response, but got none. "Good day Ma'am. Sir." He put his hat on as he stepped through the door. Grandpa followed the deputy, and watched him return to his vehicle and pull out of the driveway.

Grandpa rejoined Benzler's Mom in the kitchen. She had her elbows on the table, head in her hands. Streaks of grey hair showed through her black locks. Grandpa observed her with caution.

"Now what?" he asked.

Her voice faltered. "I don't know."

"I think that boy's right about that doctor," Grandpa added.

"I know, I know," she said. "I'll start making him go." They remained seated for a couple of minutes until Grandpa stood again.

"Well, I guess I'll be agoing then."

"Thanks so much for coming down here Cecil," said the daughter-in-law.

He bundled up in the anteroom, but before he left he asked, "What about you, Rose?"

"What about me?"

His eyes rested on the floor a moment, and he noticed the grime built up on the linoleum. "I mean you've been having a hard time yeself. Maybe you could do fer some help too."

The tension mounted back up in the air. She responded, metered, "What kind of help do you mean exactly?"

Grandpa stopped and thought a long time. "Rose, I don't want to play word games here. Marshall's been through a lot and so have you." He stole a glance into her eyes. "We all have. All I'm sayin's maybe you could use a doctor, same's Marshall."

Benzler's Mom's ire erupted again. "Don't you come down here to tell me that. Don't you come down here and tell me it's my fault." She raised her clenched fist, and then she broke down in tears and laid her head on the kitchen table.

Grandpa returned to her side and placed his hand on her head, stroking her soft curly hair. "Alrighty now. It's not your fault. I just want what's best for you and Marshall." She whimpered softly.

She remained like that long after Grandpa departed. Through a tremendous act of will, she pulled herself together and got up. She went back to the TV room, where both of her younger kids lay asleep on the floor. She put Nancy in her bedroom, but just covered David where he lay on the couch. She felt guilt about ignoring them tonight. She hadn't even cooked any dinner for them.

She trudged up the stairs, and drew near her older son's bedroom. She hesitated outside the door, hand on the knob. Hearing nothing, she cracked open the door and peered inside. When her eyes adjusted to the dark room, she observed the disaster area first hand. But all she really saw was the gangly form that lay still on the bed fully clothed. She entered, took off his shoes, and pulled up the blankets. She watched him sleep quietly for many minutes, and softly stroked his hair. Then she exited, closing the door. He slept soundly through the night, but she didn't.

*   *   *

Chapter 31

I'd never been ice fishing before, but Benzler, the avid fisherman, talked me into it. My Dad only allowed me to go because Benzler's Mom had called and begged. Doctor's orders, he needed stable friends. Dad couldn't say no; besides, he didn't think we could get into any trouble fishing.

Benzler's Mom swung by this morning to pick me up. Once inside our house, he pulled his jacket hood off. "Hey Diggerman, you ready?"

"Man, you cut your hair." His hair stuck up maybe a quarter inch long all around.

He rubbed the stubble with his hand. "Mom butchered me."

"Do I smell Aquavelva? Did you shave your peach fuzz too?"

He puffed out his chest, and faked a pose. "It's part of the new, clean cut me."

"I like it." I pulled on my parka and grabbed my fishing gear.

"You would." He opened the front door and headed out. "I know how you like things nice and square Digger."

"Shut up." I elbowed him in the back, and followed him into the backseat of their Blazer.

"Hi Donny," Mrs. Benzler said, with bright eyes and a broad smile.

"Hi Mrs. Benzler," I replied, a bit shocked. I hadn't seen her smile in I didn't know how long.

336

She gave us a lift to one of our favorite summertime fishing holes. A little pond named "16B" hid in a remote area a few miles south of us in Delaware County. The pond lay on state property, a nature reserve of some sort. The state numbered all of the numerous ponds and lakes, and sometimes when there were clusters, they each received a suffix such as, "A or B."

We'd fished here dozens of times, but never in the winter. We even stayed overnight here once last summer, catching bullhead.

Ice fishing was unlike regular fishing in so many ways. First off, it was cold. In mid-February the daytime temperature averaged about 30 degrees, though at least the sun shined today. About six inches of packed snow lay on the ground.

We couldn't ice fish every year, because it needed to be cold for long enough for the ice to freeze 6 to 8 inches thick. That allowed us to walk on it without cracking.

Finally, the actual fishing was different. Most fish wouldn't bite, and live bait didn't work too well. About everything changed. One good thing however, there were no bugs. No pesky mosquitoes, no biting flies, nothing.

We were out in the middle of nowhere, with nobody around us, certainly no other fishermen. In every direction absolute white surrounded us. Our feet crunched through the unruffled blanket of snow that smothered everything. We spotted wildlife tracks, and the occasional scat. It was weird to think of all the dormant things buried beneath: the seeds of plants and weeds, insect larvae, smaller animals in burrows. The bigger predators eked out a living on fall leftovers, and the rare careless prey.

We picked a random spot out on the pond, brushed away a patch of snow, and took turns chopping a hole in the ice with a hatchet. Each chop echoed, and shattered the utter silence. We geared up, baited our hooks with simple dough balls, and dropped our lines. We caught nothing at first, and stared disillusioned into the hole we'd made.

Benzler related the details of his turbulent past month. He got grounded for trashing his room, and he and his Mom started back with the psychiatrist.

"Everyone at school's calling you 'the Weed,'" I told him.

"I know." He paused. "My Dad used to say a weed was any plant you don't want."

I nodded. "Yeah. I heard that one."

"I guess that means Rustin's right." He grimaced and yanked his pole back, impatient. His bait hung on the hook, unchanged, though now frozen. "I hate that fucker." He dropped the dough ball back in.

338

We carried on, but we didn't even get a nibble. I doubted whether any fish could live in that black forbidding opening. Meanwhile topside, the air thickened and a light snow began to fall. A breeze picked up and as the clouds blocked the sun, the temperature dipped.

To fight the cold I wore the proverbial layers: thermals, t-shirt, sweatshirt, and my down parka. Ski mittens kept my hands warm, and a stocking cap covered my head. Benzler wore his Dad's same old dull Army jacket. No matter how you sliced it, it was still cold. Whenever I breathed through my nose, it felt like tiny icicles grew on my nose hairs.

Out of the blue Benzler said, "You know, I wanted to kill you last month."

"What?" The hairs on the back of my neck rose.

"Yeah. That Saturday you guys were hangin' with Rustin."

I looked at his face to check his sincerity. His eyes held no humor. "You're serious?"

He didn't respond, he just gazed at his red and white bobber on the water.

"Man, I explained that whole thing to you," I continued.

"I know." He raised his eyes back to meet mine. "Besides, you stood up for me the next day." He leaned over and hugged me, a giant bear hug. "I didn't do it did I? I don't feel that way now." The act touched me, but I still felt odd embracing out in the boonies in these noisy stuffed coats. That plus he had just said he wanted to kill me.

"All right fagboy," I said and pushed him away. "That's enough."

"Sorry," he apologized. "I just..." but he didn't finish. Our lines tangled, so we struggled to separate them.

"Shit, where'd the sun go?" I said, noting the dark storm clouds forming in the west. "What time's your Mom supposed to pick us up?"

"I don't remember." He shrugged. He pushed up his jacket sleeve away from his glove to show me a bare watchless wrist. "I don't know what time it is anyway." I didn't even own a wrist watch.

He went on. "It's getting pretty damn cold. What should we do?"

"Wait right here for your Mom, that's what," I responded. "What choice do we have?"

"We can walk home," Benzler piped in. He stomped his feet to knock off some snow.

"You're crazy man. That's too friggin' far." I watched the tops of some pines bend just before a gale blasted across the open pond, and whipped snow into our faces. We huddled down and pulled our jacket hoods close over our heads. It dawned on me that I had just called him crazy. I peeked out to see if he'd caught it. Maybe not.

When the wind momentarily calmed I repeated, "It's too far." My fingers and toes already felt numb.

He glared over at me. "Don't call me crazy."

Sheepish, I looked back at him, and then realized he was joking. "Sorry man, it slipped." He patted me on the back and laughed.

He said, "Maybe we can stop at a house on the way and call my Mom."

"Sure, which house though?" I waved my arm in a dramatic arc. He followed the motion full circle. "Who the hell lives out here anyway?" I added.

He pulled his line out of the hole, and set it on the ground. "OK, why don't we just sit here and freeze to death then? Sound good?" He started to stow his gear. I kept on fishing with him behind me, arms crossed.

After about fifteen more minutes, the icy air further seeped into my bones, and I changed my mind. "You know what? Great idea man. Let's get outta here!" I announced. I packed up my tackle box, and together we trudged through the snow, heads down.

As we backtracked up the trail, conditions worsened. I blamed our ancestors for settling in a place with such a harsh climate. Idiots. We struggled uphill to the trailhead where Benzler's Mom had dropped us off. The gravel road we came in on hadn't seen a snowplow all winter. We followed the sole tire tracks left earlier by his Mom, so we made out the path easily. Two hundred year old oaks and maples lined each side, and thankfully cut the wind or it could have beeen even worse.

We stopped talking, as we both looked down, and kept our faces inside our jackets. The fur lining inside my jacket collar got wet as I breathed on it. I'd eaten nothing since a light breakfast, and now I tasted the stomach acid, and smelled my stale breath. The unpaved road led us out onto State Route 229, a rural two-lane highway. We hiked only about a quarter mile to get there, but in this weather it took forever. We'd made a good decision to walk, just to get moving, and get our blood pumping.

"Which way?" I asked when we reached the highway. "You remember any houses?"

Benzler pointed with his gloved hand to the right. "I think that way." I gripped the handle of my tackle box with one hand and my pole with the other, and we pressed on. I didn't think I could straighten my stiff, curled fingers again. They'd plowed this highway, but apparently not in awhile. Two foot high mounds of snowpack fenced in the road, and about an inch of new snow covered it now. We walked down the center of the empty right lane, and not a single car passed in either direction. Only a fool would have come out in this weather. Or a crazyman. I guess that made me the fool.

As the sun set, the sky darkened further, and the wind made a hollow whistle above us in the bare trees. The highway created a forest gap, which acted as a wind tunnel. Wind flecked with snow barreled down the road, and bit at my exposed chapped face. The wind chill factor had to be below zero.

"We should have gone the other way," Benzler said after some time. "At least then the wind would be at our tail."

"Too late now," I replied.

The highway emerged from the forest to some hibernating farm fields bracketed by snow fences. Drifts built right before our eyes.

We spied a light aways down, and Benzler said, "I think we know the people that live up the road there. Maybe we can use their phone."

"Hold on," I replied. I had to raise my voice to cut through the howling wind. "Let's stop here a minute. I'm beat."

"C'mon man we gotta keep goin'."

"I'm too tired man, and too friggin' cold." I took a knee on the frozen roadside. "I gotta sit down."

"Man, my Grandma got stranded in a snow storm a long time ago. She lost some fingers and toes to frostbite. We can't stop now." Benzler pushed me on. He looked scared. "C'mon man, just a little further."

Midwestern parents often used horror stories like that to teach kids to respect winter. I'd heard them my whole life. "Maybe someone will come by with a sleigh, like on the Walton's Christmas." I let out a hollow, breathless laugh.

He shook his head. "Now you're getting delirious John Boy. Let's go." He pulled me up by the arm.

I didn't want frostbite or to freeze to death, so I got back up. As we drew closer, we saw the house materialize. The relief that it wasn't some kind of mirage gave me the extra boost to move on.

"Who lives there?" I asked.

"I'm not sure," he said. "But I think my Dad knew them."

"You're not sure?" I snapped. "We do the Bataan Death March to get here, and you're not sure?"

Benzler kept plodding toward the house slow and steady. "Have you got any better ideas? I'm freezing my ass off too you know."

344

We approached the old, brick farmhouse. Thank goodness they'd built it fairly close to the road. On the porch, we tried, but couldn't see through any of the weatherproofed windows. Benzler knocked on the door, but with the wind and his padded gloves it seemed to not make any sound at all. I yearned to feel warm. The dull ache in my toes, fingers and face faded to no feeling at all. The wait seemed long, and I squelched a desire to curl up right there on the stoop.

Finally the door cracked open, and my heart leapt when I see a familiar face. I didn't know the woman's name, but recognized her as an acquaintance of our parents. She was my Dad's age with auburn hair pulled back tight into a bun. Her quizzical expression showed her surprise. I bet we looked like a spectacle all bundled up, strangers at her door at dusk in the middle of a snowstorm.

Her soft voice squeaked, "Can I help you?"

Benzler spoke up. "Excuse me M'am. We got stranded. Can we bother you to use the phone?"

She hesitated for a split second then responded, "My goodness, please come in before you catch your death." We entered, and the warmth instantly overcame me like melted butter. She invited us to remove our icy garments in the foyer. My dead fingers made disrobing a chore, but Benzler and I helped each other as much as possible.

Benzler's beet red face glistened in the light. We tossed our outer clothes onto a rubber runway that divided the hardwood floor.

She came back with some towels, and exclaimed, "Why you're Marshall Benzler. I'm sorry, I couldn't tell before. C'mon in."

She escorted us into her kitchen, and offered us hot chocolate. Benzler asked for coffee, but she ignored him and soon brought the cocoa back to the table. She wore an apron, and a worn plain dress. I wondered if she was a Mennonite.

When Benzler ran off to the next room to make the phone call, she asked in a West Virginia drawl, "You're Coach Eidegger's boy ain't ya'?" Nope, not a Mennonite. They didn't have that accent.

"Yes'm." I savored both the heat and the rich flavor of the beverage. She had even put a marshmallow in.

"You're the spittin' image of 'im. How are your folks?" Her hazel eyes sparkled with none of the fear I had seen at the door.

"Fine, thank you." I sniffled, and wiped my nose with my sleeve.

The old farmhouse made a warm and cozy retreat. I could hear a fireplace crackling in the next room. We sat at the kitchen table, and I rubbed my palms on the macramé place settings. I picked up the warm mug with both hands. My fingers looked like pink raw sausages.

346

The friendly woman flitted around me like a finch. "What in heaven's name were you boys doin' out in this blizzard?"

"We went fishing over at the state park, and then the weather turned," I responded. She nodded, and flattened her apron.

Benzler returned to the table. "No answer."

"Maybe I should call my Dad then."

"Can't hurt nothin'," Benzler replied.

"Go ahead honey, I don't mind," the woman agreed.

With the chill gone, my limbs began to throb as they thawed out. My skin always got itchy too, so I fought the urge to scratch.

I placed the call, and Les picked up the phone. I argued with him to get Dad.

"Daaaaaad." I pulled the phone away from my ear, but could still hear him yell, "It's Donny."

"Where the dickens are you?" Dad blurted when he took over.

"We're over at... hold on a minute." I stretched the phone cord to its length, so I could direct my question to our host. "Excuse me M'am, what's your name?"

"Rita Steinbach."

I repeated that to Dad, "We're at Rita Steinbach's house."

"I heard. What on earth are you doing over there?"

347

"It's a long story Dad. Can't you just come get us?" I pleaded.

"Us. Who's us?" Dad barked into the phone.

"Me and Benzler," I replied softly. I wrapped the phone cord around my wrist. "Remember?"

He paused for a second. "Dammit son, it's snowing to beat the band out there."

"I know. That's why we need a ride," I said flatly.

During his next pause I wondered if maybe he'd just leave us here. "Well," he finally said. "I suppose I better come get you. Where does Rita live?"

"I'm not sure exactly, hold on." I set the phone down gently on the wooden counter, and returned to our host, "Mrs. Steinbach, I need directions for my Dad."

She hopped up out of her chair. "Let me tell him honey."

I heard her in the other room, "Coach?"

*   *   *

He arrived in about half an hour, honking his horn as he pulled in. We thanked Mrs. Steinbach, and got into the station wagon. The

348

snow came down much harder, but the wind had eased. The huge flakes looked like falling ashes.

At Benzler's house, we parked next to his Mom's Blazer in the driveway. Two other cars and a sheriff's cruiser unexpectedly filled the rest of the lot.

"Uh oh," Benzler said when he saw the other vehicles. "Can you come in with me?"

"What? No way?" I protested. I just wanted to go home, and I'd seen his Mom rage before.

"My Mom's gonna be pissed." I watched him squirm, but I still didn't want to go in. "You can help me explain. C'mon," he begged.

I looked up at my Dad and hoped for rescue. He crammed a cigarette into the car ashtray and frowned. "Go on, make it quick."

We found his distraught mother on a chair in the living room surrounded by his Grandparents, Benzler's uncle, and Deputy Jameson. The way they hovered and supported his Mom reminded me of his Dad's funeral.

The group overreacted to us as soon as we enter. "Where were you? We've been looking everywhere!" they sang in chorus.

Benzler shrank back as if he expected some kind of brutal attack. He mumbled, "We got too cold with the storm n' all. We hiked out to Rita Steinbach's house."

To my surprise, his Mom was not angry. She came over and hugged her son. "Thank goodness you're all right. I was worried sick we'd lost you."

"Sorry Mom." Benzler's words were muffled in her ample bosom. "We didn't know if you were coming."

"Of course I came. When I couldn't find you I just didn't know what to do." She rocked him back and forth, not letting him go.

I stood quietly behind them, and with the happy reunion I stated, "Well, my Dad's waiting outside. I gotta go." I snuck toward the back.

"Donny." Mrs. Benzler looked up from her son. "Please tell your father thank you for me."

I rejoined Dad back in the car. He waited, smoked, and listened to the storm report on WMRN. He glanced at me as I got in. He left the car engine on to keep the old station wagon toasty even though he rolled his window down to let smoke escape. I bet he didn't want to risk it not starting as well; otherwise he wouldn't have wasted the gas. He put out yet another Winston butt in the overflowing ashtray. He blew out his last exhale.

"Donny, what the hell were you thinking?"

I watched the smoke tendrils spiral up from his dispensed cigarette. "I don't know."

He pulled off his deer hunting cap, and scratched his full head of brown hair.

"You guys could've frozen to death." I looked down at my gloved hands.

He put the car into drive, and crawled around the circular path through the deep snow. "You're lucky you didn't at least get frostbite." I didn't answer, but I noted his harsh response in contrast to Benzler's Mom.

He went on. "That sonuvagun means trouble. If it isn't one thing, it's another."

The rear wheels spun for a moment as we pulled onto Benzler Rd. He steered carefully, hands at 10 and 2 o'clock. I held onto the handle as he regained control.

"Dad, it wasn't his fault."

"Pshaw," he blew out. "Where've I heard that before?"

"Seriously Dad, if he wasn't there, I don't think I'd have made it."

*   *   *

Chapter 32

I scrubbed the curry comb across the muscular haunch. Only when I stood on a wooden stool could I reach the top of this tremendous draft horse. The comb ruffled her short hairs, while my other hand drags behind and smoothed them back down. Oily gray-white dander coated the tool and my hands.

"Feels good doesn't it Beauty girl?" The horse stomped her foot and shuddered as if in reply. I put my cheek up against her, and breathed her rich animal smell. I stole the name made famous by Anna Sewell's novel, but though she was the color of coal, we just called her Beauty. Dad wanted to call her Sox because she has white stockings on each hoof. I won out; she was my horse.

"Whaddya know, it's Mister Ed." Benzler jutted his head through the open upper half of the stable door. Since his buzz cut, his hair had reached that untamed length where it stuck up in all directions. He visited at my house again on this Saturday, the first day of our spring break. This was the first time Benzler had been back in our barn since that fateful day last year. To tell the truth, I didn't come out here all that often anymore either, except for my chores. It just wasn't the same.

"That's one fat friggin' horse," he said.

"She's pregnant you idiot." I tenderly stroked the swollen belly. Even with me up on the stool Benzler looked me in the eye. He'd grown at least 2 more inches since he came home, and meanwhile I seemed to stand still.

"She looks like a tick about to pop," he exclaimed. I threw the comb at him, but he ducked down and the comb clanked off the door.

Soon I wound up my chores, closed up the tack room, and we headed up to the house. The fresh outdoor air purged the barn odor stuck in my nose. Springtime bloomed all around us: shrubs, flowers, trees, and weeds. Benzler sprouted like his nickname, "the Weed." As we walked, he stood a foot taller than me, with all the length going into his arms and legs. He looked ostrich-like with his head still stuck in the sand.

We passed Mom's newly tilled and planted garden, and he said, "Hey man, I moved out to the barn."

"What does that mean?" I loop both thumbs under the straps of my overalls as we walk.

"Dad had his office fixed up nice. There's already a bed, and a heater. Even a fridge." He sniffled, and produced a red and black checked bandanna from his back jeans pocket to wipe his nose. Like every spring, his allergies acted up again. But at least he had a snotrag this time. "So I moved a bunch of my things, and I'm livin' out there now."

"What for?"

"Keeps Mom out of my hair."

"I thought you guys were gettin' along better."

"We are." Our boots sliced through the grass as we walked in step. "But it gives us some space. She's cool with it, and so's Doc Stevenson."

I broke stride to stamp down some mole holes that had resurfaced. "I thought you said that place creeped you out."

Benzler joined in on the stomp. "Yeah, it used to. But I'm over that now."

"Sounds cool."

Back at the house, we stretched out on our back deck chairs. Mom delivered us some cookies and glasses of her prize lemonade to wash it down. She retreated to her kitchen perch, the source of that constant whiff of baked goods. Benzler pretended the lemonade was booze and staggered around like a drunken fool or two until he spilled some onto the deck's 2 by 4 floorboards.

Mom watched this from the kitchen window that looked out on us. She shouted, "Marshall, don't you dare break my glass."

Benzler dropped his head. "Sorry Mrs. E." She pulled her head back away from the screen.

"Nice job," I said. He shoved me, and more liquid sloshed out of his glass.

I reclined with my hands behind my head, and stared out over the lake behind our house. Tiny circles appeared on the surface, and grew larger. Fish made those I guess. "What about those nightmares you were having?"

His serious face returned. "They stopped." he said.

I drained the last of the lemonade, and wiped the dribble off my chin. I crunched on a piece of ice, with some lemon pulp stuck on it. "So what do you want to do?" I sat up quickly and added, "And don't say you want to ride the horses."

"Ha ha, very funny." Benzler moved to the edge of the deck, and gazed at the water. "How 'bout fishin'?"

"Ha ha yerself," I replied.

"I don't mean ice fishing. C'mon."

"Nah, I don't feel like it. Besides, the fish won't be bitin' at this hour." I thought hard, while watching the clouds drift past, white and fluffy as cotton. "Let's go back out to the barn then."

"And do what?"

"I don't know. Hang out in the loft." His expression remained flat, so I upped the ante. "I got some chew."

Benzler blew out a raspberry, and responded with an unenthused, "OK. Yer the boss."

Funny, Benzler acted more subdued this year. At least when it was just the two of us. Sure he still goofed off, but it was a matter of degree. He always used to jabber on non-stop and sang aloud with his awful screechy voice. Now he didn't talk as much and he definitely didn't sing.

As we approached the barn from the east side we could see twelve stable doors in a row. Eleven were open, some with horses visible within. Door twelve, conspicuously closed, still drew my eye. Gypsy's. I glanced at Benzler, and caught him looking at it too.

We rounded the corner to the west side where an earthen driveway ramped right to a set of second story double doors. Inside we clambered up a peg ladder into the loft. Afternoon set in, and shadows casted into the corners. We crossed the bare wooden center aisle, which extended from the ladder to a window. Stacked bales lined each wall of

the loft, hay on one side, straw on the other. Loose strands of straw and

hay dust littered the floor. Caught in the sun's rays, particles floated on

the air, barely moving. I wondered that we could even breathe up here.

We sat down at the upper loft window, and dangled our legs out.

A hook the size of a man's hand hung outside on a pulley. We loaded

and unloaded here during baling season.

Once settled, I revealed my stash of Red Man, and we molded

chunks of the broad leaf into oversized balls, and forced them beneath

our cheeks. It was fun to chew up here, since we launched our excess

saliva three stories down. The spring evening came early before daylight

savings time, the colors deadened, and quiet descended over the valley.

Cardinals chased one another, and a robin with the tell tale red breast

whistled at us. Despite the serenity of the scene, twilight put me on

edge. It gave me an empty feeling, like the brink of life and death.

We watched our Shire Beauty tear purposefully across the

pasture. She galloped back and forth at full speed. Back and forth from

one end of the grassy field to the other.

"What's the heck's the matter with that horse?" Benzler spat,

leaving a trail of brown spittle on his chin.

"Remember I told you she's pregnant? Horses act weird when they get close to foaling. For some reason Beauty likes to run."

Benzler looked at me sideways, eyes slanted. "That is weird," he said, mouth full. He spat again, and then finally wiped his chin with his flannel sleeve. We observed the horse's unusual behavior a minute longer. "You mean right now?" he asked, eyes wider this time behind his glasses.

"Well, it could be any time."

The horse returned at a trot and entered the barn directly below us. Benzler tried to spit on her but missed. I thumped him on the shoulder. Moments later we heard her begin to bellow loudly from below.

"Now what's she doing?" He rubbed the meat of his arm where I had just hit him.

"I don't know. Maybe now's the time." I stated this calmly, feeling proud of my knowledge.

"Uh oh. What should we do?"

"Let's go down and check her out." I jumped up and crossed the loft.

Benzler trailed me. "Aren't you nervous?"

"This happens all the time Benzler."

358

We slid down from the loft all the way to the first floor on an old

firehouse pole my grandpa rigged in the barn years ago.

"Run and get my Dad," I told him. "I'll stay here with the

mare."

Benzler just stared at me, stupefied. "Where will he be?"

"Check his basement workshop. He's always in there." Benzler

ran off in the general direction of the house. I carefully stepped into the

pregnant horse's stall. Beauty lay on her side, and her great belly

heaved, long, pained breaths. She rested quietly for now, her body

taking up most of the space.

I kneeled beside her and pet her wiry mane. "Good girl Beauty,

you're gonna be fine old girl," I whispered. Her ear twitched with my

breath. She stared at me with one deep brown eye, but I knew she

couldn't understand. "We're gonna take care of you, you just hold

tight."

My Dad hurried into the barn with Benzler right behind. He

wore his filthy hunting cap and jacket, his weekend attire. "Donny,

how's she doing? Has the water broken?"

"No Pop. She's just laying here." I wondered what Benzler had

told him. Dad tiptoed into the stall and crouched beside me. He rubbed

the mare's neck, and gave her a quick once over.

"She seems OK for now. You boys stay here, I'm gonna call Chuck Parker." Chuck, the large animal veterinarian took care of horses, cows, and such, not the typical dogs and cats. He lived in Waldo, three miles south.

"What do want us to do Dad?"

"Just stay here and watch her." He unlatched the gate, and it creaked as he stepped out. "Why don't you talk Marshall through the foaling process?"

"What? But Dad, I've never done it by myself." Anxiety quickly replaced my earlier cockiness.

Dad laughed as he tapped a cigarette from his pack. "Calm down. She's not ready yet."

"But what if something happens?"

"Relax, I'll be right back." He cupped his hands to light up, and then blew out the first smoke. "Anyways, it's easy son, you've seen it before." He slammed the gate shut, and left us there alone.

Sweat dripped off my forehead, so I wiped my eyes with my t-shirt. Benzler climbed in next to me. "What about 'It happens all the time?'" he whined, mocking me.

"Shut up," I replied and gave him a shove. He lost balance, and his knee fell into some horse crap. He began to wrestle with me, but then Beauty started to groan again. We froze. Her water broke with a gush.

"Called the vet." Dad came up behind us outside the stable door. We both jumped, startled by his voice. "He wasn't there." He leaned his elbows on the closed lower portion of the door. "Left a message with his answering service. They'll track him down."

"Dad, the water broke, I think."

"Oh. That means it's time then." Dad entered the barn, and turned on the light. He disappeared into the tack room, and returned with a foaling kit filled with items that we'd need. "OK boys, I'll talk you through it. When the time comes Donny, you and Marshall can handle the birth."

"But how Dad? What do we do?" We followed Dad outside of the barn to the water pump on the side.

Dad set his jaw, and pumped up and down on the handle, which squeaked with each crank. "For Pete's sake Donny, you've seen this a dozen times. Don't worry, the mare does all the work. You just help guide the lil' critter out." We each washed down with the cold well water. Benzler held his hands out like he was a TV doctor ready to operate.

As soon as we returned to the stall, Beauty kicked out and let out a noise that was half neigh, and half squeal. A single small hoof emerged from the mare then disappeared again. Dad saw this and his face went white. "Dammit, it's breach."

"What do we do?" I stood back on the verge of losing it.

"Hold on a minute. Calm down." He looked back toward the house, paced, and kicked at the dirt. "Where the hell's that vet?" The horse let out another strange guttural noise. "I guess we're on our own. We're gonna have to help pull it out now. I'll steady her head. Come on Donny, hurry up!"

"What?" I asked weakly.

He raised his voice. "Reach up in there and grab it. Now come on what's the matter with you Donny?" He furrowed his eyebrows, and his forehead crease deepened.

I rolled up my short sleeve over my shoulder. Then I meekly attempted to push my hand into the horse. Beauty lifted her tail and let out a stream of gas right in my face. Benzler giggled hysterically, and even Dad chuckled. "Stop it you guys." I could hardly bear the stench.

Dad clapped his hands twice, just like he did when he was coaching. "C'mon Donny, chop chop." I gave it another try.

"No, no, not like that," Dad yelled. "Get your hand in there."

Finally, I reached into the birth canal. My arm slipped in easily up to my forearm.

Dad said, "Marshall, get up there closer. You need to check this out." I felt around to find anything to grab. Failing, I removed my hand.

"What're you doing? You gotta keep trying."

"I can't grab it Dad. It's too slippery." I stood there, the panic rising, unable to move. Poor Beauty, lay on her side the entire time, and her bellows reminded me of last summer when Gypsy broke her leg. Eerie. I saw Dad's mouth move, but I just stood there mesmerized. The barn spun.

Benzler jumped in, and knocked me aside. He inserted his arm into the horse, and grabbed a hoof and began to pull. The two rear hoofs came out, but got stuck at the hips. I came back to my senses and got beside Benzler to help. We pulled as a team, but the foal wouldn't budge any further.

"Come on, you gotta pull down, not straight. Guide the hips out," Dad hollered. "For the love of Mike hurry up, she's hurting here. The foal could die."

"It won't come Pop. It won't come out."

Benzler looked at me and said, "We gotta do this together. Come on, one, two, three, PUUUULLL."

We braced our feet against Beauty's rear, and we pulled in unison. I gritted my teeth, and the tendons of my neck strained. My shoulder and back muscles burned. Dad stood at Beauty's head, and shouted encouragement.

With one last pull, finally the dark black foal flopped out. With the resistance suddenly gone, Benzler and I tumbled backward with the newborn animal onto the straw covered floor. Benzler embraced the foal around the neck, a miniature version of the mother. Benzler wore the first genuine wide smile I'd seen on his face in a year. Wet with blood, sweat, and fluid, dirt and straw clung to both he and the foal.

Benzler tried to pick up the newborn in his arms. Hands out, my Dad stopped him. "Whoa, Marshall. Don't pick it up. You need to give the mare a few minutes to clean it up first."

Benzler backed up and grinned, his crooked canine teeth askew. "All right, I made a horse, I did it."

Dad returned the smile, and patted him on the back. "You sure did son. Good job Marshall."

"We did it!" Benzler cried. "We did it!"

While Dad bent down to check out the foal and mare, the vet arrived. Dr. Parker, sandy haired with a reddish beard, had been the practicing livestock vet in these parts for a dozen years. He wore a Polo shirt and Bermuda shorts, as if we had interrupted his golf game or a bar-b-cue.

"Am I too late?" His cologne clashed with the usual barn smells.

"It's a boy!" Dad replied. "It came breach, but it looks like they're both OK."

Dr. Parker examined the animals. "Breach huh? You guys were lucky. Seems like they're both doing fine though. Good job fellas."

The colt attempted to stand up on its unsteady legs, but wobbled and fell. We all laughed at the pure spectacle, the miracle. The colt rose to stand again, and this time he stayed up. Benzler gave me a high five, then one to my Dad as well.

"Let's get cleaned up," Dad said and we left the colt alone with its mother. Benzler continued to beam despite being a mess. The four of us exited the barn, the two adults in front, and the boys behind. Benzler broke into the song "Ring of Fire" by Johnny Cash.

I put my arm around him, and joined in belting it out. Dad turned to look at us and to my surprise he too picked up at the chorus. By the time we reached the house, even the veterinarian sang along with us. As we approached the back door, the yellow porch light beckoned us to come in out of the dark.

*　　*　　*

Chapter 33

I watched the horses as they grazed in Dad's field. I hadn't been home in a long time. Too long. A soft drizzle fell, more like a mist, and my black Armani suit began to dampen, as a herd of horses strode for the cover of the barn. I should have had enough sense to go inside too. I heard footsteps behind me on the wooden deck.

"Donny, I've been looking for you." I turned to find Benzler, a look of concern on his careworn face. "I'm sorry for your loss." He extended his hand, and I took it. Funny, I didn't remember seeing him at the funeral. "Donny, you should come inside." Hand on my shoulder, he escorted me into Mom's kitchen.

She slumped in the corner on her favorite chair, broken by her loss. Several of her elderly friends gathered around to console her. The living room remained the same, unchanged since the 70's, except for the stale smell of age. I searched for something to drink, but no, Mom wouldn't have that. I settled for one of Dad's cheap beers leftover in the fridge, and brought one to Benzler.

He and I stood and chatted, leaving the chairs to the old folks. I saw my wife and kids in the next room. My ten year old son fidgeted stiffly in his new suit. He talked with another boy who looked exactly like Benzler did at that age.

"That your boy?" I asked, nodding in their direction.

"Yup." He took a swig of beer. Benzler still stood a head taller than me. And he never had picked up his parents girth. "Got two of 'em. That's my wife over there." He pointed with his beer bottle to an attractive brunette woman.

"You have a nice looking family." I took a drink, and relished the cool, hoppy taste with the hint of a burn. The mood and setting brought me back to when we were kids, best friends. I recalled the junior high years most vividly. One day emerged clearly, the day Beauty had delivered the breech foal.

After that day, Benzler had turned things around. I wouldn't say that the foaling "cured" Benzler. He still endured tough times following that event, and he struggled throughout his teenage years. But that momentous incident seemed to spark a change in him. Perhaps he had a catharsis. Maybe somehow the new life replaced something dead inside him. In any case, he became more positive and freer with his own life.

After the colt, Benzler permitted others to help, and many did. Maybe the foaling just opened a door that had been closed.

In the years following the colt's birth, Benzler took a keen interest in its development. Dad allowed him to name it, and he chose the name Magic. You know like Black Magic without the black. He came over constantly to help care for it, and he learned to ride it. I think animals definitely help stabilize people.

He had lived in his Mom's barn through the rest of that summer, while he and his Mom grew to have a certain understanding. That fall the family worked out a solution in which he stayed at his grandparent's home next door. That enabled some breathing space between him and his mother. Subsequently, they established a commitment to live in harmony and build rather than destroy their relationship.

They both continued to see Dr. Stevenson for therapy, only now Benzler had a new mission. He found that the doctor could indeed help him. His Mom also thrived with therapy, and later she eventually went on to become a counselor herself.

Benzler made it through school, and got decent enough grades to graduate. He kept out of trouble; not only did he avoid further suspensions during the next five years, but he actually created a solid reputation with the faculty. He even forged a positive relationship with

Principal Schecter. Rustin more or less left him alone after their fight in 7th grade. Rustin's family moved away in 8th grade, but others still called Benzler "Weed" for a number of years. However, the negative nuance faded with Rustin.

The two of us remained friends for many years. Through high school, despite our varying interests and growth, we stayed close. After high school, Benzler enlisted in the military and I enrolled at Ohio State. We kept in touch until I moved west for good, and he got stationed overseas. When his military stint ended, he returned home.

After the colt's birth, my father gained a new understanding and empathy for Benzler. He provided some much needed male mentoring, and treated Benzler as his own son. After I left and Benzler returned, he and Dad grew close. Benzler came to the funeral out of respect for my father, not for me.

When all was said and done, all of this possibly might have happened anyway. But it occurred to me that the life cycle of the horses triggered a life change for Benzler. After the rebirth, he himself could be reborn. He still said so, and I believed it too.

THE END

Made in the USA
Lexington, KY
11 May 2014